Jarrod and the Demon's Knight

P N BURROWS
AUTHOR

Jarrod and the Demon's Night
Book One in the Jarrod Series

First published in 2022
P N Burrows

Copyright © P N Burrows 2022

ISBN-978-1-913091-26-2

DEDICATION

This book is dedicated to my wife Cath, she endures my madness. She is my world.

Chapter 1

Jarrod gripped on to the handle as the harsh Mancunian wind threatened to lift his umbrella into the heavens. The wizard looked at the throng of people rushing below and sighed. He disliked humans: collectively they were destructive, spiteful, deceptive and downright disgusting. There were a few – just a handful – that he did like; those rare humans filled with good intentions whose auras remained relatively untarnished. To Jarrod they were beacons of light, shining brightly amidst the putridness of so-called humanity. His left hand rolled a coin over and under his knuckles. The process was something Jarrod had performed for so many years it was no longer a conscious effort. But this was no ordinary coin; it was one of many magical talismans Jarrod possessed. The coins stored energy for when situations arose that required prompt action, a magical battery for a better analogy. It was one of four that Jarrod carried at all times, and as he was doing now, he would draw in the ambient energy from the universe and imbue into the finely crafted metal disk.

Another year or so, Jarrod promised himself with a sigh,

then I — no — we can go home. Jarrod corrected himself, referring to his long-lost son. Decades earlier, baby Arbon had been smuggled to Earth following an accident that killed Jarrod's wife and almost killed Arbon too. Jarrod could never prove the supposed accident was meant for him, but he had powerful enemies. With the aid of his friend Swalon, Jarrod had hidden Arbon on Earth for his safety. Disaster striking shortly after, Swalon disappeared, taking with him the only way to reach his son. By the time Jarrod had learnt the skills necessary to locate Arbon, he had grown into a man, an adult who had no idea about his heritage or true father.

'I'm sorry Mr Wentworth, the police won't allow anybody in,' a uniformed guard said as he joined Jarrod at the top of the building's steps, startling Jarrod out of his reverie.

Jarrod turned towards the security guard and sighed. He could see recent events were troubling the man. 'It isn't your fault Barry. Tell me what happened.' He sighed once more at the futility of living on Earth. *How do I tell my son that he is not just from another world, but another dimension, one where magic prevails?* It wasn't the first time Jarrod had pondered over the problem. Arbon had been raised as a human, flawed and frail.

'They tasered Martin and then hit him on the head, knocking him unconscious. The ambulance took him away shortly before you arrived, Mr Wentworth.' Barry's usual pallid face was flushed red, his heart raced at the retelling. 'I was on the third floor working my way down, Martin was checking the ground and we should have met up for a brew in the office. His head's a mess, Mr Wentworth. There was blood everywhere.'

Jarrod tried to calm the man, worried for the overweight guard. 'Barry, he'll be ok. Head wounds bleed profusely and always look worse than they are. Now think, what did you see and what have the thieves taken?'

'They took the gold from the shop, the stuff we sell to the tourists.' Barry leaned against the wet railings, shielding himself with a faded umbrella. Jarrod did not recognise the motif emblazoned upon it.

'So, they didn't steal any of the relics upstairs?' Jarrod looked back at the building, the stone facade resembling a museum to entice passing tourists to part with their cash.

Barry looked downwards, embarrassed.

'Barry, is my consignment untouched?'

'I'm sorry. They came in at the back. There's a building being renovated on the far side of the warehouse and they used the scaffolding. The police are saying it's an inside job, Mr Wentworth. They knew when we would start our patrols, where the cameras are, and they bypassed the sensor on the upper window.'

'They're not professionals if they walked past the relics in the sorting house,' Jarrod snorted, 'not if they stole the rubbish in the shop.'

'I had to take a detective to the office to look at the camera footage. It was kids, a street gang by the look of it. They wore hoodies and face-scarves. They timed their route to coincide with the start of our patrol, then left through the front door when they'd finished. It was the door that set the alarm off,' the guard muttered, his knuckles white as he gripped the rail.

'My consignment Barry?' Anger flicked at the back of Jarrod's voice, not at Barry — for Jarrod knew he was an honest man — but at the intrusion.

'I don't know for sure, they asked me to leave the office once I had shown the detective how to access our system. I'm a suspect, too.' Barry's voice broke a little with the realisation. 'But before they kicked me out, I saw one of the hooded figures look at something on your shelf. A statue, I think.'

As a professor of ancient sorcery, Jarrod's official mission on Earth was to discover what magical knowledge the humans had once possessed. Fortunately for him, his in-depth study of Earth's ancient civilisations provided him with enough insight to build the cover persona of a boring purveyor of antiquities. Massaging the tension behind his temples, his left hand over his forehead, Jarrod mentally worked his way through the inventory of his latest consignments. Barry's description of the stolen item didn't narrow down the possibilities; his current shipment from the Far East contained a multitude of figurines and statues.

'Was there anything important?' Barry asked, knowing that few of Jarrod's imports held any personal significance for the old man.

'There are a couple of items for my studies. You know me, Barry, forever the optimist.' Seeing the worry in the man's eyes, he patted the guard's arm in a friendly manner.

An attractive woman momentarily stepped out of the doorway behind them, quickly stepping back as the rain lashed at her. 'Mr Wentworth?'

'Yes,' Jarrod replied. He stared warmly into the woman's hazel eyes. She was strikingly beautiful. *Indian origin, no sign of a foreign accent, possibly third generation British,* he surmised. Jarrod cast a quick glance over her and took a mental snapshot of her appearance and physique. Examining the image in his head rather than staring at her, he studied the detective. She was dressed in matching jacket and trousers, a dark blouse and sensible boots. She emanated an air of competence — he hoped it was competence and not arrogance. Jarrod unfocused his real vision for a millisecond to visualise her aura with his mind's eye. Underneath the swirling clouds of everyday feelings and health, he could see that she was fundamentally a good person. True she had some dark stains in her aura, but who didn't? She wasn't a shining flame of purity and innocence, but she was a rarity; she was honest. Jarrod smiled.

'That's the detective that kicked me out of the office,' Barry whispered to Jarrod. 'Detective Constable Widcombe.'

'Could we have a word inside?' the detective asked.

'Sure, I'll be there in a minute,' Jarrod replied. Turning to Barry he asked, 'So, how are you getting on with the last book that I lent to you?'

'Well, slowly. It's in Spanish,' Barry complained. 'Couldn't I just buy the English version?'

'No! No, no, no...,' Jarrod shook his head chuckling, 'You should always read the original manuscript, unadulterated. So much of the nuance is lost in translation.' Turning away he added, 'Keep at it. The Labyrinth of Solitude or El Laberinto de la Soledad as it's really called, is worth reading. It will help you understand the Mexicans when you go there.'

'When?' Barry muttered under his breath, an air of regret enshrouding him.

Detective Widcombe insisted that Jarrod sit while she stood to take his details. She saw his shoulders sag as he sighed; he recognised it as a power ploy utilised by police forces all over the globe, a way of keeping him submissive. *Interesting, he's been interrogated before,* she thought. *Nothing on his records though.*

'I have told you everything I know Detective, I am not sure how you think I can be of help?' Jarrod questioned.

Why do I also get the weird ones? Someone up there hates me...

she shook her head at the notion. 'They have assigned you a dedicated area in the clearing house, Mr Wentworth. You must be a valuable customer?' She knew exactly how valuable. Archie Randle had let slip how much Jarrod imported through their establishment. The Cambridge toff didn't meet many women in his line of work; he'd babbled inanely in her presence. She may have twiddled her hair a little, to urge him on.

'Caster and Randle have been very considerate, Detective.'

'How much would you say you spend here?' She watched him as he answered. People lied all the time, unaware that their body language gave them away.

'Last year, it must have been close to a million pounds, Detective. Caster and Randle source, purchase and import all kinds of antiquities on my behalf. They have access to lucrative auctions and collections that I do not. I fail to see the relevance of this.'

Damn it, he told the truth. She was sure this was an insurance scam. Someone had tipped off the crooks and this man, in his retro burgundy suit, was hiding something. She could smell it. He wasn't fazed by her questioning. He was too calm and he'd conveniently turned up after the break-in.

'I like to know the facts, Mr Wentworth. I observe and I learn. I'm sure you've seen it on TV, it's called police work. It helps to solve cases.'

'Please, call me Jarrod.' Jarrod smiled up at the detective. 'Close your eyes and describe me.'

'What?' She stared at the man, wondering if she should ask one of the uniformed officers to join her. *Weirdos, I always get the fucking weirdos,* she thought.

'I want you to prove that you are as observant as you claim.'

'No,' she answered, as a uniformed officer knocked on the open door. The policeman proffered a computer tablet. *Should she ask him to join them?* 'Thank you, John.' She rolled her eyes at her colleague and dismissed him. She could put this creep down if he got handsy.

Closing the office door, Detective Widcombe could feel the old man staring at her. A shiver went down her spine. *Ew, he's creeping me out.* Still facing the door, she took a deep breath and said, 'Male, five foot eight in bare feet, mid-fifties, short, cropped beard matching the greying hair, you still have the odd brown hair amidst the grey. Your clothes belie the fact that you are more athletic than your appearance suggests. The two flights of steps to this office didn't even cause you to miss a beat in our conversation. You suffer from arthritis as you wear a copper bracelet. Your clothes are tailor made, expensive … burgundy is not a colour I would have chosen for you. You appear to be right-handed, but the dexterity in your left indicates that you could be ambidextrous.' She turned and stared at Jarrod. 'You play with a sobriety token when you are nervous.'

Jarrod stopped rolling the coin from knuckle to knuckle and flicked it towards Detective Widcombe. She caught it, unsure if the speed of the toss was a test of her reflexes or aggression.

'It's heavier than I expected. Warmer too, you must have hot hands.' She turned the coin over unsure of what she could perceive about the metal. It felt odd... it was steel, but heavy like lead or gold and the warmth from Jarrod's hands didn't fade as she examined it. As she rotated the coin, the delicate leaf pattern seemed to draw her in; she found herself mesmerised by it.

'It's meteoric iron. I had them commissioned years ago,' Jarrod informed her as she ran her finger around the edge, tracing the vegetative vines.

'The leaf pattern is an old family emblem from many generations ago.' He answered her unspoken question as he plucked the coin from her hand.

Startled, she stepped back; she had not heard the man rise from the chair let alone move towards her. Her hand felt empty without the coin, it was oddly comforting. Shaking her head to snap out of her stupor, she thrust the iPad into Jarrod's hand. 'They stole an item from your last assignment.' She scrolled through images of his consignment. 'I'd like you to tell me what's missing.'

'It would be easier if I could see my items in person, Detective.'

'I'm sorry, we're waiting for forensics to arrive.'

Jarrod studied the image, zooming in and panning across the width. From his old-fashioned appearance, Detective Widcombe was surprised that the old toff was computer literate.

'It all seems to be here, Detective,' he said.

Detective Widcombe tilted the screen towards her and scrolled to an image of a youth lifting a foot-long artefact from one of Jarrod's boxes. The miscreant's face was hidden by a hoodie and face-scarf. 'Really?' *This has got to be an insurance fraud,* she thought. *The old boys club banding together. He probably went to Cambridge with the insurance appraiser. Idiots!*

Chapter 2

'It's been over twenty-four hours. I was told my items would have been processed and cleared by now,' Jarrod snapped at Johnathan Caster, one of the proprietors of Caster and Randle.

'I'm sorry Jarrod, we haven't been told anything,' Johnathan complained. 'The police have made as much of a mess as the thieves.' Nodding to his secretary he continued, 'Jane will call Detective Widcombe and ask if your items can be released.'

'Thank you.'

'Let's go into my office old boy, I could do with a cup of tea. I've just received some bad news from our Malaysia office.'

'I'd prefer to watch the CCTV footage of the theft if that's okay?' Jarrod ignored Johnathan, not feeling the desire for small talk. Jarrod was grateful that Caster and Randle had persuaded the police to call in a specialist to perform the forensics. Even so, he was still concerned that the fingerprint powder may have left stains on his consignment.

'Yes, of course, I don't see any problem in that. We can

access the system from my office.' Johnathan held up two fingers for his secretary to see and mouthed: *two teas and biscuits.*

'There you go Jarrod. It's a fairly straightforward system.' Johnathan Caster handed Jarrod the wireless mouse and turned the large monitor. 'I've set the date parameters. You can enlarge the thumbnails by clicking on the camera you require. The system saves all the camera feeds for three months; if there was any movement on a camera it shows it on the timeline bar at the bottom.'

Jarrod watched the grid of thirty cameras. At ten minutes past midnight the two security guards left their office to perform their assigned routes. Barry walked up to the third floor and swiped his ID card on a sensor to inform the system that he had arrived. Martin — the less fortunate guard — did the same at the ground floor.

'They have to swipe at key points around the building. Their patrol is timed and if they miss a scheduled swipe, the other guard is notified that there might be something wrong,' Johnathan explained.

Jarrod sped up the footage to sixteen times, making the guards look comical as they whizzed around the building.

'The break-in first occurred at ten past five. May I?' Johnathan gestured for the mouse. 'See here, this camera just about shows the buggers on the scaffolding at the back.'

Jarrod watched as the gang of youths swung planks from the scaffolding to a window ledge on the antiquities warehouse. One of the hooded figures ran across and could be seen waiting, looking at his watch.

'They knew Barry's routine?'

'Which is why the police said it was an inside job. We've put Barry on paid leave until the police clear him,' Johnathan confirmed.

'You know he wouldn't do that!' Jarrod protested.

'Well, I agree old boy, but the police don't, and the insurance people were quite insistent,' Johnathan apologised. 'There's more, watch.'

Jarrod watched as the gang followed Barry's route, always a couple of minutes behind him. At the stairway security door, they bypassed the lock with ease and once on the second floor disappeared off camera.

Johnathan held up his hand to prevent Jarrod's question. 'That door has a smart lock, a key with an embedded chip is required to access it. All the keys have different ID numbers. Once opened, the ID number is sent to the security system so we can track who opened and closed what.'

'Are you saying Barry left the door unlocked?'

'No. The system logs show the door was locked after Barry passed through. You can even see him checking it locks as he always does. Detective Widcombe took great delight informing me how useless our security is and even showed me a video on YouTube on how to open that particular lock. They knew what locks we use and they brought a tool to circumvent them.'

'And so do any number of clients and delivery personnel, myself included,' Jarrod snapped. 'Why have they disappeared?' he asked, gesturing at the screen.

'We only have cameras at strategic locations; the building is too large for full coverage. They're hiding off camera at the moment and reappear on the next security sweep. They knew there would be no one in the office watching the cameras.'

Fast-forwarding, Jarrod watched as Barry and Martin

exited the office once more, the timestamp on the recording showed ten minutes past six. A few minutes later the youths re-appeared on screen; it was here that Jarrod saw a youth dart back and pluck a figurine from one of Jarrod's boxes.

'That's Selgroch's idol!' Jarrod blurted out.

'Who?'

'But it's still in the box, I saw it in the police photo. The woman with a snake.'

'I'm sorry old chap, I think there was a mistake regarding that fertility statue.' Johnathan sat forwards in his office chair and offered Jarrod a copy of the auction listing. 'I called Mario in Malaysia to see if there had been a misprint in the catalogue. Mario's our buyer out there, he purchased the statue on your behalf. Maybe it was part of a set and that's why one is still here? It was during the call that I heard the bad news, the thing I mentioned earlier.' Taking hold of a now cold cup of tea he continued, 'Mario was a dear friend of mine, I got him the job in Malaysia. We went to Cambridge together.'

'Was a good friend?' Jarrod questioned as Johnathan paused to drink his tea.

'They found him dead a couple of days ago. A gardening accident. Apparently, he was clearing a patch of bamboo when his digger overturned. He'd managed to cut the damned stuff down and was about to use the digger to remove the roots when it tipped over, pinning him to the ground. He was there for four days before they found him. He would have lived if it had been any other plant. It was the height of the bamboo that indicated how long Mario had been trapped. The embassy told me it was over seven feet when they cut it down to release him — it had grown right through his body. A terrible way to die.' Johnathan's voice broke as he spoke.

'I'm sorry Johnathan. I never met Mario myself. We'd emailed a few times.'

'So, I don't know,' Johnathan said, pulling himself together. 'There could have been a mix-up. I've sent another man out there to deal with things, hopefully he'll get time to look into it for you.'

'There was only one idol of Selgroch. I have been after her for a long time.'

'I'll go and see if I can rustle up another pot of tea,' Johnathan said, not listening to Jarrod. 'Hell of a way for Mario to die, poor blighter,' he muttered as he left the room.

Jarrod watched the rest of the heist unfold on the monitor. The guard called Martin reacted to something offscreen — a noise perhaps — and ventured off his predetermined route. On the periphery of a camera, a hand appeared from the shadows and Martin crumpled onto the floor. A figure stood over the fallen guard. Jarrod replayed the footage again and studied the man's gestures... he was sure a conversation had occurred. *Man, not youth*, Jarrod thought to himself. It was hard to be sure at this distance, but the figure emanated confidence and his stance suggested an experienced fighter. Jarrod played the rest of the footage. He saw an arm gesture reminiscent of extending a collapsible baton, the weapon itself was too thin to show up properly on the long-distance footage. This motion was quickly followed by a vicious downward strike. Jarrod realised this was the cause of the head wound Barry had told him about. The youths, on the other hand, quickly made their way to the display counters in the shopping area, ransacked the place and left via the front door, only then setting the alarms off. Martin's assailant did not — in Jarrod's opinion — exit with the group, the body language was incorrect. The hooded figures were hurried and less confident.

Jarrod sat back perplexed as he waited for Johnathan to return with a fresh pot of tea. He left the CCTV system playing in grid mode so he could watch the rest of the scene unfold. Upon hearing the sirens, Barry had rushed to the control room, walkie talkie held to his face, presumably calling for Martin. The security office itself was not displayed on the screens and Jarrod assumed that Barry saw the ransacked shop and called the police. Soon after entering the office, Barry ran downstairs and secured the shop front. Upon the police arriving, Barry and the police searched the warehouse for Martin. Amid the turmoil, the calm shadow of a man appeared at Jarrod's shelf. After a moment of riffling through Jarrod's items, the man's composure changed to one of anger. Placing an identical looking figure to the one that was recently taken into Jarrod's box, the man then moved out of the camera's field of view. Jarrod was still searching for further footage of him when a more perky Johnathan reappeared holding a tray of tea.

'Good news Jarrod. You can collect your items,' he beamed.

Jarrod filled the screen with the image of the man placing a replica statue back into his box and declared, 'You had two break-ins that night. Only, this chap's a professional.'

'She doesn't look Malaysian,' Johnathan commented as Jarrod lifted the figurine out of a shipping crate.

'She isn't,' Jarrod answered as he examined the exquisite piece. 'She was also wrongly identified by the seller as a fertility idol.' Jarrod carefully held the foot-tall statue with one hand along her back and the other supporting the head and neck, as if she were a new-born baby. With reverence, Jarrod carried the statue to a nearby examination table.

'She's beautiful,' Jonathan said, in awe of the craftsmanship. 'Don't let her body fool you, she's as evil as they come.' Jarrod switched on the table lights and stood back to admire the idol. Carved from stone, the ancient twelve-inch high figurine somehow epitomised the trending standard of modern beauty.

'Voluptuous breasts, childbearing hips and leggy. Tastes haven't changed much over the centuries. She is stunning,' Detective Widcombe said as she approached from the shadows.

'You would not like her, Detective. Her worshipers were cannibalistic by nature. They would suck out and eat the eyes of their victims before forcing them to walk back to the coven for sacrifice.'

'What does the snake symbolise?' the detective asked, regarding the large serpent clinging to the figurine's left leg and shoulder, its head held firm in the idol's hand.

'A snake is often used throughout history as a symbol of fertility,' Johnathan informed the detective as he walked around the table to examine the rear of the statue.

'And you bought this for...?' The detective asked, her notepad out already.

'Research, Detective. It's what historians do.'

'What I don't understand is why did the man put her back...?' Johnathan commented, to ease the tension between Jarrod and the Detective.

'He didn't,' the detective interrupted, 'he was here to swap this for the original.' She stared at Jarrod, defying him to argue with her.

'Oh, I don't think so, Detective. She's genuine, I'd stake

my reputation on it.' Johnathan smiled at the detective.

'How much do you have this insured for, Mr Wentworth?'

'Detective, you are relentless.' Jarrod beamed his most disarming smile at the woman. 'Caster and Randle paid one hundred and thirty thousand pounds, on my behalf. Plus expenses, which I might add are sometimes excessive,' Jarrod smiled at Johnathan. 'Until the item is cleared, it remains the property of Johnathan here.'

'You are free to use other companies, Jarrod,' Johnathan replied, quite used to Jarrod's banter over the company's fees. 'We are not the only importers of historical artefacts, you know,' he retorted, defending the company.

'You are the only one I trust Johnathan, as you well know.' Jarrod turned to the detective. 'I vet the people I deal with, Detective. You might say I have trust issues. Caster and Randle are the reason I am in Manchester and not London, Paris or New York,' Jarrod lied.

'Really?' Johnathan smiled.

'Besides your taphophilia, Johnathan, you are as straight as they come.'

'Steady on old boy! No need for name calling, you know.' Johnathan's cheeks flushed as he spoke. 'Gravestone rubbing,' he explained to the detective. 'I collect rubbings from the graves of heroes and people who changed history.'

'If you two have finished,' the detective huffed, 'is this or is this not your statue?'

'She matches the description, old boy.' Johnathan fetched the inventory sheet from Jarrod's shelf.

'This is over two thousand years old and is as authentic as Johnathan expressed earlier. Certainly worth every penny that I and he paid for her. She matches the description except for one vital flaw: she is not the figurine from the auction.'

'I don't understand,' Detective Widcombe said as Jarrod riffled through nearby shelves for something.

'Jarrod, do be careful,' Johnathan fumed at the man's rudeness.

'This is perfect,' Jarrod explained, flourishing a bronze mirror, sending packaging nuggets tumbling to the floor.

Before placing the mirror behind the statue, Jarrod drew in the ambient energy left over from the creation of the universe. It permeated everywhere, ebbed and flowed like water. As a wizard, Jarrod had trained for decades to enable him to convert the universe's energy into other forms, such as light, heat, force, movement and more. Silently casting a small cleansing spell, minute vibrations displaced the grime and a swirl of air movement scoured the metal polishing, enhancing the reflective properties of the bronze surface. The detective shivered visibly as he did so.

'A chill,' she gasped, pulling the front of her jacket together.

Jarrod smiled at her. *Interesting, she felt my use of magic. In another time and place, Detective Widcombe, you'd control a modicum of power yourself,* Jarrod thought.

'Jarrod, I saw her posterior when I walked around the table,' Johnathan complained, as the bronze mirror was placed behind the statue. 'Please can you put the mirror back? You know as well as anyone how valuable it is.'

'Watch,' Jarrod instructed, as he turned the statue around.

'My God!' Johnathan gasped, bending closer to inspect the reflected image.

'What?' Detective Widcombe enquired, leaning closer, bewildered at the man's response.

'Certain cultures throughout history burned, killed and

even tortured those who dared worship any deity that wasn't in vogue at the time,' Jarrod said. 'This provocative statue was designed to blend into any ancient household as a trinket or fertility idol. Look at the reflection, Detective, and tell me what you see?'

'The mirror image of what I saw a minute ago,' she snapped, irked at his question.

'The snake is now wrapped around the right-hand side of her body, it's now held in her right hand. The woman's face looks menacing in the reflection. Who is she?' Johnathan spoke in a hushed tone, totally in awe of the statue.

'This statue is no one, the reflection is an evil deity called Selgroch.'

'Who?' both Detective Widcombe and Johnathan asked, almost in unison.

'Selgroch. She is evil incarnate. In all my research, this alluring creature is the most heinous. In her heyday on Earth, long before Christianity, she slew and devoured thousands of humans.'

'So did Christianity,' the Detective humphed.

'Selgroch is a demon, Detective. She is far worse than any human could ever be. Humans do not have true power over life and death. They do not wield magic to heal a body, only to torture it to death, again and again and again,' Jarrod said.

'Myths and legends,' the detective sighed, only partially interested by the history lesson.

Jarrod picked up the statue and cradled her once more. 'The owner of this would worship the reflection, not the statue, of course. Only in the sacred temples would the true idol be on show. It was one of those idols that I bought.'

'Jarrod, how did you find her?' Johnathan's head swivelled from Jarrod's craggy face to the voluptuous figurine and back again.

'Research Johnathan. This should have been one of the Selgroch's original figurines. Her sect has persisted throughout history. This is a mirror replica, as I have said; the statue I bought should have been from one of the original covens. It was a devil of a job finding information about them.'

'The pattern on the snake, the spaces in between, is that writing?' Johnathan enquired.

'I don't see anything,' the detective answered.

'It is.' Jarrod smiled, happy that his friend had recognised the pattern in the reflected swirls.

'I can only make out a few words, do you know what it says?' Johnathan's face flushed with excitement.

'It's an incantation to call forth Selgroch,' Jarrod explained. 'A sacrifice must be offered, with the blood spilling over the idol. Not this reverse replica, but the original from the temple.'

'Watch,' Jarrod instructed, as he turned the statue around.

'She is beautiful,' Johnathan mewed over the figurine.

'She's evidence in an ongoing investigation, Mr Caster. Please wrap her to go.'

'Detective!'

'It's okay, Johnathan, the statue is useless to me. But if she can aid the police in their investigations...' Jarrod shrugged, indicating for his friend to drop the matter.

'I will require a receipt and confirmation that your insurers have been made aware of the valuation before I relinquish it to you,' Johnathan demanded.

From the protective shadows of an alleyway, a hooded

man watched Detective Widcombe leave Caster and Randle. Inhaling the last of his Turkish tobacco, he flicked the cigarette butt onto the ground by his feet. Slowly exhaling, filling the surrounding air with the rich fragrance of aromatic smoke, his thoughts were disturbed by an annoying voice.

'I'm gonna have to give you a ticket for that, fella,' a pathetic looking man dressed in a city uniform announced. 'Fixed penalty notice for littering is fifty quid, more if you don't pay up on time.' The man took great delight at informing the stranger of this. As if this modicum of power was the only thing in the man's life that gave him purpose. 'Right, I'll need your name and address.'

'Yes, of course.' The stranger opened his jacket as if to retrieve his identification. Instead, he whipped his hand out to reveal a long ice-pick-like instrument. With a precise and controlled motion, the stranger pushed the weapon through the warden's left tear duct, leaving the eye undamaged. The thin shaft slid deep into the man's head, stopping only when the stranger's knuckles touched the warden's face. The needle-like instrument transferred a cocktail of chemicals into the brain tissue: anaesthetics to mask the immediate pain, Rohypnol, to induce amnesia and necrotising fasciitis to ensure a prolonged and painful death. Whispering something into the man's ear, the stranger extracted the weapon and replaced it back into his jacket carefully. A single droplet of blood seeped out of the tiny wound and rested in the corner of the warden's eye. Steadying his half-lobotomised victim, the stranger forced the man to stumble further into the alley. Sitting him on the ground, the stranger removed the warden's body camera and once again whispered into the dying man's ear, before quietly walking away.

Chapter 3

'I'm sorry about your statue Jarrod, from what Johnathan tells me, that was some find,' Archie Randle said as he shook Jarrod's hand. 'An idol from some sort of satanic cult. Well I never.'

'Selgroch is an entity of her own Archie, nothing to do with Satan. She had — and I now believe still has — a very small and select following.'

'Has?'

'Who else would want to steal her? Another collector would have driven the bidding up at the auction, far higher than what we paid for her.'

'Well, I hold judgement on that.' Archie chewed at the end of his pipe, annoyed that UK laws and regulations prevented him from smoking in his own office.

'I've come to ask if there have been any developments in the investigation. It's been a week and the delightful Detective Widcombe is refusing to discuss the case with me.'

Laughing, Archie replied, 'Yes, I heard she had egg on her face about the CCTV footage. By finding the second burglar on our system, you made her look bad, Jarrod.

21

Neither she nor the police will let that pass lightly.' Archie returned the end of the pipe to his mouth and gave it a puff. Annoyed at the lack of smoke, Archie tossed the unlit implement on the desk. 'There has been no development as far as I am aware. You know how it is old bean, the constabulary are merely a token gesture at enforcement. They're stretched so thin as to be useless. Unless a criminal stumbles at the scene and knocks himself out, they don't have the manpower to solve it,' he ranted.

'I see Barry's name on the roster. Has he been cleared for duty?' Jarrod nodded at the white board on the far wall.

'Tomorrow. He was never a concern, you know that. He's upset, but he got a week's paid leave out of it.' Archie huffed, 'I'd be so lucky. Mind you that female detective was on his heels from what Barry was telling Johnathan. Seems Barry has a second income and he's spent a fortune in the last couple of years. The police were onto that straight away. But it turns out our Barry is quite the hobbyist in his spare time, producing metal and wood craft items. All legit, pays his taxes, has receipts and everything.' Archie picked up his pipe and started filling it with tobacco. 'I must warn you: she didn't like it when she found out how much money you've been sending to Barry.' There was an unspoken question in Archie's voice.

'As you said, he is quite the hobbyist, wasted here as a watchman,' Jarrod said.

'I'm surprised she didn't come knocking at your door Jarrod. Barry said she was furious when your name came up.'

'And the other guard, how is he?' Jarrod asked.

'Ah, that's another matter.' Archie lit a match. 'You don't mind, do you?'

'Not at all.'

'Martin's gone. I went to see him in the hospital,

thought it only right to visit the poor fellow. He was conscious by then, but heavily sedated. The nurses said he was having severe panic attacks. Whatever that bounder said to Martin, it scared him half to death. He discharged himself from the hospital the next day and hasn't been seen since.'

'So, was he the inside man? For the first break-in?' Jarrod quizzed.

'That's my train of thought. His background check was clean. Whenever a new guard comes on board, we receive a copy of their personnel file from Johnson Security. But that woman detective, what's her name, er... Willows, Widows...'

'Widcombe.' Jarrod suggested.

'Widcombe, right. She did say something about Martin's stepbrother being in prison for burglary.' Archie shrugged, 'Could be a coincidence.'

Chapter 4

'Mr Wentworth, how nice to see you.' Barry greeted Jarrod with a firm handshake. 'Come in. I'm sorry, the place is a mess. I've been using the time to finish the next batch of leaves for you.'

Stepping through into the lounge, Jarrod noted Barry's idea of a mess was today's newspaper left open on the settee and a half-full cup of tea sitting by the armchair. The book Jarrod had lent to Barry lay next to a Spanish dictionary. A piece of paper hung out of the book about three quarters of the way in.

The room was as it always had been on previous visits: spotless. Barry, a widower of five years, kept the house the way his late wife, Irene, had left it. The routines they had formed over nineteen years of marriage continued, only now Barry performed Irene's duties as well. Her feminine touch was still present in the room, a little chintz here, a throw there. Jarrod knew that Barry had learnt woodwork and craft skills in order to repair the furniture he and his wife had bought together. He had even re-upholstered the settee and repaired the curtains. The only new addition was a framed Mexican print above the fireplace. Once a month

Barry would take down the old print and replace it with a new one, as their routine dictated. Irene had always wanted to visit Mexico; she died a week before they were set to leave on their twentieth wedding anniversary. A drunk driver had fallen asleep at the wheel, crushing the small economy vehicle that Irene drove.

'Tea?' Barry offered. Seeing Jarrod smile, he continued. 'Come on through.'

The kitchen was as immaculate as the rest of the house; the linoleum floor was faded, but serviceable. Jarrod knew what would be in the fridge before Barry opened it. Wednesday night was Indian night. Barry had never learnt to cook; instead he ordered take out each night, eating half and leaving Irene's half for breakfast. Jarrod shuddered at the man's sodium consumption.

'That detective lady came around the other day, erm... Widcombe. She was asking a lot of questions about you, we had to answer her. I'm sorry.' Barry apologised as he poured water into a mug. He slid the brew across the counter to Jarrod, the tea bag string still wrapped around the handle.

'I heard, it's okay, Barry. There's nothing to hide,' Jarrod lied. His whole life on Earth was a lie. 'I'm looking for Martin. He's disappeared.'

'Martin? Why?' Barry became defensive about his colleague.

'The police seem to think he may have been involved with the theft. His disappearance isn't helping.'

'I don't know... I told the police everything,' Barry confessed.

'No, no one tells the police everything, no one likes being interrogated.' Jarrod removed the tea bag and blew on his tea.

'Well, it might not be anything, but Martin's sister's away. He mentioned having to look after her dog.' Barry shrugged. 'That's it. I only thought of it after Detective Widcombe had left. I would have called her, but it's like you said, it's the accusatory tone she used.'

Jarrod opened the cab's door and stepping into the passenger side, he instructed Bert the driver of his destination. Resting a heavy cardboard box on his knees and placing his ever-present umbrella point first into the footwell, he said: 'When we get there, I'll need you to wait again and look after this for me.' Jarrod tapped the box.

'As long as there's nothin' illegal in there, Mr Wentworth,' Bert nodded, never taking his eyes off the road. 'You know me, 'appy to oblige where I can.'

After a few minutes of jostling in the Mancunian traffic, Jarrod pushed his seat further back and placed the package he had received from Barry on the floor. Bert worked for Jarrod, or for one of the taxi companies Jarrod owned. Even though Jarrod's licence declared that he could drive vehicles with up to eight passengers, Jarrod had never learnt to drive. The real owner of his identity had.

'If you don't mind me saying, sir, we 'ad the popo around the office yesterday, asking about you. Guvnor sent them packing, mind. The detective wasn't 'appy. She swore she would be back.'

'She? Pretty Indian woman?'

'Legs up to 'ere,' Bert indicated with one hand. 'She was a scorcher for a copper. Just thought I'd mention it is all.'

'A Miss Widcombe, Bert. She didn't take to me for some reason. I think I'll ask her out for dinner.' Jarrod smiled at the thought.

'You be careful, sir. She'll still be a copper in the sack, lookin' for stuff even when on 'er back, she will.'

Chuckling, Jarrod replied, 'I doubt I would get that far, Bert. I'm old enough to be her father.'

'Nowadays, women like a bit of silver on their men. A bit of experience, if you know what I mean? Respectable looking fella such as yourself Mr Wentworth, you'd 'av no trouble.'

Chapter 5

Bert drew the cab to a stop beside a large laurel hedge, which defined the grounds of the house Jarrod had requested. Adjusting his rear-view mirror, he said, 'That detective I mentioned, Mr Wentworth. She's in the car behind us.'

'Shit!' Jarrod swore as he moved the rear-view mirror to see behind him. 'Wait here for me, Bert. If anything goes awry, keep hold of my box until I pick it up.'

'Right you are, Mr Wentworth,' Bert agreed as he pulled a broadsheet newspaper and a flask from beneath his seat. 'I'll be waiting here.'

Before Jarrod could open the car door, Detective Widcombe's knuckles rapped on the window. Jarrod didn't attempt to wind the window down, instead, he forced the detective to step backwards as he opened the door.

'Do you know what we call people who insert themselves into an active investigation, Mr Wentworth?' Not waiting for an answer she added, 'Suspects. I don't like you, Mr Wentworth. There is something wrong about you, I can feel it.'

Ignoring her with a smile, Jarrod asked, 'Detective, are

you following me?'

'What are you doing here?'

'Am I under investigation, Miss Widcombe?' Jarrod saw the annoyance in her face at the omission of her working title.

'That's Detective Constable to you,' she snapped. 'What are you doing here? If I find you are interfering in my investigation, I'll have you hauled into the station. Do I make myself clear?'

'Hostility, Detective? Really?' Jarrod tried to calm the woman with his disarming smile.

'You insert yourself into my investigation, you omitted to inform me that you own forty percent of Caster and Randle, where your item was stolen from. With inside information on the building's security, I might add. And you own this taxi firm. Does that sound like an honest man to you?'

'For a self-proclaimed astute observer, Detective Widcombe, you have learnt nothing about how money works. Money is made to be used, not spent. Why would I spend millions on another man's business when I can own that business and pay myself? Assets and liabilities, Detective, make your money work for you, not for someone else.' Seeing the detective's nostrils flare, Jarrod decided to elaborate. 'Never spend your own money, always use the money from one asset to pay for the liability of another. It's why the rich stay rich and the poor stay poor.' *My goodness, as pretty as she is, she is exquisite when she's angry.* Jarrod tried to hide his smile.

Gritting her teeth at the pompous financial lecture, the detective's eyes narrowed as she declared, 'And your real name is George Mannering. You conveniently forgot to mention that.'

'I don't see how that is relevant to your investigation or

any of your concern.' Jarrod's annoyance rose into his voice. 'If you must know, I changed my name to prevent an unwelcome suitor from harassing me.' This much was almost true. George Mannering — whose identity Jarrod was borrowing — had filed restraining orders against a former girlfriend, something the detective would have uncovered in her investigation of him. Jarrod had changed his name as he had not wanted any of George's former acquaintances turning up proclaiming him to be an imposter. Choosing the family name from George's great grandmother seemed prudent and Jarrod was his real name.

'Smoke and mirrors, Mr Wentworth, or whatever you are called. I suggest you get back into your taxi and leave.'

'It's a free country and I am here to see if Martin is ok. I was hoping he might have some information that might lead to the whereabouts of my missing idol. We can walk up together if you like.' Seeing the anger in her eyes, he added, 'You have no authority to prevent me.' Pulling a candy bar phone out of his pocket, he asked, 'Do you wish to speak to my solicitor? He can remind you of your legal limitations if you like. I have him on speed dial.'

'As if I would trust your solicitor. You probably own him, too.'

'I am on the board of directors, yes. But if you have done your research as I know you will have, then you already know that. Having money is not a crime, Detective.'

'No, but using a bloody Nokia thirty-three-ten should be.' She took Jarrod's proffered phone out of his hand and shook it at him. 'Do you know who uses these phones? Do you?'

'If they are like me, anyone who is concerned for their privacy. The masses may have no problem spreading their private lives over social media and allowing their phones to track their lives, but intelligent people shy away from the limelight, Detective. It's called a private life for a reason.'

'Bullshit. When I see a Nokia like this, I think drug dealer. I can't tell you how many of these I have confiscated in the course of my investigations. The more I learn about you, the worse you look. You couldn't dig yourself into deeper shit if you tried.'

Snatching his phone back, Jarrod walked up the laurel enclosed drive. 'Those are preconceptions, Detective, not observations.' Jarrod referred back to the conversation they had in Johnathan's office.

'Do you mind?' Detective Widcombe said tersely.

Jarrod paused with his finger above the doorbell. With a dismissive chuckle and shake of his head, he stepped back. 'Please,' he gestured with his hand, 'after you.'

The dual-tone doorbell chimed and the pair waited.

'You do know that Miss Bagnall is on holiday, don't you?' Jarrod teased.

'What? How do you know that?'

'It's precisely that tone that prevents you from being a great detective.' Using his umbrella as a support, Jarrod squatted down to look through the letterbox. As soon as he lifted the flap, the smell assailed his nostrils. 'Oh!'

'What?' Detective Widcombe demanded as Jarrod walked to the side gate. She too squatted down and peered through the letterbox. 'I can't see anything.' It took a few seconds for the aroma of decomposition to register. 'Jarrod, wait!'

She caught Jarrod at the rear of the property peering through the kitchen window, head held in his hands, shielding out the low evening sun. 'I think I have found Martin. It's a little hard to tell.' He stepped back for the detective to see.

'What the hell?' The detective wasted no time in whipping out her phone to call for backup.

Jarrod returned to the window, looking for clues. Martin's body lay on its back across the width of the kitchen table, his hands and feet secured by short lengths of rope to the wooden legs, forcing the man's back to arch. The pain must have been excruciating. Jarrod removed a small torch from his pocket, the tiny device was incredibly bright. Holding it against the glass to reduce the reflection, Jarrod studied the scene inside. Small spots of light reflected off the man's body.

'What are they?' the detective asked, peering alongside Jarrod.

'Acupuncture needles. The body has bloated so much that only the heads of the pins remain visible. I studied Chinese medicine while in China, including acupuncture.' Jarrod answered the detective's question before she could ask. 'Those needles are situated above nerve clusters and a few other painful areas,' he added.

'So, you returned to the crime scene and you know about Chinese torture? I think we need to have a chat down at the station, Mr Wentworth.' The detective smiled at Jarrod.

Without taking his eyes from the scene, Jarrod passed his retro mobile to Detective Widcombe and said, 'I've pressed speed dial. Mr Jenkers would like a word.'

Jarrod tuned the detective's conversation out as he continued to study the scene. The interior kitchen door was shut, trapping most of the smell within the kitchen. The shadows and discolouration of the body made it difficult to see properly from outside, but Jarrod was sure he could see a second set of taser marks on the man's chest, almost in the same location, suggesting the perpetrator was the same height as the man who attacked Martin previously. *Probably the same attacker,* Jarrod thought to himself.

'I will need you to make a statement Mr Wentworth, then you are free to go. I apologise for my rudeness,' Detective Widcombe said handing back the phone. Her facial expression didn't reflect the sincerity of her words.

'The killer shut the inner doors. He didn't want the postman hearing Martin's screams or smelling the aroma afterwards.'

'So?' the detective queried.

'This wasn't torture for an interrogation, Detective. The discolouration around the needles indicates they were the source of an infection.' Jarrod pointed though the window, angling his torch to the nearest needle. 'I'd say he died of sepsis; his own body killed him trying to fight the infection. He would have taken days to die.'

'So, we're looking for a sadist,' the detective murmured. 'Great. As if this case wasn't bad enough.'

'We've gotten off on the wrong foot, Detective. Could I buy you dinner tomorrow night and maybe start over?'

Sirens grew louder as the emergency vehicles approached. Jarrod saw the flash of blue reflect off the far chimneys as the police entered the street behind.

'Go home, Mr Wentworth. A uniform will call to see you for your statement.' She shook her head and exasperation filled her voice.

Jarrod lifted a hand to touch her arm, the ice in her eyes convinced him that it would be unsafe to proceed. With a shake of his head, Jarrod suggested. 'Look for the dog, Detective. Miss Bagnall had a dog, that's why Martin was here.'

Several police cars pulled up, their sirens turned off as they entered the street. Blue light reflected off the pallid gawping faces that appeared in the neighbouring windows.

Chapter 6

Jarrod closed the door to his apartment and sighed. Brushing his hand over the copper branch he smiled, happy to be home. The volume of police that had encircled the crime scene was quite impressive. Unfortunately for Jarrod, the Senior Investigating Officer insisted that he remain to give a statement, which was then verified by Detective Widcombe.

Leaning with his back against the apartment's wall, Jarrod closed his eyes and breathed in, held his breath for a second and breathed out. He was home, his small sanctum amongst the turmoil of this dangerous world. His calm and safe place. *Breathe in, breathe out.* Jarrod allowed his mental guards to fall, pushing the stresses of the day out of his mind. With his eyes still closed Jarrod held out his umbrella and hooked it onto a gnarly tree branch, the vibration caused the copper leaves to chime as they jiggled. It wasn't a real tree of course; it was one of seven metallic sculptures scattered around his home, encompassing the exterior walls with their branches.

Jarrod placed the heavy box that he had received from Barry onto an oak table. It landed with a thud. Peeling back the tape from the lid, he lifted the first copper leaf from the packaging. Holding it by the stem, Jarrod lifted it towards the light, appreciating Barry's craftsmanship. Gently flicking the metal object with his fingernail, the intricately crafted leaf rang out with a perfect D-flat tone. It was a work of art all on its own. Barry created each leaf in his workshop and while he could not play the piano, he could match the sound of the leaves to the keys on his wife's old keyboard. 'Perfect Barry, absolutely lovely,' Jarrod commented aloud. The quality of work was far beyond his own meagre skills.

Removing a coin from his pocket, Jarrod pushed his mind's eye outwards, towards the talisman, feeling for the energy stored within. Touching the coin to the leaf, Jarrod shaped the magical energy with his mind, focusing the raw brutal energy from the universe, changing it, reshaping it, moulding it into a delicate spell. With precision honed over many decades, Jarrod transferred the energy into the copper leaf. The spell was an adaptation of the first incantation they teach new students at the University of Magic, a protective ward. The fragile leaf hummed at the infusion of magic and metal. Pressing the stem of the leaf to the branch, Jarrod used the energy to forge a bond fusing the two together. The leaf glowed and the nearby foliage chimed, almost as if welcoming the newcomer. The fragile talisman joined thousands of others around the apartment, all protecting Jarrod from intrusion, whether it be magic, demonic or electronic.

As he picked up another leaf, Jarrod reminisced back to his student days. On Prushal, where he came from, all people have the ability to perform magic at some level. Some may only be able to ignite tinder or form an orb of light on a dark night. Others, like Jarrod, have abilities that go far beyond this. Each magician, sorcerer or those with a predilection or gift to magic, was born with an affinity to two metals: one to be used for passive spells, such as protection, or items that needed to be invoked at a later date. The other metal was for active spells, where the output was apparent and manifested itself at the time of casting. In the younger adolescents, active incantations were frequently seen during playful duels. As children, they were all taught that the power of magic comes from the universe itself, the primordial energy that created everything. All children are taught how to tune themselves into that power and how to focus and shape it for casting. Spells, incantations and tools are all designed to tune the wizard's mind, to focus it to a specific point where it can accomplish the task. Over time, those adept at magic can cast the spells without the flamboyant accessories, their minds remembering how to focus, a cerebral muscle memory. Performing magic also depletes energy from the user; those who practice the darker forms steal this energy from those around them.

Jarrod had unfortunately been born with an affinity for the low-class metals of copper and iron. His mental ability for magic far outstripped his birth metal's ability to hold or focus such energy and so his spells often burnt through the receptacle or focusing tool that he had been training with. It was unheard of in Jarrod's society for anyone at the level of wizard to be hampered with one base metal, let alone two and yet Jarrod had attained that level and more. Stumbling across a meteorite while out walking, Jarrod felt his energy course into the charred fragment. Like a sponge, it absorbed his magical energy and then some; Jarrod had passed out, drained.

With the aid of metal from the heavens — and much work — Jarrod found that he could forge and cast spells with ease. He never told a soul about his discovery.

At two in the morning Jarrod was awakened by his summoning stone. In the real world, it neither glowed nor vibrated and yet in Jarrod's mind it performed both actions. Donning his traditional cloak, he prepared to perform the Wayfarer's Step. This conjuring had once been lost and forgotten for centuries, the act of Stepping from one place to another using a non-existent area called Nowhere. Not just on his home world, but to places that existed outside of his reality, other dimensions. Earth was one of many planets he had visited, but the only place he had spent more than a year studying. Magic energy was pervasive, omnipresent, but the ability to use it was not inherent in all life forms. Humans had had it once and still did, to a much lesser extent. This was the official reason for him staying. As a professor at the University of Magic, he was encouraged to research and explore ancient forms of magic.

Jarrod tuned his mind to the cosmic energies, with the mental acuity of a chess master, his thoughts shaped the energy, the fabric of reality and space to do his bidding. With a confident step forwards, Jarrod disappeared from his Earthly home and entered the dull grey void of Nowhere. Time slowed. A person neither aged nor became hungry in Nowhere. A candle flame glowed but the wick never burnt down, or the tallow dwindle. The flame never flickered. A man could walk a thousand years and never find the other side, for it had no substance. Jarrod felt with his mind for the opening leading to his home, feeling for weakness in the membrane of this non-reality. He had found many weaknesses in the past, many of them led to certain death. More than a few of the test vegetables he had partially pushed through returned twisted, mutilated, or worse. Like most magic, nothing was tangible, it was ethereal feelings and thoughts, like holding a cloud of smoke — if he grasped at it, it would disperse between his fingers. After decades of practice, Jarrod could sense the thin membrane, to feel if the other dimension was suitable for visitors from his domicile before Stepping through.

A feeling of warm familiarity crept over him. He had found the entrance to his home world, the membrane worn thin by his many trips through it. He'd once described it to his sister, one of the few people he trusted, as walking though jelly. The subsequent trips were easier as the passageway had already been made; even if it sealed over again, it became weaker than before.

Jarrod Stepped through, exhaustion causing him to slump and grab for the nearby wall, his fingernails scraped along stone blocks as he floundered.

'Brother.' Firm feminine hands grabbed at his arm, steering him towards a table and chair. A tankard appeared before his lips and he swallowed the hearty beverage.

'Chandice...' Jarrod called for his sister, his eyes foggy, his energy spent.

'I'm here Jarrod, the chancellor will be here in a moment. It is he who demanded that I summon you.'

Lifting his bowed head, he whispered 'Why?'

'He wouldn't say.'

Feeling his strength returning, Jarrod examined his old quarters. Home. The air smelt fresh and the energy levels of the university buzzed all around him. The magic induced heat in the walls enveloped him, teasing him with a tender and familiar embrace.

'Jarrod, you don't have time to sleep,' Chandice said, admonishing him. Thrusting a smaller glass into his hand, she instructed, 'Drink.'

Jarrod complied, the stimulant in the drink energising

him instantly. He laughed, 'I haven't tasted that since my college days. I thought it had been banned.'

'For students, yes. You're a professor. You can do what you like.'

'How are you, Chandice? And the family?'

'We are all fine. The children have grown up while you've been away. You missed both of their initiations in the College of Magic.' Her tone indicated that Jarrod was in trouble, but Chandice recognised that this was not the time for an argument.

'I'm sorry Chandice, you should have summoned me.' He held her hand and received a little squeeze in acceptance.

'I might need to speak to your lodger soon. I have an investigator asking questions about my... his past.'

'George? Oh, he moved out ages ago. I organised an apprenticeship at a bakery for him. He has a natural talent for food and has since opened up his own eatery. He's doing well, people like his alien cuisine.'

Jarrod smiled in appreciation of what George Mannering had accomplished. Jarrod had found him over ten years ago on the verge of suicide. The conversation had been complicated by the fact that Jarrod had initially learnt Earth's most prevalent language for his trip to the planet. George had used an app on his iPhone to translate the Mandarin into pidgin English and back again. With this convoluted method, Jarrod had offered him a new life away from London. Eventually George acquiesced, and moved away from the bridge's precipice. Jarrod Stepped him into Nowhere and then 'ack to his university quarters on Prushal. After a period of weeks to calm himself and get acquainted with the transition to a new world, George taught Jarrod English and the foibles of living on Earth.

Jarrod took George's identity, changed his name via

deed poll and toured Earth looking for ancient magic. More importantly, he searched for his lost son. Ten Earth years later he was still there. Having found Arbon, he was unsure how to approach the man.

'Jarrod.' A deep baritone voice boomed as the door opened.

'Chancellor.' Jarrod stood up, still a little shaky from his trip.

'Sit, sit down, before you fall,' the newcomer roared, taking a seat of his own.

'Sir.' Jarrod smiled at his old mentor.

'You are well?'

'Yes, sir.'

'Your beard is so short, are you sure?'

'It's fashionable where I am, sir,' Jarrod explained.

'The cocoa plants you brought back last time have gone down well. The university is doing very well on the royalties. The Bursar sends his regards.'

'Chocolate is very popular on Earth,' Jarrod replied. 'Chancellor, if I may ask, why am I here? Why did you summon me?'

'I need you back here soon, Jarrod. I want you to finalise your affairs and take up your old position as professor or your tenure will end. I have kept it open for as long as I can. I'm sorry but the pressure from the council is mounting. You know they are suspicious of your motives for being away.'

'Jealous, you mean,' Chandice interrupted.

'That too, Chandice. None of us possess the ability to perform the Wayfarer's Step and so, some grow suspicious. They fear what they do not understand. They are frightened of you, Jarrod.'

'Then why do they want me back?' Jarrod shouted in anger. 'I have more to learn on Earth. They had powerful magic in the past, I can still feel its presence.'

'You are a mage with base metals and yet you wield sorcery at a level of the ancients. Your affinity metals should have held you back and yet you have risen to the position of a full professorship at the university. No sorcerer alive uses iron, but you. There are rumours that you have turned.'

'What?'

'Chancellor! You can see Jarrod's aura; you know he is in balance. Which is more than many on the council!' Chandice chastised the old wizard.

Jarrod felt the gaze of the chancellor's inner eye on his aura. He knew what the chancellor would see. Jarrod's aura was split equally between good and bad, the deeds of his youthful indiscretions still staining half of his aura midnight black. As a youth, Jarrod had been bullied and picked upon for his low-class metals and poor-quality magic. A soft target for bullies. Shortly after his meteoric discovery, in his first year of university, Jarrod fell prey to three hot heads from rich and important families. They were known in the university as tormentors and their previous antics had put several freshmen into the infirmary. Money — and their family's influence — smoothed matters over, their victims had been quietly transferred to other universities, all fees paid as a recompense. Jarrod had not been so fortunate that night. The three rowdies urged each other on until their mostly Harmless pranks became flamboyant fireballs of flesh-eating lava, lightning and fire. If not for Jarrod's store of magic in his meteoric iron, he may have perished that night. His protective warding spells imbued into the copper threads woven into his clothes would have fizzled under the first attack. Years of fine-tuning his magic incantations to compensate for his low-class metals had honed Jarrod's mind into finding simpler alternative methods. He improvised and thought up unconventional methods to marry the two affinity metals together, passive and active working in unison. Previously, the ideas had only provided him a slight improvement, but with the added power of the meteoric iron, the performance was tenfold. Jarrod's defensive spells in his copper amulets and the threads woven into his clothing drew power from his iron — lots of power — his warding spells nullifying the incoming threats, enraging the three attackers even more. Jarrod had spent years learning unpretentious, low energy, delicate spells because he was unable to summon power-hungry fireballs. He struck out, out of anger, out of years of frustration. A small, simple and deadly spell, it passed through the aggressors' shielding, destroyed their protective wards, overloading and physically melting the affinity metals they were imbued into. The three died before their bodies hit the ground, each suffering from multiple brain aneurisms. A small spell — not flamboyant, delicate — honed smaller still through necessity, invisible, a thin stiletto of a spell, piercing through conjured armour and instantly fatal. The families of the three boys were enraged and brayed for Jarrod's blood; they insisted on the death penalty for the slayer of their angelic sons. The university stepped in, realising Jarrod had acted out of self-defence. Although, at the time they did not understand how a freshman had bested three skilled and powerful post-graduates. The fiasco was covered up as a duelling incident, legal killing under Prushal law. Jarrod however had known that he was more powerful than the three adversaries and that he could have easily subdued the hotheads without hurting them. Their needless deaths cast his aura into blackness. The condition of a person's aura also affects his or her personality. Dark thoughts filled

Jarrod, vengeance, greed, hate, murder. If it hadn't been for the love of his sister and mentoring from the university's chancellor, he would have been lost.

It took a long time to bring his aura into balance. A good deed for the sake of reward is not a good deed and therefore would not reduce his burden. It was a thoughtless act of sacrifice that eventually liberated him from the foreboding negative influence of his dark aura. A five-pronged Arkbille escaped from the university's collection of magical creatures. Jarrod found it by chance in the infirmary. He was there for his own selfish reasons, trying to find a way to beat his affliction. The creature was stalking a baby in a crib as he entered the hospital ward; without thought Jarrod stepped between the Arkbille and the baby as it struck. Jarrod died that day and was brought back from the brink of death seventeen times as the infirmary staff laboured valiantly to save him. He hadn't thought about his action, he had reacted purely on instinct to protect the new-born. He died painfully over and over again. During the interlude between life and death, Jarrod found religion. Jarrod could never describe to anyone what had turned him from an agnostic to believer, only that he sensed that something had happened while he was dead. He had awoken on the seventeenth revival a different man.

The head of the university waited while Jarrod caught his breath, then stood to leave. 'Walk with me Jarrod,' he instructed.

The wind above the university's battlements whipped at Jarrod's short hair. The fresh air invigorated him. In the distance, the picturesque vista of magic and technology working in union was breathtaking. Jarrod's mood lifted as he gazed at the once familiar sight. Large mechanical transportation carriages floated above pre-set lines of magical energy, as if hovering above multicoloured threads of whisper-like clouds. Jarrod watched crop harvesters trundling through swathes of brightly coloured vegetation. Part mechanical, part magical, the huge contraptions were owned and run by the university's horticultural department. Magic had many applications, but it was rarely used as a power source. Friction-free spells prolonged the mechanical infrastructure, while the sun's radiation powered the mechanisms. Jarrod smiled, remembering his childhood, working on similar machines for pocket money.

'I miss this place,' Jarrod confessed to the chancellor; a small tear formed in the corner of one eye. *Just the wind,* he lied to himself.

'What news on the other matter?' the chancellor whispered, fearful that the breeze might carry his words.

Jarrod bowed his head, hiding within the hood of his cloak. Steadying his voice to hide his shame at having to lie to his friend, he said 'I have seen no sign of Swalon, Chancellor. If he is on Earth, he is not using magic, or at least nothing strong enough to ring the leaves on my trees.' Jarrod referred to the copper protection and magic detection leaves in his home. 'I do not think he's on Earth.' *Hide a lie within a truth.* The humans had taught him that.

'He has to be there, you said so yourself ten years ago.'

Jarrod nodded. Swalon, the chancellor's son and Jarrod's closest friend, had been the university's brightest student. It was he who rediscovered the fabled Wayfarer's Step. Shortly after hiding Jarrod's son, Swalon disappeared. The Wizards' Council, angry that no other Wizard could perform the incantation for the Wayfarers Step, and hungry for power and prestige, forced Swalon to experiment, to find new worlds, new resources. One day, nearly forty years ago, he failed to return. He reappeared disfigured and deformed fifteen years ago. He had not returned sane. His incoherent rambling at the time talked of other dimensions filled with demonic creatures. It transpired that he had been captured and tortured for decades before making his escape. Swalon's aura was totally black. The chancellor and the Wizards' Council never found out what deeds had turned it such, only that Swalon ranted that they had been necessary for him to survive. In his infrequent coherent periods, he refused to Step again, not even to retrieve Arbon from Earth. Swalon became enraged when he discovered that his father and Jarrod had been studying his academic papers on the Wayfarer's Step. He warned of the perils beyond their realm and that they needed to prepare. His warnings went unheeded and eventually Swalon turned on the Council and his father. He swore to dominate Prushal and subjugate all that stood in his way, for their own protection. His power was incredible, amplified by the blackness of his aura, it took the combined force of the Wizards' Council to thwart his plans. A wounded Swalon Stepped out of their trap, into Nowhere and had not been seen since. The chancellor and Jarrod continued researching through Swalon's old notes and the transcripts of his insane rantings for years. After half a decade of toil, Jarrod felt the barrier between Prushal and the other dimensions; the passageway led to a place the ancients had christened Nowhere. Initially the members of the Wizards' Council were furious to discover that Jarrod had learnt to perform the Wayfarer's Step. No one else, the chancellor included, could master the complexity of the spell nor had the mental acuity and dexterity to locate the ethereal membrane between realities. With practice, Jarrod managed to carry two other members of the council through with him. After that, the Wizards' Council restricted the research papers on the Wayfarer's Step to council members only, stating the ability was too powerful and could destabilise society.

'I shouldn't need to remind you, Jarrod, Swalon is dangerous.'

'He's your son, Chancellor.' Jarrod placed a hand on the old man's arm. The conflicting concern for his son and the safety of Prushal, twisted the old man's face.

'I... I know Jarrod, but what he did... the Council... they will never allow him back, not alive.' The chancellor looked at Jarrod with weary eyes. 'I am frequently questioned about his whereabouts, you know. Even after all these years, my loyalty is questioned. He's dangerous, Jarrod and so are you. They fear you will kill them in their sleep.'

Jarrod held the old man's arm and gave it a gentle squeeze. 'You know I would not do that.'

'I do Jarrod, but fear makes them foolish. You must be careful.'

Chapter 7

Jarrod walked through the gift shop and entered Caster and Randles' restricted area. Barry, the guard, was back at work and greeted Jarrod happily, with a hearty handshake for the support he had shown during the week of enforced leave. Barry was, like all the employees at Caster and Randle, unaware that Jarrod was a major partner in the business.

'That detective's here, Mr Wentworth. She arrived first thing this morning. I had to walk her through the robbery again. She's annoyed because she can't figure out how the other thief gained entry.'

Chuckling, Jarrod asked, 'Where is she now?'

'Loading bay, out back.'

Jarrod found himself smiling at the thought of seeing the antagonistic detective again, not that he expected such feelings to be reciprocated. It had been a couple of days since their encounter at the house owned by Martin's sister and Jarrod was eager for news on the investigation, especially the pathology report. He realised that he would have to surreptitiously use his abilities to loosen her tongue.

As Jarrod turned the corner, the smile fell from his face. The scene before him did not bode well for Detective Widcombe. She was sprawled out beside a white van, a muscular man leaning over and holding a stun gun against the detective's chest. The voltage surged through the woman's body causing her to convulse and Jarrod was concerned about her head as it repeatedly bashed against the concrete floor. With the tip of his umbrella in hand, Jarrod strode forward and swung the brolly, striking her attacker below the ribs on his right side. The weighted wooden handle struck the man's soft tissue, transferring the impact into his liver. The sound of the crackling energy from the stun gun ceased as the thug folded over against the van, dropping the weapon on the floor.

Upon arriving on Earth nearly ten years ago, Jarrod had obtained detailed knowledge of the local's anatomy and the fragility of the human body. Life was often cruel and short-lived for those adept in magic and training in non-magical self-defence was always high on a magician's list of priorities. Momentarily flicking to his inner eye, Jarrod watched the man's nervous system as it went into overload, his vascular system was dilating and at the same time his heart rate dropped. With his blood pressure low, his body's immediate reaction should have been to lie on the ground, the fact that he was semi-upright attested to the man's fitness and experience as a fighter.

The side door of the van swung open and the burglar from the CCTV footage appeared. The man looked at the unconscious body of Detective Widcombe, to Jarrod, to his accomplice and then with a look of annoyance back to Jarrod. Quickly regaining his composure, the man dragged his stumbling cohort into the vehicle and closed the door.

Jarrod fought hard to not unleash the full force of his magic upon the occupants of the vehicle. He felt impotent;

he was possibly the most powerful person on this planet and yet he feared being discovered. Dragging Detective Widcombe away from the van, Jarrod prevented the vehicle's rear wheel running over her leg. The van's tyres didn't screech as it drove away, the driver was too experienced for that.

Jarrod sat on the floor cradling Detective Widcombe to keep her warm. He pinched the bridge of his nose and huffed at the thought of giving more witness statements as he dialled 999.

Focusing his inner eye to examine the detective's injuries, Jarrod was grateful that he could not detect any damage to her skull. Focusing on the magical energy in one of his coins, he transferred it into the detective. Jarrod was not a physician, nor a mage of medicine and so he could not magically heal the woman's injuries. Instead, he focused on speeding up the body's own healing process. With a sigh, Jarrod noted that the swelling in Detective Widcombe's head was slowing. Moving his thoughts to her chest, worried that the electoral charge might have damaged her heart, Jarrod blushed as his mind's eye wandered over her small, pert breasts. 'You'll be ok, Detective,' he whispered, happy there was no damage to her vascular system. With a blood-soaked hand, Jarrod moved a strand of hair from her half open eyes. Aware that his ministrations will have shocked her body almost as much as the attack, he instructed: 'Sleep now,' casting a spell of healing sleep.

The gash on the back of the detective's head, like all head wounds, was bleeding profusely, the blood matting in her soft brown hair. Pulling the silk handkerchief from his breast pocket, Jarrod applied pressure to the wound.

The background hum of everyday life became more frenzied as the emergency vehicles raced to the scene.

Jarrod could hear a mixture of sirens converging on his location. The heavy security door behind him burst open and the staff of Caster and Randle rushed out.

'Jarrod, are you ok? Barry saw what happened on his screen, we've called the police,' Archie Randle gasped breathlessly.

★ ∘•∘ •∘ ∘• •∘ ∘• •∘ ∘•○∘• •∘ ∘• •∘ ∘• •∘ ★

Tired from hours of police questions, Jarrod sat in Archie's office. He'd managed to wash the detective's blood off his hands, but not off his jacket and trousers.

'I thought you were very brave, old bean,' Archie said for the umpteenth time as he rewound the CCTV footage to view the incident again.

'I didn't think about it, she was on the floor and needed help,' Jarrod replied, slumped in a cosy leather chair that Archie had dragged from the director's lounge. Leaning across the desk, Jarrod picked up the man's leather tobacco pouch. Extracting a pinch, Jarrod rolled the leaf strands between his finger and thumb, a hint of honey and fruit emanated from the crushed leaf.

'Sorry Jarrod, it's a filthy habit, I know.' Archie's jaw dropped, then turned into a smile as Jarrod pulled a pipe from the recesses of his jacket. Jarrod's family leaf adorned the lip of the bowl, the fine copper contrasting against the black wood. 'Oh, by all means help yourself. That's my go-to pouch for emergencies, Davidoff Red, damned expensive stuff,' Archie added, picking Jarrod's umbrella from the stand. 'This faired reasonably well old boy. I thought it would be bent out of shape with the whack you gave it.'

Jarrod chuckled. 'Well don't tell the police, but that version is sold primarily for self-defence. The advert shows it taking the weight of a man. I even took the lessons in bartitsu.' Archie looked at Jarrod with a raised eyebrow. 'The Victorian martial art of defending one's self with a walking stick... a sturdy umbrella is adequate for the task.' Pipe smoke billowed around him as he lit the pipe.

'Damned shame we can't make out the man in the van though. The police said he must have had an array of infrared lights around the door frame.' Archie paused the footage where a bright glow began to fill the screen as the van's side door opened. 'I take it you have given the police a description of the fellow?'

Jarrod pulled a copy of a sketch he had drawn for the police out of his jacket. The man's eyes were mostly hidden behind the peak of his baseball cap, he was clean shaven with prominent cheek bones and wearing a loose-fitting jacket.

'You drew that old boy? I'm impressed,' Johnathan Caster spluttered as he entered the office. He wafted at the smoke with exaggerated movements. 'The police are leaving now. I overheard one of their radios; they have found the van, abandoned a mile or so away.'

'When you have drawn as many diagrams of historical digs as I have, a face is nothing.' Jarrod smiled, comfortable in his lie. 'A tool of the trade.' Jarrod was an excellent artist. All students of magic had to master the ability to produce incantation diagrams, many of which were finely detailed and some included anatomy.

'So, what did the bruiser look like, Jarrod?' Archie pumped his friend and co-partner in the business for more details.

'I only saw him from behind Archie, he was leaning over Widcombe with his back to me; when I struck, he fell forwards against the side of the van. Before I had time to step over the detective's body, the side door opened and he fell in.'

'The blighter knew the position of the cameras. There isn't a clear shot of him; the cad kept the peak of his cap down.'

'Is there any news about Detective Widcombe?' Jarrod asked Johnathan as he settled down in the seat next to him.

'One of the constables mentioned that she'll be okay, nasty crack to the head and burn marks on her, er... bosom.' Johnathan blushed as he thought of the detective's chocolatey coloured breasts.

'Do the police know who this fellow is?' Archie brought up the original footage of the robbery. 'Swapping Jarrod's idol is one thing but assaulting a police officer...'

'Attempted kidnap, Archie,' Jarrod corrected him. 'Also, I believe he's the person responsible for Martin's death.'

'Martin? Our security guard, Martin?' Archie frantically tapped his pipe on the desk, his hands shook as he filled it with fresh tobacco. 'Good Lord, why?'

'I believe he's still looking for the idol.'

'Lord!' Johnathan exclaimed. 'Are we in danger?'

'Did you hear about the attack on the litter warden the other day, across the road?' Archie asked, bellowing out a huge cloud of fragrant smoke.

'Nasty affair, Jarrod. The man was half lobotomised.' Johnathan put a finger to the corner of his eye. 'Thin blade right here. Poor fellow is still in intensive care, some sort of secondary infection I believe,' Johnathan added.

'No, I've been preoccupied.'

'It's been all over the news old bean, how could you have missed it?'

'I don't have a television.'

'Good Lord!' Johnathan looked even more surprised at this than the news of Martin's killer. 'No TV? I wish I could get rid of ours, Jarrod. I'd much prefer to listen to Radio

Four at night. The lady-wife wouldn't allow it of course.'

'I have matters to attend to. Before I go, I'd like to propose that we upgrade our security,' Jarrod said as he rose and gathered his belongings. Seeing the vacant stares from his partners, he added, 'We have had two break-ins, an attempted abduction and there is no useable surveillance footage.'

'Jarrod, the expense,' Johnathan huffed.

'And if word of our ineptitude gets out and the fact that we have not addressed the problem... think of your reputation.'

'But those cameras are less than six years old, Jarrod. There is nothing wrong with them,' Johnathan protested.

'They're outdated and too few. We need a high-profile installation, lots of vans outside to let the local thieves know that we are no longer an easy mark,' Jarrod replied in a stern voice. 'Contact Johnson Security and tell Matt Johnson that we want the Business VIP Package.'

Chapter 8

Detective Widcombe stood in the long corridor leading to Jarrod's front door. She was impressed by the quality of the apartment building — it was high class and even included a security guard at the front desk.

Looking down at the plush carpet, she moved the plush pile with the toe of her boot. Commenting to no one, she muttered, 'I thought the service charge on my apartment was high. I'd hate to pay for this place.'

Jarrod's front door looked ancient, in style for the relic expert, but out of context with the building. Approaching the door as she strolled along the corridor, it appeared to be made from a solid block of copper, the leaf design she had noticed on his sobriety token was etched into the door and inlaid into the brown painted walls. She was less impressed with her reflection in the polished metal. A slight curvature of the door distorted her image from lithe to downright rotund.

Halfway along the corridor she could see no knocker or bell on the door, nor was there a lock or handle. A high-tech palm reader sat on the wall, the juxtaposition of old decor and new technology gnawed at the detective's sensibility.

Walking back to the lift, Detective Widcombe couldn't help but wonder why a building designer would waste so much space on a such a long corridor for one door. Running her hands along the leaf pattern in the walls, she was surprised to find that the metal felt warm to the touch. Reaching the elevator doors, Detective Widcombe looked around the small waiting area on the off chance she had missed seeing another apartment's entrance. Her eyes had been transfixed by the polished copper door after all. She asked herself: *One apartment for the whole floor and he wastes space on a long corridor... why?*

Feeling foolish, she turned and walked back towards the copper door shaking her head at her silliness. Ahead, Jarrod's door opened and a petite Chinese woman exited.

'Oh, you have got to be kidding me?' Detective Widcombe said aloud as she saw the Chinese woman's face. The oriental woman's beauty was marred by two black eyes and bruising on one side of her face. 'Did he do this to you? Miss, did he just do this?' Detective Widcombe shouted. Holding up her police credentials, she ran the last few metres.

Jarrod appeared in the doorway and smiled at the detective — an innocent smile that she greeted with a sneer. 'Did he do this to you?' She spoke slower, unsure of the Chinese woman's vocabulary.

'Jarrod do this?' The woman mumbled from her swollen lips.

Detective Widcombe missed the sarcasm in the woman's pidgin English. Pulling her handcuffs from beneath her jacket, she strode towards Jarrod. Placing one booted foot into the doorway, she asked, 'Well Mr Wentworth, what do you have to say for yourself?'

'He too slow, long arms, clumsy,' the Chinese woman

explained, her accent somehow elongating her vowels. 'He could not hurt me.' With that the small woman pushed past Detective Widcombe, shouted at Jarrod in Chinese and attacked him. A flurry of kicks, punches, chops, jabs and elbows flew in quick succession, forcing the detective to step back into the corridor. Detective Widcombe was surprised that Jarrod held his ground, somehow managing to deflect the majority of the blows. Those that did strike struck only with enough force to prove the woman had the advantage. After an intense thirty seconds, the woman stepped back, her breathing normal as if nothing had occurred. She bowed towards Jarrod, who returned the formal gesture. In the light of Jarrod's apartment, Detective Widcombe realised the woman could only be in her early twenties; the recent injuries to the woman's face belied her youth.

'Detective Widcombe, I'd like to introduce you to a good friend of mine: Wang Xiu Ying.'

'So, you didn't hit her?'

'Hit me? Jarrod?!' The woman laughed, 'He gentleman, never hit me.'

'Xiu, you speak impeccable English, cut it out.'

'She thought I was a hooker, I play the part.' Seeing Jarrod's disapproving look, the young woman offered her hand to the detective. 'Nice to meet you, Detective Widcombe,' she said in perfect English with no trace of a foreign accent.

'Xiu is a postgrad at the university. She's finishing her master's degree in Economics and Philosophy. She is also training me in various martial arts.'

'I apologise if I offended you Miss...'

'You can call me Xiu, pronounced shee-you.'

'Miss Xiu. May I ask how?' Detective Constable Widcombe indicated the woman's face.

'Airbag.' The woman shrugged. 'I am sorry, I have to go or I'll be late for class.' Smiling at Jarrod, Xiu bowed once more at Jarrod and retreated down the corridor.

'Mr Wentworth, I came to thank you for saving my life.' Detective Widcombe's cheeks turned crimson as she spoke. 'I seem to have made matters worse.' Thrusting out her hand she sighed, 'Sorry.'

Jarrod smiled and took her hand in his for a firm but gentle shake. 'It's fine, Detective, please call me Jarrod.' Stepping backwards he offered, 'Would you like to come in?'

Jarrod placed a cup of tea in front of Detective Widcombe. 'Milk? Sugar?' he asked.

'Just milk, thank you.' Oddly, the detective felt at ease in Jarrod's kitchen. The apartment had a calming and tranquil atmosphere. 'I'm sorry about Xiu, I didn't mean...' Her words faltered as she didn't know why she reacted so badly. Jarrod had done nothing wrong but he always managed to put her on edge. She knew there was something about him that wasn't right, but she couldn't put her finger on it. *Frustration manifesting as distrust?* she queried herself.

'She's a big girl. I'm sure she has shrugged it off by now.'

Sitting at a huge and rugged kitchen table, Detective Widcombe felt underneath to see if the solid looking slab of copper was real or just a veneer. Not finding an edge or groove, she tried to lift the table a little with one hand. 'Is this a solid block of copper?' she asked as she ran her finger along the delicate copper branches etched into it.

'Yes.'

'Sorry.' She apologised for being inquisitive. 'Look,

thank you for what you did the other day. If you hadn't stepped in when you did...' The detective paled at the thought. Her head turned as she followed copper tree branches around the exterior of the room. *What is it with copper leaves?* She didn't like to ask for fear of offending him.

'Have you come up with any leads? Was your attack related to Martin's death?'

Looking at Jarrod, she felt a sudden chill; hugging the warm cup to her chest she decided to chance confiding in him. *He seems to care, and he did save my life,* she thought. 'I'm not on Martin's case, I am only a Detective Constable, I investigate burglaries, not murders.' She took a sip of her tea, pausing, collating the information in her mind before saying it out loud. 'They found the man you hit with your umbrella. He hid his face from the cameras, but I saw it when he attacked me.'

'Is he talking?'

'No, he's dead. It's the violent way that he died that makes us think the driver of the van was also the person who killed Martin.' She sipped from the cup once more, not for the refreshment but to hide the slight tremor in her hand. The thought of how close she had come to being the killer's captive made her heart race.

'I gave a sketch of the driver to your colleagues.'

'Yes, it was quite impressive.' She smiled at Jarrod.

'We do believe that it was he who broke into Caster and Randle and placed the fake statue in your box.'

'I agree, the body shape and the way he moved was the same as the CCTV footage.'

'I think he is still after it and has been since it first appeared for auction. You heard about... erm...'. Detective Widcombe pulled out her notebook and flipped through the pages. 'Mario Smithe, the overseas buyer in Malaysia?'

Jarrod nodded. 'Yes. Johnathan Caster was upset about

it. Apparently, they were friends.'

'He told us too. Not because he thought it had any relevance, I think he was in shock and was just telling everybody. Anyway, Johnathan said that he had died a slow and painful death. The SIO in charge of the two murder investigations sent out a request to the Malaysian police asking if they suspected foul play.' Seeing Jarrod's eyebrow rise she added, 'Senior Investigating Officer. A report came back detailing the death of him — the auctioneer and seller in Malaysia.'

'How?' Jarrod looked up sharply.

'The seller was killed by Paraquat poisoning. Local officials were annoyed as it transpired the seller had a large stock of the herbicide and it's been banned in Malaysia since '02. I didn't catch his name as I only saw the despatch for a second. The auctioneer, a Mr Pappas, died from something called Scaphism. I couldn't see the details and I haven't had time to look it up,' she explained.

'It's an ancient Persian torture designed for the Greeks. Pappas is a Greek name meaning Priest. I'm not going to describe it Detective, it isn't very nice.' Jarrod pulled a few utensils from a nearby cupboard. 'I was about to eat before going out, do you want anything?'

'I could murder a bacon butty,' she confessed.

'Sorry, I'm mostly vegetarian.' Jarrod shrugged as an apology.

'Mostly?'

'Another time, it's a long story. I'll whip up something quick for us both,' Jarrod said as he measured some chickpea flour into a bowl. 'Sorry, this might smell while it cooks but it's worth it,' he said, waving a sachet of Kala Namak salt.

'Mum uses it all the time. She still holds to the old traditions. She always cooks traditional Indian cuisine when I visit. I'm more a product of western culture, nothing wrong with a bucket of chicken thighs if you ask me.' Detective Widcombe pulled a face as the familiar eggy aroma from the sulphur salt wafted across the room.

'How did your attacker die?'

'Your blow damaged his liver and would have hospitalised him, but he died from complications caused by a half lobotomy. There was another similar death last week, a council warden. He was found not far from Caster and Randle.'

'Quite a productive killer you have there, Detective.'

'Not mine Jarrod. I'm only a DC, as I said. And, call me Sarala. I'm not on duty.'

'Sarala, meaning honest and also pine tree.' Seeing Sarala's questioning look at his knowledge of Indian culture, Jarrod explained, 'I spent a year exploring India. I learnt to speak Hindi and a few other languages, including Sanskrit of course. Most important in my profession.' He dished up a plate of vegan omelette in front of the young woman and said, 'Bon appétit.'

'If you don't mind me asking,' Sarala said between mouthfuls, 'what's with all the copper?' Then, pointing at her plate with the fork: 'This is really good.'

'Copper? Well, I like it,' Jarrod shrugged. 'It's been used for thousands of years for its durability and antibacterial properties. The branches around the outside walls also form a faraday cage, preventing any electronic signals from entering.'

Concern showing on her face, Detective Widcombe extracted her mobile phone and grunted at the lack of signal. With a puzzled expression she asked, 'Why?'

'Why not? I don't have a TV. I can pick up missed calls when I leave the apartment and those who are important in my life will visit me in person.'

Shaking her head, as if she couldn't imagine life without a television she asked, 'Netflix?'

'What?'

'Streaming TV over the Internet?'

'No. I read and I listen to music. This is my quiet place.'

'So, you stream your music then?'

'Vinyl, Sarala. No TV, no Internet, no phone,' Jarrod replied. 'Peace and quiet.'

'You're a hermit.' *Explains why you're so damned odd.*

Ignoring her comment Jarrod replied, 'You have miscalculated one thing, Detective. The auction was a closed, private affair. I could only obtain the catalogue through Caster and Randle. I suspect if the killer had known of the auction, he would have stolen the idol there. He obviously found out after the event and followed the trail here.'

'I agree.' Holding a fork of food up, the Detective nodded as she gulped down another mouthful. 'This is really nice. My mum would love you.'

Smiling, Jarrod commented, 'You never said how Martin died... did you manage to read the coroner's report?'

Sarala's face sagged as she thought of Martin's body. Looking at the last mouthful of food on her fork, she replaced the cutlery on the plate, suddenly no longer hungry. 'You saw as much as I did. He was tied over the width of the table to arch his back and stretch his muscles and tendons. The glistening pin heads were acupuncture needles, as you suggested. The body had bloated so much that they had been absorbed in. That's where it gets weird. The needles were contaminated with dog faeces, which caused the body wide infection and again, as you guessed, his body's immune system went into overload and destroyed itself.'

'Sepsis?'

The detective nodded as she moved the plate toward Jarrod. 'Martin's tendons in his arms and legs had ripped, his shoulders had been dislocated. We couldn't see that through the window, not with the angle of the body and the bloating. He died in pain, Jarrod. A lot of pain.'

Cleaning the plates in the sink, Jarrod said, 'I'm meeting Ronnie Bagnall in an hour, Martin's stepbrother. He has agreed to see me. The sister contacted him on my behalf.'

'Strangeways?'

'HMP Manchester, yes. When I phoned for advice on how to proceed, the officer on the phone became agitated when I called it Strangeways.'

'Yeah, they would. That's not a nice place, Jarrod.' The detective frowned. 'It's category A, meaning it houses the worst of the worst.'

'So why is Ronnie there then? He's just a thief.'

'Locals waiting for trial are sent there.' She waved Jarrod's next question away before he had a chance to voice it. 'I don't know, Jarrod. They just do.'

Chapter 9

As the taxi drew nearer HMP Manchester, Jarrod became quiet, almost sullen as he studied the exterior of the Victorian facade. A century and a half of corrupt souls had left a psychic mark on the area, the weight of which seemed to bear down on his shoulders.

'He won't tell you anything, Jarrod. You're wasting your time,' Detective Widcombe said.

'Someone killed his brother, Sarala. He'll want answers, he'll talk,' Jarrod replied in a gruff voice, the tension permeating from the prison seeping into him.

'Stepbrother,' the detective corrected.

'Best leave your brolly, sir,' Bert stated as he pulled the taxi to the kerb. Turning around in his seat, he handed Jarrod a deep tray. 'Your items will be safer here, sir.'

'Do you come here often, Bert?' Detective Widcombe asked.

'Regular miss. Never been in myself, nor do I wish to. There's an essence that clings to people when they leave, you can smell the prison on them. Sweat, fear, desperation, drugs and disinfectant — similar to hospitals, but more menacing, if you know what I mean.'

Detective Widcombe nodded watching as Jarrod emptied his pockets. Four coins with his leaf design, a copper torch, an ornate pipe, a retro phone, a large bar of mint cake and a moderately full money clip. Jarrod peeled a wad of notes from the clip before tossing it onto the tray.

'See you in an hour, Bert. Please take Detective Widcombe home.'

The evil atmosphere inside of the prison tugged at the dark areas on Jarrod's aura and a headache formed as soon as he stepped out of the taxi. He could feel the depravity of the inmates, almost taste the corruption of their souls. Emotions flashed through his mind as he fought to control his inner demons, his dark past loomed up wrestling once again to take control. Jarrod steeled his will against such notions and continued forwards, stepping over the threshold. The light from the sun seemed to fade and wither as it too passed through the doorway. Bright incandescent lights illuminated the interior with a sickly off-white radiance. To Jarrod, the room was still dark and foreboding.

The process of entering the prison was as he had been informed by Ronnie's sister. After an identity check he was patted down for contraband, the dog paying no attention to him after an initial sniff. Jarrod deposited fifty pounds into Ronnie's prison account, as requested by his sister. He was led with the other visitors through a maze of passageways and a multitude of locked doors. The guards were neither polite nor rude but perfunctory, not caring about the visitors, only seeing them as a hinderance to the daily prison routine. Each visitor had the potential to upset an inmate. Not all inmates could drop their hard prison persona they'd developed to survive in such a brutal environment. This then caused confusion when their loved ones arrived: instead of love and gratitude, a cold empty void would sit between husband and wife. Anger often flared from frustration and from there, violence often ensued.

Jarrod was shown to a table in a communal room. A selection of inmates talked to their visitors with hushed tones. The odd bark from the guards prevented the couples from holding hands. Ronnie Bagnall entered the room, escorted by a burly guard. Jarrod knew he was Martin's stepbrother, the resemblance was uncanny. Ronnie's face was swollen, his lip split and the right eye bruised and bloodshot.

'Mr Wentworth?' Ronnie asked as he sat down.

'I'm sorry about your brother, Ronnie. I talked with him on several occasions.' Jarrod refrained from asking about the recent injuries.

'We didn't always see eye-to-eye, Mr Wentworth. But he was my brother.'

'What have the police told you about it?'

'Nothing much. They came swaggering in, as they do, wanting to know who he was mixed up with. The bastards didn't even bother to offer condolences or anything.'

'I'm sorry, I don't know much but as promised, I will tell you what I do know.' Jarrod paused for a second, only continuing when Ronnie gestured for him to do so. 'There was a break-in at Caster and Randle, where he worked, and it may be that he gave the thieves the information they needed to bypass the security. Camera locations, types of locks, you can guess the rest. Nothing has been proven. Unfortunately, that same night a professional thief struck, too. It was the thief who tasered your brother. I saw the footage. He questioned Martin before knocking him unconscious. He was after a certain item, one that the first set of thieves took by chance, a statue, an ancient relic. I believe this second thief killed your brother, trying to find out the whereabouts of the first set of thieves. I am convinced he would have returned and killed Martin on the night of the burglary if he had found the statue.'

'What do you want from me?' Ronnie asked, his voice broke at the thought of his stepbrother dying.

'I need to know the name of the gang that broke in that night. I believe that Martin's killer is after them. If I can find them first, I can set a trap for the killer.'

'Why do you care? You said it yourself, you only spoke to Martin a couple of times.'

'It was my statue, Ronnie. Caster and Randle bought it on my behalf from Malaysia. I feel responsible.'

'You just want your fucking statue back, you fucking bastard! Don't give me all this crap about finding Martin's killer. You're just as bad as the pigs.' Ronnie fell silent, his hands on the table-top, fists clenched tight.

Jarrod remained silent, giving Ronnie time to ruminate on the situation. Looking around the room, Jarrod didn't wish to view the other prisoners with his mind's eye as he knew most of them would have black auras. A few like Ronnie stood out, run-of-the-mill thieves on remand, all battered and bruised. Jarrod shook his head as he guessed which of the inmates were murderers. *They would not be alive on my world,* he thought to himself. Killing was permissible of course, if done legally: duelling or self-defence. Nor would Ronnie's attackers have managed to inflict such wounds on a fellow prisoner. Prisons on Prushal used Spectral Guards to maintain order and prevent violence. The wraith-like guard was usually an experienced prison officer who was near retirement, brave men and women who volunteered for this special duty. The volunteers were medically killed to release their spirit, which is then magically bound to the prison. The body of the volunteer guard is held in a state of suspended animation for three years, after which the guard is brought back to life, commencing their retirement with a substantially enhanced pension. The Spectral Guard can feel anger, rage, violence and hatred as it occurs in the building and instantaneously appear at the beginning of altercations. The ghost serves out rough justice, which is equal or greater to the offender's intended infraction; the mere touch from the spectre causes physical damage to living tissue. Only new inmates are ignorant or foolish enough to risk the wrath of the Spectral Guard. They are often goaded into physical violence by the prison's lifers as a form of entertainment.

'Ronnie, anyone in possession of the statue is a target for the killer. He has killed six people that I know of and tried to kidnap a young detective the other day.' Sensing that he had caught Ronnie's attention, he added, 'He's looking for the person who stole the statue. He's dangerous and he must have thought Detective Widcombe knew how to find the gang.'

'Does he?'

'She,' Jarrod corrected. 'No. The thieves wore hoodies and hid their faces from the cameras. The police have no idea who they are.'

'I can't help you Mr Wentworth,' Ronnie said as he rose from the prison bench.

'Can't or won't?'

'I don't know who the thieves are. Martin owed money is all I know. I was caught doing a job to bail him out. He was not a bad person Mr Wentworth, but he liked his Greyhounds. Spent all of his money on the races.' Before asking the prison guard to be taken back to his cell, Ronnie turned and asked, 'What did they take? The thieves, besides the statue?'

'Jewellery and trinkets from the shop and storeroom. A lot of gold, cheap historical replicas for the tourists. They knew where to look and how to bypass the security. Like I said, they had inside information.'

To the prison guard's annoyance, Ronnie returned to Jarrod. 'The gold, Mr Wentworth, would have been melted and sold to any number of shops. You don't get as much that way but it's safer. I'm sorry I can't help. I honestly don't know anything. It may be worth checking the local pawn brokers to see if they were offered any of the jewellery. One or two of the scrotes might have kept a handful of items to sell privately.'

Jarrod rose to leave as Ronnie started to walk away. 'May I ask how you sustained your injuries?' Jarrod casually pointed at the man's face.

'Shower, Mr Wentworth. I slipped in the shower.' Ronnie's head turned to sweep the room looking for eavesdroppers. 'There are plenty of ways of hurting yourself here.' Ronnie didn't look back as he left, leaving Jarrod standing by the bench table feeling as if he had wasted his time.

Chapter 10

The sun was high in the noonday sky when the taxi dropped Jarrod off at the gates of Alexandra Park.

'I'll be 'onest Mr Wentworth, there was a time I would have refused to bring a man such as yourself to Moss Side,' Bert the driver said as Jarrod alighted the cab.

'I've been in worse places, Bert.'

'You don't normally see this down here.' The driver nodded towards a man wearing a religious placard. People entering the park were veering away from him and his *"Jesus died for you"* sign. 'Takes all sorts I suppose.'

'I'll be an hour, Bert.'

'Right oh, sir.' Bert tipped his flat cap. 'I'll be back at 1 p.m. sharp.'

The street preacher ranted from the height of his portable step. 'The Bible says Jesus Christ came to call sinners to repent. If he were here now, he would tell you sinners to repent. I ask you to repent. One day you're all going to die! You're going to die and you're going to Hell!' The middle-aged woman he pointed at quickly shuffled her two children to the safety of the park's gate. 'You're all going to die, repent while you have the chance!' Turning towards Jarrod, the man held his Bible high. 'I am preaching the word of God. Sir, you in the burgundy suit, are you a sinner?'

Jarrod, unafraid of the self-righteous man on the step, was walking the shortest route to the gate. 'I am!' Jarrod sensed a collective sigh from the other pedestrians. They had been given a reprieve while the zealot homed in on Jarrod.

'The eyes of the Lord are on you. You must repent!' The man waved his Bible at Jarrod. 'The Bible says the Lord is angry at sinners, you must repent before it is too late!'

Jarrod stopped before the man and stared. He did not wish to use his inner eye to see the man's aura; those who shouted the loudest were normally either empty of knowledge or trying to hide from their own sins. Instead, he reached out and took the man's book. It was an old Bible. Jarrod recognised it as a rare edition, which proved to him the preacher was an idiot for bringing such a valuable item into the street and that he coveted material objects. Jarrod spoke calmly, as if he were instructing a child. 'This is a man-made construct.' Jarrod waved the Bible back at the irate preacher. 'This was written by man. It is a tool of subjugation. Your God did not write this!'

'Blasphemer!' The preacher screamed and grasped with futility at his book, almost losing his balance and falling off his prominent perch.

'You are not worthy of preaching! What gives you the right to come here and preach to me?' People turned as Jarrod's words bellowed.

'I have dedicated my life to God. I serve the Lord. I am his scholar and have studied the good book for over thirty years,' the preacher shouted back, not sure if he was glad for Jarrod's interaction or not.

'You have studied one book and call yourself a scholar? A *scholar*? Do you think those students —' Jarrod pointed at a group of late teenagers who had stopped to watch the spectacle, with phones held high, recording the drama — 'would pass their courses if they only read one book?'

'The Bible is the only book I need to read because it is the book of God.'

'And so were the ones before it. Have you studied the Codex Cairensis, the Aleppo Codex or the Dead Sea Scrolls? Have you learnt the ancient forms of Hebrew, Arabic and Greek?'

'The Bible is the only book I need to read. It is the book of God. It shows the way,' the preacher repeated even louder.

'It is one book written and controlled by a pervasive organisation that has dominated the populace of Earth for two thousand years. You should have read the original texts for yourself, learn to think for yourself. The events of your Old Testament were written down in Mesopotamia four thousand years ago; learn to read Cuneiform and study the Sumerian tablets — discover your true history for yourself.' Jarrod dropped the man's Bible on the floor, ensuring it fell flat as not to damage the tome. 'This is nothing more than a pyramid scheme. The heads of your churches languish in luxury while millions of parishioners starve. Find your *own* faith, man! If God is in your heart, you should not need to be told right from wrong. God does not need grandiose altars and churches; the true God will hear you wherever you go.' Jarrod reached out with his mind and drew in some of the ambient energy, allowing it to flow through his thoughts to be shaped into a spell. The repurposed energy was released towards the preacher, carrying Jarrod's commands. Jarrod inserted the desire to research, to learn, into the zealot's psyche. It was not a spell he could normally cast with success, but the man's mind was already gullible, open to suggestion and used to following blind instructions. Proper magical mind control was a doctrine all of its own — unpredictable and unreliable at best — Jarrod had only ever learnt to insert suggestions and reinforce them with persuasive conversation.

A few people clapped in appreciation of Jarrod's tirade on the preacher.

'You will burn for your sins!' the street preacher shouted as Jarrod walked away. 'Jesus died for you! Repent, before it is too late!' Retrieving his Bible from the floor, the preacher wiped it clean and held it to his chest for comfort.

'Quite a speech,' the now familiar voice of Detective Widcombe said from behind Jarrod.

'Detective Widcombe. Or may I call you Sarala?'

'Sarala,' she conceded. 'I'm officially on sick leave.' The detective held her hand out to greet Jarrod. 'I wondered what you discovered yesterday at the prison.' Confusion clouded her face as Jarrod placed something in her palm instead of shaking her hand.

'It's the phone you accidentally misplaced in Bert's taxi. The one you used to track me here.' Jarrod smiled. 'I would have invited you, but the gentleman I am about to meet will not be happy if I turned up with a policewoman in tow.'

'I'm not sure you should be telling me that.' Concern crossed Sarala's face.

'Nothing untoward, Miss Widcombe.' Jarrod tested the title to see if Sarala corrected him. He knew many police who refused to wear wedding rings on duty.

'May I ask who?'

The inner smile at not being corrected broke on to Jarrod's face: *Not Married.* 'Barlow. Joseph Barlow,' he replied, trying to hide his grin.

'The fence? Jarrod! I'm trying to trust you and now you're meeting with a known criminal, a receiver of stolen goods and a thug to boot. Why? How do you even know him? Argh!' the detective wailed.

'Funny story really.' Jarrod pointed at a park bench. 'Let's sit. I have five minutes or so. Joseph brings his niece here every Thursday to feed the ducks.'

'Joseph Barlow brings his niece here to feed ducks. Are you kidding me? Joseph the Hammer has a niece?'

'Yes. He's a changed man. Although I believe he still hits people with a hammer if they break his rules.'

'Jarrod, for Christ's sake, you can't trust this man. He's dangerous.'

'Do you want me to tell you the story or not?'

Detective Widcombe fell silent with a stern look on her face and nodded.

'Good. About six years ago I was politely asked by two large men to attend a meeting with Mr Barlow. He had a dubious relic that he believed was cursed. The item was embellished with a crude back-story, which stated that whoever defiled the temple of Hurbar would wither away starting with the hands and feet. It was total nonsense of course. There is no Hurbar and the terracotta statue was a forgery, the sort of thing created in Victorian times for gullible tourists. He insisted on showing me his feet. It was clear to anyone who studied any form of medicine that he was suffering from the onset of gout. You must remember that back then, Joseph was grossly overweight.' Jarrod paused while a couple walked past. 'I performed a moderately good rendition of a Tibetan ritual for good health, broke the statue and informed him that he needed to adhere to the Buddhist way to ensure the curse never returns. I also enforced a strict Indian based vegan diet on him. He lost ten stone and is much healthier for it.' Jarrod omitted the fact that he also used his magic to alleviate the gout until the diet brought it under control.

'Jarrod, he still hurts people and he still orchestrates burglaries and sells stolen property.'

'He's always going to be a criminal, Sarala. But now he only hurts people who deserve it and he will no longer take items from a job if someone gets injured. I'd take it as a win if I were you.'

'You're unbelievable. You lied to Joseph Barlow, a man who will bludgeon you to death with a hammer if you so much as sneeze in the wrong direction. Are you mad?' she hissed.

'Keep your voice down!' Jarrod patted her knee as he spoke. 'I'm trusting you with this, it's confidential. So, no passing it on to your colleagues,' he warned.

'So why are you meeting with him?' Sarala asked, trying to contain her annoyance.

'I'm hoping he knows who stole the items from Caster and Randle. I'm sure some of the jewellery will have come his way.'

'And you're okay with this? You're a director of Caster and Randle and you're happy for Barlow to be selling your items?'

'No, I'm not happy. But the recovery of the items is in your hands and if you fail, well, we have insurance to cover the loss. I don't care about the gold trinkets they stole — it's the idol that worries me. Someone believes it's genuine and they are willing to go to great lengths to obtain it.' Standing, Jarrod declared, 'It's time to see Joseph. I need you to leave,' Jarrod indicated with his hand towards the park's gate.

Nodding, the off-duty detective stood. 'Will you tell me what he says?' She fixed her hazel eyes on Jarrod's.

Jarrod smiled. She was truly beautiful and relentless. 'I promise that if there is anything tangible to report, you will be the first to know.' Jarrod studied her form as she walked away. When not on duty the cut of her civilian clothing accentuated her figure. 'Sarala,' he shouted. 'Meet me at Caster and Randle in the morning!'

Raising a hand above her shoulder to indicate she had heard Jarrod, Sarala continued walking away.

She walks differently when not on duty, Jarrod noted to himself, watching as the detective's hips swished delicately from side to side.

'Jarrod, nice to see you again.' Joseph the Hammer greeted Jarrod as he approached the park bench. Joseph did not stand or offer his hand. 'I'm glad to see you came alone.' The man's tone changed, almost threatening.

'Miss Widcombe had a couple of urgent questions. She has left the park.'

'I hope the detective has recovered from her ordeal, Jarrod.' Joseph moved his paper off the bench and offered the space for Jarrod to sit down. 'Don't be surprised, Jarrod. I keep a close eye on the current affairs, more so if I know the people involved.'

Jarrod mocked a humbled expression. He had seen Joseph's man pretending to read a newspaper near the main entrance. The stooge lacked the necessary covert skills for such a task and his surreptitious use of his phone to photograph Jarrod and Detective Widcombe had been laughable. 'She's eager to find her attacker,' Jarrod explained.

'Does she know why you have come here today?'

'She took your name seriously Joseph, there was no point in lying.'

Joseph chuckled. 'I bet she did.'

A young girl with pigtails ran to the bench, waving a small paper bag at her uncle. 'The duck ripped my bag,' she complained with a pout. Her forlorn look eliciting another parcel of bird food from the nefarious criminal. Another of Joseph's men stood near the pool, watching the girl like a hawk.

'She's growing,' Jarrod commented.

'Too fast,' Joseph nodded in agreement. 'I have met with one of the men that attacked your detective friend. I assume that's why you're here?'

'Who and when?' Jarrod took a deep breath to calm himself, surprised as his emotions flared. He felt a primordial rage at the mention of men who had hurt the detective.

'The one that turned up dead, he visited the office last week asking for jewellery that matched the items from the Caster and Randle job. Flashed some money around, pretending to be a PI. We couldn't help him, not that I wanted to. I recognise a crook when I sees one. Plus, my associates know not to hit your gaffs or if they do, not to bring their stuff to me.' Seeing a raised eyebrow on Jarrod's face, he explained. 'It's good business etiquette, Jarrod. Plus, I've seen you fight. And I don't mean that night you brought my men back to me all bruised and feeling sorry for themselves. I've seen you deal with thugs. I saw what you did to that mugger last year. Vicious you are, Mr Wentworth. Under that veneer of civility is a man I can respect. You protect what is yours with a controlled ruthlessness.' Joseph put his hand out and touched Jarrod's arm. 'Don't get me wrong Jarrod. I've watched you help an old dear across the street, dropping money in her bag and then go after the pocket robber that slipped her purse. You broke his hands. Old school you is, Jarrod. A man knows where he is with a bloke like you.'

'I like things orderly Joseph,' Jarrod said. 'Sometimes people need correcting if they've taken the wrong path.'

'You use that brolly like I use my hammer. Nobody expects that, not from someone dressed like you. As I said, I told my crews not to bother you and yours, don't want them turning up with broken hands and elbows, do I? No use to me then. Plus it would put us in a difficult position.' Joseph cast a warning glance at Jarrod.

'I would ask before educating any of your men, Joseph, to be polite.' Jarrod smiled.

Joseph burst out with laughter and slapped Jarrod's knee. 'Old school gent, Jarrod, as I said.' Tears of mirth escaped from the corners of Joseph's eyes.

'I'm also after the gang who broke into Caster and Randle,' Jarrod said.

'No idea. As I said, they all know not to approach me if they steal from my friends.'

'Damn. You don't know anything about the robbery?' Jarrod's voice was hollow with disappointment.

'No, but I do know who has disappeared. Haven't seen or heard anything from the Razor Crew for over a week. Word is they've gone to ground. I'll get their last known location sent to you in the morning,' Joseph promised.

The little girl returned with an empty bag. 'All gone, Uncle. Can we go to the swings now, please?'

Chapter 11

The three Razor Crew youths squirmed in their bonds when they saw their captor returning, the man's peaked cap shading his eyes. It was a fruitless exercise; their hands were fastened behind their backs with stout cable ties and their ankles and thighs bound with silver duct tape. The man never smiled whilst in their presence, never raised his voice. He made no threats and was devoid of all emotion. For some unknown reason that their adolescent minds couldn't fathom, this scared the young men even more.

Placing a cardboard box on the table, the capped man pulled a kitchen chair forward and sat facing the three. He watched them for a minute. The air in the kitchen smelt of sweat and urine, the middle one of the three having defiled himself. The man in the cap removed the gag from the first in the row.

'The Razors are gonna kill you, man! You stupid messing with us! We gonna cut you, you'll bleed out and we'll leave you to die.'

The tirade of threats continued for several minutes. They meant nothing to the man in the cap. Empty threats from an ignorant uneducated imbecile — bravado nothing more. 'Whose house is this?' he asked, his accent declaring him foreign.

'Gonna slice you up man! Gonna feed you bits of yourself.' The young captive continued shouting threats, ignoring the question.

With a sigh, the man in the cap stood up to retrieve a wide hose and a funnel from the box. The hose was lubricated with engine oil, the smell was a pleasant distraction from the scent emanating from the young males. 'Eighteen, nineteen? How old are you?'

The sight of the hose shook the young man for a second, 'Seventeen,' he replied, staring at the hose.

'I asked you a question before and you didn't answer. You are now going to serve as an example to your friends.' Lifting the youth's chin, he held the boy's nose and mouth to prevent him from breathing. When the youth's struggle became frenzied, the man in the cap released his hold on the young man's mouth and forced the tube down his gasping throat. The capped stranger paid no heed to the choking sounds and tears streaming from terrified eyes. 'You live by the blade you die by the blade.' A jar of craft blades in a viscous liquid was ceremoniously tipped into the funnel. The man made sure the other two captives could see what fate was befalling their friend. Pulling the funnel from the young man's throat, he re-inserted the gag to prevent another tirade of inane insults.

Placing the funnel and the empty jar on the kitchen table, the stranger pulled two more jars from the box and placed them at the edge of the table, making sure to rattle the contents in the thick poisonous liquid. The smell of urine in the room increased as the third captive wet himself. The man walked over to the middle youth and removed his gag. 'I am going to ask you a few questions in a minute and I expect you to be truthful and polite. Do you understand?'

The young man nodded, too afraid to speak.

'First, I have to attend to your friend.' Kneeling down the man cupped the first captives head and whispered into his ear. Firstly, he spoke in Canaanite — an ancient language that predates the pharaohs of Egypt — and then he translated it as best as he could and spoke it out loud for the Razor Crew members to hear. 'Selgroch, Mistress of the dark, defiler, most unclean, devourer of children, I send you this sacrifice. May this soul sustain you, may his torment please you. I worship you. I prostrate myself before you and whimper at your feet. I am unworthy.' The youth screamed into his gag as the capped man repeatedly punched him in the stomach. 'May my efforts please you.'

Minutes passed as the man remained kneeling next to the crying youth, his hand still cupping the back of his head. With his eyes closed, the stranger's lips moved in silent prayer. The two other members of the Razor Crew stared and squirmed on the floor, straining to break the tape holding their legs.

Selgroch didn't manifest herself into the pitiful dwelling. The man was not surprised. She rarely appeared outside one of her sanctified chapels and then only when the sun was below the horizon. He would obtain the lost idol for her soon and receive her bloodied blessing. Of the original thirteen unholy statues, only six remained in possession of the sacred order. The others were either destroyed or obscured from detection by their proximity to other religious relics or hidden away on ground consecrated by the false gods that came after Selgroch. Each graven effigy of his Mistress contained the blood of her enemy Priestesses, each surviving idol formed the heart of an unholy church. In the old days, when the world was forming, many creatures of the dark stirred amongst the fledging humans, each competing for dominance. Snapping out of his reverie, the unholy disciple asked, 'Whose house is this?'

'His sister's.' The middle captive nodded his head towards his dying companion.

'She is in the front room, dying. She cannot help you. Do you understand?'

'Yyyess. Please mister, we didn't do nothin'. Arghhh!' The captive choked as strong fingers dug into the soft flesh of his throat and squeezed his trachea, the sensitive nerves around his windpipe overloading his mind with pain.

'Be quiet,' the man ordered. 'Who has the statue that you stole from Caster and Randle?'

'I wasn't there, I don't know. Please, Mister. I don't know,' the bound captive pleaded. Seeing the strange man lift the funnel and jar off the table, he screamed. 'The fucking dyke, she took it! I wasn't there, it was Hellcat! Please, don't hurt me.' Tears streamed down the young man's cheeks as the funnel advanced.

'You had one chance and you lied,' the unholy man said as he held onto the youth's nose and mouth. 'Selgroch, Mistress of the dark, defiler, most unclean, devourer of children, I send you this sacrifice. May this soul sustain you, may his torment please you. I worship you. I prostrate myself before you and whimper at your feet. I am unworthy.' The stranger didn't wait before he started punching. As soon as the jar's contents were deposited, he struck his victim's stomach. The youth screamed into his gag, blood frothing around the rag. 'May my efforts please you.'

The funnel and jar were returned to the table and the third victim's gag removed.

'She lives in Piccadilly, in the abandoned buildings behind the station. She moves around a lot as there are builders there. Please don't hurt me, Mister. Please...' he pleaded.

The man in the cap closed the UPVC door of the house and listened. The faint whimpering of three Razor Crew members could be heard if there was no passing traffic. Pushing the door open once more he entered the lounge where the woman lay on the sofa, turned the television on and choosing a music channel, he increased the volume.

Pulling the door closed once more he was satisfied that those inside would not be discovered until it was too late to save them. Locking the door with the woman's keys, the stranger tossed them into the bushes. Pulling a crinkled hand-rolled cigarette from his pocket, the man walked along the garden path enjoying the coolness of the evening breeze against his light olive skin. He was a Knight of Selgroch, he performed her bidding. In return, she fed him in the blood blessing and his life was extended.

Chapter 12

'Please take a seat,' Archie Randle offered as he showed Detective Widcombe into Johnathan's office.

'Jarrod,' she greeted, seeing him sat behind the desk.

'Sarala.' Jarrod stood, a broad smile lighting up his face. 'Have you seen the news?'

'News?' Jarrod looked puzzled.

'For God's sake get a TV and keep up with the world,' Detective Widcombe admonished him. 'Three Razor Crew members were found near death last night and the sister of one of them has been lobotomised. Sound familiar?'

'Joseph was right then... he said it might be the Razor Crew. He said they've gone to ground.'

'Or they're all dead.' Widcombe sat down in the proffered chair. 'Did he give you an address?'

Before Jarrod could speak, Johnathan Caster entered the room.

'Some scally dropped this off at the reception for you.' Johnathan handed Jarrod an unprinted business card containing two lines of handwritten text. 'Cheeky devil had the audacity to compliment us on the new security we're having installed. *"Tough to crack they is,"* is what he said to

Betty on the front desk.'

'I'd take that as high praise Johnathan and no, I won't explain.'

'What does it say, Jarrod?' Detective Widcombe asked.

'Under Mayfield station and a post code.' Jarrod turned the card over then lifted it towards the light hoping for something else to appear. Disappointed, he handed it to Detective Widcombe.

Turning her phone to show the others the google map, Detective Widcombe proclaimed, 'The post code doesn't match the old railway station. It's an old factory, north of Mayfield near the canal. That area's been abandoned for years,' she said.

Archie Randle pulled an Ordnance Survey map of Manchester from his desk and marked the two locations in pencil for them all to see. 'When are we off then?'

'We?' Jarrod asked.

'Come on old boy, this is dash-exciting you know.'

'You're all staying here,' the detective instructed, pulling out her phone.

'We should be safe enough, Sarala. We can have a scout around the outside and call in your colleagues if we see anything.'

'Are you kidding me? They're thugs. They don't have the moniker of the Razor Crew because they are clean shaven. They'll cut you for so much as looking them. I'm sorry Jarrod. I'm going to have to hand this over to the SIO.'

'Senior Investigating Officer,' Jarrod explained to the other two.

Detective Constable Widcombe stood and paced the office as she passed the information back to the station. Whomever she was speaking to was not amused when she could not explain where the information had come from.

'They're too busy to chase up a lead from an anonymous source.' She fell back into her seat, deflated. After a moment's thought, she looked up. 'Recce?' she asked Jarrod, apologetically.

Chapter 13

'I can't see them using this place Jarrod. It may be derelict but it has a steady footfall of train buffs,' Detective Widcombe commented as the taxicab pulled up outside the two storey building. 'It's hard to seal off a place like this: the main building, maybe, but not the yards.'

'The Manchester International Festival used this place for a music event a couple of years ago,' Bert said, looking in the rear-view mirror. 'I dropped many a scantily dressed lass off that night. I took two of them to the hospital shortly afterwards.' Bert's bushy brows dropped as he remembered the events. 'They don't watch their drinks, Mr Wentworth. Spiked they was.'

'It's a familiar story nowadays, Bert,' the detective agreed. 'Boys are too lazy to wine and dine a lady. Why bother when you can drug her. Bastards.'

'Bert, are there any tunnels under here, catacombs maybe?' Jarrod asked.

'It's Manchester, sir. There's always tunnels, cellars, and the station has arches under the tracks, of course.'

'This place is huge, Jarrod,' the detective commented. Shivering suddenly, she asked, 'Can you turn the heat up, please Bert? I'm chilled.'

Jarrod smiled. Sarala had picked up on his use of magic again. A small un-obscuring spell, he could not tell Detective Widcombe what it revealed as it would cause too many questions.

'Drive us round the block Bert. Slowly,' Jarrod instructed.

The cab turned down the side of the dishevelled train station, following the poster clad brickwork which eventually gave way to a steel gate and fencing. The interior of the yard was immense and Jarrod called for Bert to stop the car.

'Jarrod?' Widcombe questioned.

'Look at the graffiti.' Jarrod nodded to a freshly sprayed tag. The obscure wording of the artist's insignia was irrelevant, it was what it was covering that caught Jarrod's eye. This painted vandalism was simpler than the one he had seen at the front. He hoped Detective Widcombe could discern the underlying image.

'They're not here,' she said after a few seconds. Someone had sprayed over the Razor Crew's tag.

'If you don't mind, sir, what are we looking at?' Bert turned, hoping for an explanation.

'Under the white paint, Bert. You can just about make out The Razor Crew's 'RZR' insignia. If someone has painted over it, you can guarantee the Razors have gone,' Jarrod explained.

'They cut his fingers off, Bert, and I don't think they would stop there. Cut-throat razors and fear are the Crews' weapons of choice. They're into drugs, prostitution, extortion, theft, anything that turns a profit. Did you know they use kids as young as nine to carry out their crimes? The courts won't prosecute kids, and the gang leaders get away scot-free every time. Gang stabbings are on the increase — between that and drug addiction, most of the kids involved don't live long enough to finish school.'

The detective pulled a sad grin, showing her reluctant acceptance of the situation. 'That's why I don't want children,' she confessed. 'How can I bring a child into this? It's a war zone and the public don't know it.'

'You could always move out of the city?' Jarrod suggested.

'When Mum's gone, I'm emigrating. I'm thinking of New Zealand, somewhere quiet, a small town maybe. I've signed up for a locksmith course, it starts next year. It's a trade.' The detective pulled herself together, ashamed that she had voiced her fears and aspirations.

'I studied with the Māori for a couple of months. Lovely culture, friendly people,' Jarrod reflected.

'Lots of antiques, I should imagine.' The detective's cynicism returned.

'Relics and artefacts, Detective. An antique is something your great aunt might leave you. I have no interest in bric-à-brac.' Gently tapping Bert on the shoulder, Jarrod instructed: 'Let's go to the mill, Bert.'

Chapter 14

Bert stopped on the road near the entryway of an abandoned textile mill. He refused to go any further due to the debris on the disused tracks. The building itself was a huge, brick-built structure, four storeys high with all the windows boarded up.

'It goes back quite a bit. If they're here they will be using the side away from the road,' Sarala commented as she exited the cab. 'Bert, at the first sign of trouble call the police and get out of here.'

'Do as she says, Bert. No point you getting into trouble,' Jarrod confirmed to Bert's enquiring look.

'As you say, sir. I'll just turn the car around so I am pointing towards the main road. Don't forget your brolly, Mr Wentworth. You never know when you'll need it.'

Jarrod tapped the roof to let Bert know it was safe to leave. He and Sarala walked towards the rear of the abandoned building.

As they approached the far corner, Sarala pointed at a pile of cigarette butts littering the concrete floor and whispered, 'Someone's been here recently.'

'A look out?'

'Maybe? But where are they now?'

They continued on. The rear courtyard showed signs of frequent activity, paths in the weeds were worn down by frequent footfall.

'Road,' Jarrod pointed towards a track at the rear, the rough concrete was clear of debris.

'Come on, let's have a look inside. There's nothing here to report back to my colleagues.' She pulled a torch from beneath her jacket and Jarrod did likewise.

Inside, the building stank of stale urine. Graffiti adorned the walls as they followed a path that had been cleared through the detritus.

'Someone chased the crackheads away — those needles have been here for a year at least,' Detective Widcombe commented.

The clear walkway took them past a flight of stairs and deeper into the building, where what little sunlight shone through the boarded-up windows failed to penetrate. Jarrod peered up the stairway but it was blocked by machinery and rubble.

The next stairway was clear and the corridor beyond was filled with debris. Detective Widcombe shone her touch up the stairway, nodding to confirm that it was clear. The pair climbed upwards silently. On the second flight of steps, a cable with unlit lamps festooned the handrail. The landing to the first floor was blocked by large barrels of liquid, smaller containers were stacked along the walls of the stairwell leading up.

The detective sniffed the surrounding air. 'Smells like a chippy... Making bio diesel?' she questioned aloud. 'There's always a demand for cheap fuel.'

They climbed higher, up to the third floor. The nearby rooms were full of boxes that were stacked high. Fuel, drain cleaner, acid. Other rooms were full of old oil drums, the smell emanating from these made the duo dizzy.

'There's a meth lab around here, these are the waste drums. They create five times the amount of toxic sludge as they do meth.' The detective pulled her phone from her coat. 'Shit, no signal. We'll need to get closer to the windows. Should be this way,' she said, dashing off.

As they moved nearer to the outside wall, weak shards of sunlight pierced through the window boards illuminating the dust in the air. Entering a vast open room, the pair saw dirty tarpaulins suspended from the ceiling closing off a portion of the central area. The detective changed direction to investigate. Peering between two overlapping sheets, she exclaimed, 'Jackpot,' and stepped through. Light from the interior briefly illuminated the stout wooden planks of the floor.

'Sarala,' Jarrod whispered, before he too stepped through.

The interior of the tarpaulins were painted white, as was the floor. Car batteries powered the lamps. The area contained long laboratory tables full of equipment. Each had a sink that drained into a waste barrel.

'Power sockets... they must have a generator somewhere,' Jarrod commented, 'and extractors in the ceiling.'

'Jarrod, look!'

On the centre table, surrounded by paperwork, was an item about a foot high covered with a white sheet. The detective moved closer and carefully peeled the sheet back, so not to disturb any evidence.

'Shit!' She fumed when she saw the statue. It was a 3D plastic replica of Jarrod's figurine, the hand that should have been holding the snake's head had been redesigned. The middle finger was held high from a clenched fist.

Jarrod's hand grabbed onto hers a little too late, she had

already picked up the rough plastic figurine. The lamps flickered as something else drew power from the batteries.

Small blasts and whoomphs sounded around the building. Not the earth-trembling shocks of explosives; these were simple homemade devices igniting five litre containers of flammable liquid.

'That will teach you, you bastard,' Wilkins said.

The remaining members of the Razor Crew were in hiding. Wilkins — their current leader — had been on the phone with Josh when he had been attacked at his sister's house. Whatever the man was doing to the three members of his crew, it had shaken Wilkins to the core, their screams still echoed in his mind. He had listened to everything, the sound over the phone was muffled as if the device had fallen behind something. He heard Stoni cry as he answered all the man's questions, heard his screams for mercy as the man tortured him regardless. Stoni had told him everything — Wilkins heard the fear and desperation in his voice. It was Wilkins who called the police, something he'd never done before. He had initially given a false name and address when questioned and after answering endless questions, the police said they might send someone round later. They weren't taking his call seriously. Josh, Stoni, Flick and Josh's sister would die before the police acted. In the end, Wilkins called Detective Jeffers. The man was a bastard, he'd investigated the Razor Crew on several occasions. The detective hated the Razor Crew with vehemence because all of his witnesses changed their stories before they got to trial. Everyone who has a family can be manipulated. Detective Jeffers remembered Wilkins as they spoke over the phone.

He was unsure of Wilkins's motive, but he'd promised to send uniforms and an ambulance. It wasn't a pleasant conversation, but the policeman was honest and Wilkins knew he would keep his word.

It grated the leader of the Crew that he could not go and help his friends, but it would have taken an hour to get there and he had business to take care of. Hellcat had to be warned and a reception had to be prepared in the once secret lab. He'd listened as Stoni had given its location to the man, so Wilkins knew he had to act quickly. The Crew moved the valuable and irreplaceable items out of the building and setup the pyrotechnics that they had modified for another arson job. With only one stairway up to the third floor, the mystery killer would be trapped. Too high to jump, he'd die from the toxic fumes within minutes. Then Wilkins would have to deal with Hellcat, she had caused this. The girl had proclaimed the statue looked like her — she'd even stole a snake to parade around with.

Wilkins watched from the safety of a nearby building as black smoke escaped from the boarded-up windows. The upper floors were ablaze already, a huge explosion rocked the ground, blowing off the window boards, sending glass and debris flying into the air. *Biofuel and chip fat,* Wilkins thought to himself. He'd not had time to remove the drums. The huge fireball engulfing the building was impressive, but it had cost him a lot in lost revenue.

'Damn you Hellcat,' Wilkins cursed the girl.

He smiled at the thought of the murderer struggling to breathe. He secretly hoped the man tried to jump. Wilkins could finish him off as he floundered on the ground, all broken up and helpless from the fall.

A crunch of a stone behind him made Wilkins turn around. An antique Wilkinson Sword cut-throat razor appeared in his hand and he slashed at the air behind him.

High slash for the throat, diagonal across the chest and another across the stomach, forming their signature 'Z' insignia. There was nobody there.

A hand appeared from the shadows; an arc of electricity burned the skin on Wilkins's neck.

A stranger dressed in black with a foreign accent asked, 'Was that meant for me?' The light from the building cast an eerie glow to his dark-skinned face. 'Not very hospitable of you, Mr Wilkins.'

The man's booted foot struck Wilkins's head, rendering him unconscious. The capped man had discovered Josh's phone as he was preparing the third sacrifice. The phone was, as befitting a criminal, on silent, but the screen had glowed for a moment as a text message arrived. It mattered little. He'd extracted the information he needed and had left four struggling and tormented souls for his god. The cocktail of Warfarin-based rat poison would prevent their lacerated insides from congealing and poisons would prevent any medical aid from saving their lives — the medics would only prolong the suffering of his sacrifices.

The sound of a soft explosion alerted Jarrod and Detective Widcombe to the imminent threat.

'Stairs!' The detective ordered.

Using their torches to find their way back to the stairway, they stepped backwards as the beams of light disappeared into huge plumes of acrid smoke that was billowing out of the stairway.

'There must be a fire escape,' she coughed. 'Head for the back.' She shivered as if suddenly cold, not comprehending that she was reacting to Jarrod's magic.

On his own world, Jarrod would rarely use magic for

illumination or a torch unless he was being charitable to unskilled magic users. He would cast, as he just did, a simple spell to increase the efficiency of his low light receptors in his eyes. Smoke was seeping through the wood flooring; the ceiling had already disappeared in a blanket of black toxic cloud.

'Sarala, we won't make it that way.'

'We have to try Jarrod,' she replied angrily.

'Look.' Jarrod cast a spell of illumination all around them. The acrid smoke swirled around an invisible barrier, almost angry as it attempted to smother the protective globe Jarrod had put into place.

'What the fuck?' Detective Widcombe stared at Jarrod and then back towards the smoke and held her hand out. It passed through an intangible barrier from their bubble of cleaner air into the black toxic cloud, she could feel the heat on her fingertips.

'Detective, I don't have time to explain. This bubble won't sustain us for long, the air will run out.'

'Jarrod?' The detective pulled her hand back and looked at her fingertips. Sticky soot clung to her flesh, the chemical smell assailed her nostrils. 'How?'

The building groaned as the heat caused the structure to expand. The smouldering floorboards beneath their feet started to buckle under the heat. *The floor below must be ablaze already*, Jarrod thought.

'We have to go,' Jarrod stated.

'How?' Detective Widcombe's mind overloaded with the impossible information she was processing. Like a computer caught in logic loop, her actions slowed while she fought her way out of the insanity that threatened her beliefs.

'I'm sorry Sarala,' Jarrod put his arm around the woman and pulled her in close, the smell of her perfume a delight against the backdrop of toxic air. Wrapping his arms around her body, he lifted her and stepped forwards. His foot did not land on the smouldering floorboards of the meth lab.

Chapter 15

'Get off me!' Detective Widcombe shouted, struggling to free herself from Jarrod's arms. Her legs were moving, but she was not walking away from his embrace. 'Jarrod! Stop it! Now!'

Jarrod held his arms out wide and stepped back two paces.

'What the hell's wrong with you? Are you trying to cop a feel before we die?' Anger flared the detective's nostrils, her eyes wide. She fell silent for a second, realising they were no longer in the burning factory. 'Where the hell are we? Did you drug me?' Her phone appeared in her hand as she attempted to step away. 'No signal? Is that you?' she screamed, 'do you have a signal blocker?'

Jarrod said nothing, there was nothing he could do to placate Sarala, she would not believe anything he said at this moment in time. She would have to realign her thinking. *Is this what it will be like when I try to explain to Arbon that he is not human?* he thought. Stepping back another space so as not to appear threatening, Jarrod noted the detective's emotions floundered from anger to bewilderment, to gratitude at not being burnt, and also disbelief.

'Where are we?' she snapped, turning a full circle as she spoke.

'Nowhe—' Jarrod changed his answer as not to appear evasive. 'We are standing in an area of existence that my people call Nowhere. It is the space between realities.'

'What? Have you drugged me? Am I tripping on something? Is it the fumes from the mill? I'm probably on the floor dying and I'm having a hallucination.'

'Tell me what you saw at the mill, Sarala, from the moment you took the statue.'

They both looked at the crude plastic representation in the detective's hand.

'I picked this up and the lights flickered. There was an explosion... No, it was the sound of something catching fire, more of a whoomph.' She looked at Jarrod. 'The smoke came in so quickly, something held it back. It was as if we were standing in a bubble. You found the light switch and we could see the smoke swirling. What was that?'

'There was no light switch Sarala. You felt what I did, you shiver every time.'

'Are we dead?' The detective tried to walk; she felt the ground beneath her as her feet landed step after step but she was no further from Jarrod than when she started. She tried to move away once again, staring at Jarrod all the while, daring him to follow her, a deadly threat hidden beneath her creased brow. The detective's legs walked, her feet pushed off with each step and yet she didn't move. 'Jarrod, are we dead?'

'No Sarala, I saved us from the fire. The Razor Crew laid a trap for the killer and we blundered into it.'

'How?'

'There are ways to pass from one dimension to another,

from one place to another. We are in the space between places.'

Jarrod smiled at the detective's determination to move. She stood on one foot, leaned forward and pushed her other leg out. She stood, legs wide for a moment before lifting the original leg off the floor. She was now one pace further away from Jarrod.

'So, I am not dead?'

'No.'

'Why can't I walk properly?'

'You have lived with the notion that there is always a floor beneath you. And so, your mind tells you there is a floor under your feet. You have made that real for yourself. What you perceive here is up to you. Nothing is real.' Jarrod crouched backwards and sat down.

'You're floating in mid-air!'

'So are you! There is no floor, there's no gravity, no air. You are breathing as a reflex, there is no oxygen here. Nor do you need it.'

'What the fuck are you talking about?' She stamped her foot on the ground. No sound emanated, but she felt the jolt of the solid surface beneath her foot.

'Think of having a step before you. Picture it in your mind, know it is there.' Seeing her bewilderment, he added, 'Please, humour me. Picture a step. Now raise your foot and step forwards thinking of it landing on the step.'

Detective Widcombe closed her eyes as she created a mental image of a step before her. She then opened her eyes and in shock as her foot landed on a solid surface seven inches higher than the floor. She moved her leg up, moved her weight forwards and she landed on an invisible step. She was now looking down upon Jarrod as he sat, floating in mid-air.

'Jarrod, I don't understand.' A flicker of panic crossed

her face, pushed back down by her logic. 'This can't be real.'

'You are taking this better than I thought, Sarala. I have brought students and faculty members here before now and some of them had mental breakdowns.'

'Who are you?' she asked as she stepped higher.

'My real name is Jarrod Bantau. I am from a place called Prushal. I am a wizard, a sorcerer if you prefer. I am a professor at the First University of Magic where I teach and study. I am currently studying humanity and the magical powers you once possessed.'

'Are you going to hurt me?' She stopped mid-step, her fearful face looking down at Jarrod.

'No!' Jarrod exclaimed with a hurtful tone in his voice. 'I consider you to be a friend, even if you do not trust me.'

'I always knew there was something wrong. I felt it.'

'You felt the magic Sarala, you are sensitive. There are still humans who wield magic, Wiccans for example. They borrow energy from nature. There are others far worse and there are many like you, sensitive. You can't understand what you feel and so you associate it with a bad feeling, it puts you on edge.'

'Why?'

'Why what?'

'Why have you brought me here?'

'You'd have died. I saved your life — twice now — three times if you count the fact that I healed the worst of your wounds before the medics arrived. You repeatedly bashed your head against the ground during the struggle.'

'I felt you. I felt you in my head. I thought it was a dream.' The detective sat down, mastering the thought process to hold her from the non-existent floor. 'So where are you taking me? Are we going to your planet? Pushel?'

'Prushal,' Jarrod corrected. 'No, you would be missed

and there would be too many questions. I would spend far too much time answering police questions and I am on borrowed time as it is. I have received instructions to return home.'

'We can't go back into the fire!'

'I can Step us outside of the building. We can say that we found a way out before flames took hold. My problem is you. You know about me now and I can't allow you to tell anyone about my abilities.'

'I won't say anything, they would never believe me.'

'I can't risk it, I'm sorry. Before I Stepped us out of the building, I cast a spell of secrecy. I will be too weak to cast it once we Step back to the mill. It takes a lot out of me.'

'You cast a spell on me, without my permission? You bastard! How dare you?!'

'Would you have preferred that I left you there?'

'What does this spell do?' Anger enlarged her eyes as she spoke.

'You will not be able to convey my secret to anyone else. You will only be able to speak to me about it and only when you are certain it is safe to do so. I can remove it once I return to Prushal, I doubt I will ever return to Earth.'

'Never?'

'My work is nearly done. I have studied your ancient civilisations, voodoo, witchcraft, satanic cults and demon worshippers. I have a few threads of investigation left and then there is nothing left to do,' Jarrod lied. *Damn you, Sarala.* Jarrod felt pressured, he needed more time on Earth to deal with his son, Arbon.

'Demons? They're *real?*'

Jarrod pulled a face. 'There are unlimited dimensions and most of the time the denizens never interfere with each other. A few — like myself — have discovered how to Step through, we call it the Wayfarer's Step. There are creatures out there that are pure malevolence; you'd call them demons. Thankfully for you they can't exist on your planet for long. But, long enough to convince the gullible that they are gods. There are many, Selgroch is one of them. Their worshippers cannot perform magic themselves; Selgroch taps into the universal energy for them and casts their spells. The cost is hideous: they offer their life energy, their very soul to the demons, It's even worse when they sacrifice the souls of others. We are energy, Sarala. Our souls are an adaptation of universal energy and we are meant to live on after our physical carriage disintegrates, our bodies. Demons destroy the soul out of malice, often after years of torture. If the soul is destroyed, the person ceases to exist. Your journey is over.'

'Slow down. This is too much to take in,' Detective Widcombe said, squeezing the bridge of her nose with her fingers.

'I'm sorry, I thought you'd understand. You have an exceptional mind.'

'You should know, you've poked around in there,' she spat, regret flashed across her face as soon as the words passed her lips. 'Sorry, Jarrod. That was uncalled for.'

Jarrod pulled a block of Kendal Mint Cake from his jacket. Breaking off a piece, he handed the bar to the detective. 'Want some?'

Detective Widcombe took a piece and handed the bar back. 'Oh God, there's no taste. How old is it?' she moaned.

'Ah, sorry, time slows down here. It would take weeks for the enzymes in your saliva to break down the sugar molecules. Similarly, the cake will sit in your stomach undigested until we return to Earth.'

'Then why did you offer me a piece?'

'Manners. I'll be weak when we return. It'll take me a

short while to recover from performing the Wayfarer's Step. The energy from the sugar cake kicks in pretty quickly once we get back and it helps. A little.'

'This is too much, Jarrod. Why? Why have you told me all this?'

'I couldn't leave you to die. If I knocked you out, you would have had a stream of questions. If you thought that you distrusted me before, you'd have been even more suspicious afterwards. Get over it. You're alive and I promise that in the near future, I will answer all of your questions.'

Rubbing her eyes with the palms of her hands, the detective asked, 'You said demons are from other dimensions, does that mean there is no devil or a God?'

'That's a question for another time, Sarala. Let's not confuse matters.' Jarrod stood up from his ethereal chair. 'We should go, we have spent enough time here as it is.'

'Is it dangerous here?'

'No, not as such. But you can get lost. There is a tide that carries us away from where we entered. The longer we stay the harder it is to locate the position we entered from.'

'I don't feel anything.'

'No, nor can you see the pathways. I can find Earth, but the longer we stay, the more the tide moves us away from the point where we entered. It will be easy enough to locate Manchester, but the Mill?' Holding out his hand Jarrod pulled the detective in close and said, 'Come on. You need to be holding onto me.'

Chapter 16

Jarrod collapsed as they Stepped back to Manchester, dragging Detective Widcombe to the ground with him. The air was thick with smoke and shadows danced amid the orange glow of the burning building. Fire engines, police and ambulances congregated on the front car park, their blue lights illuminating the area. Police, paramedics and spectators milled around, watching as firemen fought to contain the fire to the old textile building.

Detective Widcombe struggled under Jarrod's weight. *Jesus he's heavier than he looks,* she thought. The heat from the burning building seared at her skin. Coughing, she shone her torch towards her fellow officers. Through the haze of smoke and tears she saw silhouettes approaching. Dizzy from the fumes, her head spinning, she dropped the torch as two men wearing masks appeared before her. She tried to struggle to her feet, suddenly unsure of those approaching. Her head swam, confused, her vision blurred. Strong hands grasped her and lifted her away from Jarrod, her hand reaching out towards him before she lost consciousness.

Jarrod regained his strength in the back of an ambulance with oxygen enriched air filtering through the clear mask on his face. With his energy level returning to normal now, he looked around to find Detective Widcombe.

'Sarala?' Lowering the mask, he questioned the medic taking his blood pressure.

'Easy fella, you had quite a scare. Do you remember where you are?'

'The Old Mill, it was a trap, the fire. Where's Detective Widcombe?'

'She's in the other ambulance. She's ok, just on air, the same as you.' The man attempted to prevent Jarrod from standing.

'I'm fine,' he declared, removing the armband and sticky sensors off his chest. Jarrod had purposely Stepped out near the building, close enough for the police to assume they'd exited the mill. Unfortunately, since entering the premises, the wind he had hoped would keep the smoke and heat away from them, had changed direction.

Jarrod removed the air mask and stepped down from the ambulance to the disdain of the paramedic. A uniformed police officer attempted to intercept Jarrod, only to be ignored. Jarrod entered the second ambulance. The detective's blouse was open, showing her soft brown breasts covered by a delicate black bra. A paramedic was attaching sticky sensors to her chest.

'Sir, you can't be in here!' The driver of the ambulance appeared behind Jarrod.

Sarala opened her eyes and her stare softened when she saw Jarrod. She held her hand out, which he took, sitting next to her as he did so.

'Sleep, you're safe now,' he whispered, ignoring the

medic as he attempted to examine his patient.

'Are you kidding? My head's buzzing, I have a million questions.' She shivered as a coldness briefly passed over her. 'No,' she pleaded, 'don...' she fell into a healing sleep, induced by Jarrod's magic.

'Take care of her,' Jarrod looked at the paramedic's badge. 'Harold.'

'I'm trying to, sir. Please will you step out of the ambulance and let me get on with my job?'

Jarrod complied with the man's wishes, only to be besieged by the detective's colleagues demanding answers.

Chapter 17

Several of the copper leaves in the vicinity of Jarrod's door chimed. He looked up from his work and opened his mind to detect who had entered his corridor. He felt rather than saw Detective Widcombe shiver as her sensitivity to magic was triggered by his mind's eye wandering over her. Moving to the doorway to greet her, Jarrod found himself smiling.

'Sarala,' Jarrod greeted, his smile increasing as he opened the door, causing her hand to flail in the empty air as she attempted to knock on the metal surface. He held the heavy slab of copper covered oak open with one arm — it was designed to self-close otherwise.

'Are you ignoring my calls?' the detective asked in a gruff voice.

'Not at all. I have already informed you the copper mesh around my home blocks out all electromagnetic signals and as you now know of my abilities, I can inform you it also prevents any unwanted spells from entering.'

'We need to talk. You can't drop a bombshell like that on me and disappear. I... I can't talk about it with anyone else, it's driving me crazy,' she said. Stooping under Jarrod's arm, she entered his large open-plan lounge.

'Come in,' Jarrod joked. 'Coffee?'

'We don't have long, there's been another suspicious death. Oh, for God's sake! I'm in so much trouble and this 'thing' you've told me about isn't helping.' Sitting at one end of the huge L-shaped sofa, she idly inspected the assortment of artefacts that Jarrod had been examining. 'I can't sleep! For fuck's sake, I can't think straight!'

'When did they discharge you from the hospital? I thought they were keeping you in until tomorrow morning?'

'I discharged myself last night. We both know that I didn't inhale any toxic smoke, you kept it away from us. How could I stay in there with these questions going unanswered?' Holding up a double-bladed dagger she asked, 'What's this for?'

'I was hoping it was an Egyptian sacrificial blade from the fifth century BC, but it's just a circumcision knife from the same era. You said there has been another death. Where?'

'Near Piccadilly. Uniforms responded to a reported break-in at one of the pawnbrokers. The neighbouring shops said it has been closed for a few days. It concerned them as the owner hadn't lowered the security screens. Alas, it didn't concern them enough to investigate or call the police. Needless to say, someone broke in last night. Responding uniforms found the owner dead in the back office. He'd been dead for a couple of days.'

'Specifics? It could be important.'

'I'm on sick leave Jarrod. I only know about it because one of the uniforms called me. He knows I have an interest in this case. He, Bob, that is, he, erm... he fancies me. It was a pretext to ask me out.'

'And?'

'I said I'm still too ill, I don't have time for a date. I want answers off you, and I need to catch the bastard that tried to kidnap me.'

'I meant, are there any other leads in the case?' Jarrod removed the knife from her hands and carefully wiped her moisture from the handle.

'Oh,' she blushed. 'The evidence was compromised. One of the thieves threw up all over the corpse. All I know is that when the keyholder opened the safe to see what was stolen, there was jewellery from the Caster and Randle robbery in there.'

As she talked, Jarrod indicated that she should follow him to the kitchen. 'Coffee?'

'Sod that, Jarrod. I want answers, I want to talk about what happened.'

'Later, I promise.'

'Why are we skulking around in an alley?' Jarrod looked confused.

'We know the murderer was watching Caster and Randle from the ally across the road. I'm certain he will have done the same here.'

Looking at the police activity surrounding the pawnbrokers, Jarrod asked, 'So why haven't your colleagues cordoned off the area?'

'Because they're men, Jarrod. No offence, but you're all pretty dim at times. Most of my colleagues are old and tired, near retiring. Most will be happy to see the pawn shop close. We all knew the place fenced stolen items; proving it was always the problem. Look,' the detective pointed at a pile of hand-rolled cigarette butts on the ground. She stood behind the pile, her hand motioned throwing an imaginary stump and she stepped to her left. 'He stood here.'

The view of the pawn shop was unobstructed, while the gloom of the small alley combined with piles of rotting boxes hid the observer from view. Detective Widcombe picked up a cigarette butt using an evidence bag and pocketed it. 'I'll call Bob in a minute. I want to check out the rest of the alley first. With any luck there may be a camera covering one of the doors.'

A few yards further along, Detective Widcombe knocked over a stack of boxes. Debris splattered everywhere, beetles and cockroaches swarmed the area like a black tide as they sought shelter. Jarrod stood still.

'Come on,' Detective Widcombe admonished him, 'you don't have time to be squeamish.'

Jarrod remained still.

'Oh, for God's sake! You're not afraid of beetles are you?' She walked back to Jarrod and kicked at the boxes blocking his way, cockroaches crunching under her soles as she walked.

'Please, stay still and wait for them to find shelter.'

'You're kidding?' The detective laughed. 'They're just beetles, Jarrod.'

'They are life-forms, Sarala, and you should not extinguish them so lightly,' he said through clenched teeth.

'What?' Detective Widcombe looked at Jarrod as if he had gone mad.

'You've heard of Buddhism, right?'

'I've seen the monks in town with their orange gowns. Why?'

'They believe in rebirth, reincarnation. That the soul comes back and you may not always come back as a human. You could be an animal or insect.'

'Yeah, yeah, so one of them could have been my

grandfather?' Impatience showed in the detective's face. 'I watch TV.'

'Sarala, it's not that simple. I can see the aura of living creatures. I can see their souls when they pass over. Most of my people can.' Jarrod delicately removed a cockroach from his leg and placed it on a nearby box. 'We believe that all life is connected. New souls start off as simple organisms. As they are reborn, they move up to plants, insects, animals and eventually to Prushal, like myself, or human in your case. It takes thousands of years to progress, learning with every rebirth. Every life you knowingly take causes you harm. The weight of the beetles' deaths has now joined the other foul stains on your aura.'

'You are kidding me? Are you seriously telling me that I will go to hell because I stepped on a fucking beetle?' Turning to walk away she added, 'Fuck off, Jarrod.'

'Sarala, I am not a vegetarian because I dislike meat. I love a good steak as much as the next man. But I cannot be party to that animal's death. By paying for the meat I am implicated and therefore bear a portion of the blame.' Grabbing at her arm, he surprised himself. He didn't realise how much he wanted acceptance from the woman. 'I can prove it.'

'How?' The detective turned, shrugging off his hand.

'You are sensitive to magic. I can teach you to see auras, the energy given off by all living beings. There are a lot of humans who can see auras,' Jarrod assured her.

'And what's yours like Jarrod? Will I like what I see?'

'No.' Jarrod's voice was faint now, shame clouded his face and his eyes looked down. 'I killed three wizards when I was young. They attacked me and I retaliated. My aura changed immediately. Our deeds in life accumulate in our auras. The good and the bad, the dominating colour influences us every day, every minute of our lives. I was young and typically selfish as most young men are. I had not accrued enough pure deeds in my aura to offset such a stain. I nearly lost everything for one momentary lapse of judgement.'

Silence fell between the two as Detective Widcombe processed the notion that Jarrod was a murderer. The sound of city life seemed to fade into the background.

'What happened to you?'

'It was classed as self-defence, which it was. But I knew I could have incapacitated them, I could have put them to sleep, instead I chose to kill them. I spent a lot of time with counsellors trying to bring my aura back into balance or at least learn to live with its negative influence on my life. Eventually I regained some light, enough to make life palatable. I have endeavoured to redeem myself ever since.'

'Jarrod, I'm sorry.' The detective stepped forwards, being careful not to trample onto any more beetles. 'I didn't mean to bring up such bad memories.'

'These are constants in my life, Sarala. Reminders that life is fragile and what we do affects not just this reality, but the next life and beyond. My quest for knowledge is not because I hunger for power; it is born out of a desire to never be reborn. I don't want to return, wherever we go after death, I wish to remain there.'

'Who?' Detective Widcombe asked, not able to prevent the inquisitive side of her mind operating her mouth. 'Who was she? To cause so much pain, it has to be the loss of a loved one.'

Jarrod's face sagged as he looked at Detective Widcombe. Taking a deep breath before he spoke, he whispered, 'My wife, Sarala. But that is a story for another time.' His eyes glazed at the thought of his long-lost wife and his face forlorn.

'Sorry,' the detective apologised. 'Come on,' Sarala said,

trying to change the subject. 'If the murderer stood here, chances are he came from that direction.'

'I don't see how this helps us. Even if you find CCTV footage, we know what he looks like,' Jarrod said as he followed the detective through the trash filling the alley.

'If he came this way, then the investigation will be wasting resources. They will be trawling through traffic cameras on the wrong streets. If we can find him in a car, we'll get the registration. It doesn't matter if it's stolen, the next time he pops up on camera we'll have him.'

'Sarala, wait up,' a voice from behind them called out.

'Bob, what are you doing here?' Detective Widcombe answered in surprise.

'You need to go. Chief Inspector Walker saw you enter the alley. He's fuming that you've turned up at an active investigation while on leave.'

'Shit.' Detective Widcombe handed the evidence bag to the constable. 'He was standing there. You also need to check the cameras in the next street.' Seeing Bob's condescending look, the detective apologised. 'Sorry, of course you will.' She turned to Jarrod. 'Jarrod this is Sergeant Robert Dowery. Bob, Jarrod.'

Jarrod held his hand out. 'We've met before, Sergeant.'

'That we have, Mr Wentworth. As I remember you were quite evasive in answering my questions at the time. Nice to see you again.' Sergeant Dowery took Jarrod's offered hand and shook it with a low-grade masonic indicator.

Jarrod could sense the man was not happy at seeing him with Detective Widcombe. 'Sergeant, did the stun gun produce any leads? The one Sarala's attacker dropped?'

'Grey import, Mr Wentworth. We passed the serial on to the manufacturer, who eventually reported that it was an American model, sold through an outlet in Texas. Probably stolen and smuggled here.'

'And the dog belonging to Martin's sister? I believe it was not at the house?' Jarrod enquired.

'Left outside a shelter in Bolton. Why would the murderer go to the trouble of saving a dog?'

'We need to go.' Detective Widcombe urged. 'Thanks Bob, I owe you.'

'You be careful Sarala.' Sergeant Dowery eyed Jarrod as he spoke.

'Sergeant, how did the pawnbroker die?' Jarrod asked, ignoring the tug on his arm from Detective Widcombe.

'Similar to Martin Bagnall in some ways. Tied backwards over his desk, shoulders dislocated. Coroner said there's evidence of poisoning. We won't know what with until he does the autopsy.'

'Bert, please take Sarala home,' Jarrod instructed the cab driver. 'I am going to Caster and Randle. The walk will do me good.'

'Are you sure, sir?' Bert replied, concerned that Jarrod would be walking through some of Manchester's less salubrious streets.

'I'll be fine, Bert. Pick me up from Caster at three, please.' Holding the taxi door open, he instructed the detective, 'Be at mine for nine in the morning. Bring your gym stuff.' Jarrod shut the door, with the detective mouthing *gym* at him through the window.

Chapter 18

Hellcat, AKA Melissa Long, held the provocative statue above a battered and rusty oil drum, the flames of the makeshift fire licked high, threatening to singe the fine hairs on her arms. The smoke floated up to the ceiling, eventually billowing out through the building's broken windows.

'Damn it.' Hellcat pushed the ancient relic back into her backpack and slung it over her shoulder. She could not bring herself to destroy the idol, it was a thing of beauty. She could look at it for hours, mesmerised. Wilkins had not returned her calls so something must have gone wrong in the old Mill. She had seen the smoke, as had the others of the Razor Crew. Anger flared within the group. They dealt out pain and terror but the Razor Crew were not used to being on the receiving end.

'Smash it or give it to him,' a voice from the shadows said.

'We need to kill him, set another trap,' another shouted.

None of them had dared visit the three Crew members while they struggled to survive in hospital. Fear of the killer was the real reason, not the uniformed officer stationed outside the ward. The papers declared that the three Crew members and Josh's sister had died horrific and painful deaths. Wilkins had listened to the man questioning them over the phone. He'd told Hellcat that the murderer was looking for her and the idol. That was the last anyone heard from their leader. Four other members of the crew had gone missing since Wilkins laid the trap. They were all presumed dead.

'We need to kill him,' Gunther said, pulling the slide of his newly attained pistol back for effect.

'We need to set a trap!'

'Wilkins tried that, now he's dead.'

'You don't know that,' Hellcat protested in innocence; she was only fifteen. Wilkins had been her mentor, she carried his gun for him, his stash of drugs. *He trusted her and...* she could not finish the thought. She had no interest in men, but she loved Wilkins, none-the-less. He was family.

'Give it to the police, let them capture the bastard,' another voice shouted from the shadows.

Hellcat recognised it as Moose — his deep voice was unmistakable. Turning, Hellcat left. She would not return. With Wilkins gone there was nothing here for her.

Chapter 19

The next morning Detective Widcombe was surprised when the pretty Chinese girl answered Jarrod's door.

'Xiu? I was expecting Jarrod.'

'He has asked for me to train you today,' the petite oriental replied. 'Have you brought your clothes?'

Tapping the strap of her hold-all slung across her back the detective asked, 'Training me in what?'

'Doesn't matter. Jarrod expressed the desire for you to be exhausted by the time he returns. His words were: *you should be so worn out so that your mind will be free of everyday shackles and preconceptions*.' Xiu closed the front door. 'You can change in the spare room.' She pointed to the copper covered door across the lounge. 'Third door on the right.'

'Your police training is insufficient. You would not last long in a real fight.' Xiu expressed concern as she once again assisted the detective up from the floor.

'I've held my own until now, Xiu.'

The Chinese woman huffed and changed stance once

more. She attacked the detective as a boxer: a swift jab, a feint, another jab and a cheeky hook. The final punch never landed; a sudden reduction in speed reduced the knock-out blow to a gentle kiss of her Chinese knuckles to Sarala's chin. Before the detective could counter, the smaller opponent had already backed away.

'You will encounter all manner of assailants. You must be prepared for all.'

Xiu's stance changed once again; this time she attacked Detective Widcombe with a flurry of karate punches and roundhouse kicks that grazed the detective's face, as well as a hip throw that placed Sarala on the mat.

'Do you put Jarrod on these mats at all?' the detective asked, her pride bruised almost as much as her rear.

'Jarrod is competent in many forms of self-defence. His height and strength are both an advantage and a liability. I too have learnt from our sessions. He uses unconventional tactics. He was not always strong and powerful, and his humble beginnings still guide him.'

'What are we doing, Xiu? Putting me on my arse is not helping me to...' She left the sentence unfinished. She couldn't mention Jarrod's magic or his promised aura training.

'I am assessing you. If our session is to be of value rather than mere exercise, then I need to know what you are capable of.' Xiu offered her hand to assist the detective off the floor again. 'We can rest now.'

'What time will Jarrod be back?'

'Tomorrow morning. We are to train until six a.m. tomorrow. I will feed you and you may have brief rest periods, but Jarrod's orders were quite explicit. I am to wear you down mentally and physically.'

The detective looked at the clock on the wall of Jarrod's dojo. It was only ten a.m. 'You are kidding? Right?'

Looking up at the detective, Xiu tilted her head as if examining her for the first time. 'You wish to open up the ability to see a person's aura. For many it is a gift they are born with; for others like yourself, their minds have to be expanded and freed of their preconceived ideas of the world around them. Your mind is locked within your own logic, your upbringing has shaped the cage of rationality that restrains your abilities. This is what I must break down.'

'You know about Jarrod?' The detective had to choose her words carefully, bound as she was by Jarrod's spell of secrecy.

'He is from another place, a place where the use of magic abounds. I know and that is why I am here. Jarrod and my father work on many projects together, bringing balance back into the world and staving off the onslaught of evil from beyond. Jarrod met my father on the pretext of being the pupil, but it soon became clear that they were equal, just in differing ways. I am here to watch if Jarrod turns to the *Ku*, dark magic. It is a condition of their continued collaboration.'

'Your father is from another place, too?'

'No, we were born near Loulan, the ancient city of the Taklamakan Desert in China, in an area called the Sea of Death,' Xiu answered.

'But he's a wizard...' Detective Widcombe fought to add the word *too,* but as that implied Jarrod was a wizard and so she could not vocalise the end of her sentence.

'No, not the same as Jarrod. There are many forms of magic. Jarrod often complains that we're a civilisation with amnesia, that we have forgotten most of what we once knew.'

'But your father performs magic like...' Detective Widcombe screwed her face in concentration, her mind became confused as she attempted to mention Jarrod in the sentence.

Xui smiled, 'My father is a sorcerer. Our family have been protectors against evil since the Tang Dynasty.'

Detective Widcombe slumped back to the ground. 'Jesus, you talk about it as if it was an everyday event.' Squeezing her eyeballs and the bridge of her nose with her fingers she proclaimed, 'I'm sorry. It's a lot to take in. I'm either going mad or this is one hell of a hoax.' She stood up as if to leave, annoyed at herself, Jarrod and Xiu.

'It is neither. If you wish to leave, then you must do so through me.'

'Xiu?'

'You know too much. You either join us in our quest against evil or you...'

'What? You'll kill me?' The detective bunched her fist and attacked Xiu.

Fists, kicks and elbows flew between the two, blow after blow landed on both sides, although Xiu never lost her footing or seemed out of breath. Eventually Detective Widcombe's reserve of energy waned. She threw a sloppy round house punch at Xiu's face, the momentum carrying her body around and she toppled to the ground exhausted.

'Excellent! That was much better.' Xiu smiled down at the detective.

'You goaded me. You wanted me to fight you.'

'Jarrod would never hurt you, Detective. He is a good man, plus he likes you.' Offering a hand, Xiu ordered, 'Now get up, we have training to do.'

The clock on the wall said 10:30 a.m. 'Oh, fuck!' *It's going to be a long day*, Detective Widcombe thought as Xiu assisted her off the floor.

Jarrod stood back and watched the pair through the doorway; both women were too absorbed in the combat and too exhausted to notice his presence. Xiu repeatedly attacked the detective, choosing a different discipline each time, on some occasions using the training knives and clubs. Detective Widcombe fended off the attacks, her movements instinctive, learned by rote, albeit slow and lacking in strength.

Moving back into the shadows of the hallway, Jarrod left the duo undisturbed. The smell of sweat permeated the air of his penthouse. Xiu had insisted that they turn off the air conditioning. 'The heat will wear her down faster,' she had explained as they drew their plan together.

The kitchen was a mess — dirty plates and glasses were scattered across the counter tops. Only Xiu's containers of herbs stood tidily amidst the chaos. Xiu's reverence for the sacred pots would not allow her to soil the area directly around them. They were an important part of her heritage; Jarrod knew that one of containers was made by her father when he was a little boy.

The sound of bare feet slapping on the hard surface of his floors alerted Jarrod that his guests were approaching. The pungent smell of athleticism assailed his nostrils as the women arrived.

'Well?' Jarrod asked.

'You were right. She is of good heart and spirit. She has potential,' Xiu replied. Sweat matted her hair, her clothes saturated, clinging to her petite body. Her eyes were a different matter. She was still alert, a tigress ready to pounce.

'And?'

'Sarala is ready. She is running on instinct. Her mind and body are a blank canvas. She needs food, a wash and when she thinks she can sleep...'

122

'I agree.' Jarrod placed a pulsating crystal on the kitchen top. 'Your father sends his love and he lent us this to...' Jarrod nodded, indicating Detective Widcombe sat on the kitchen chair.

'Sarala, drink this. You need to keep your fluids up and it will perk you up a little.' Xiu proffered a small dish containing a dark liquid.

'Oh, God, Xiu, it tastes green,' said the detective.

'Come on. Shower time, then you can have a nap,' Xiu lied.

'So tired. My body hurts, Xiu. I've never ached this much in my life.'

'Bring your drink, it will help.'

Sarala sat on a high stool in Jarrod's secret room. She wore jeans and a loose blouse. The detective's feet remained bare, she had trained all day without shoes and she felt no desire to put them back on. Her dark hair was dry after her shower, but she had made little attempt at styling it.

In her fatigue she hardly noticed Jarrod's magically enchanted robe was draped over a mannequin in the corner, and his staff nearby. Trays of coins crafted from meteoric nickel iron filled the shelves along one wall. Sarala could feel a warm vibration emanating from them. With her head low and her chin resting on her chest, she was too tired to ask why.

'Sarala, we are going to show you how to see auras. It is not magic. It is using the ability everyone is born with but most close off during childhood.'

'You promised me a bed.' The detective lifted her drooping head and brushed her dark hair from her eyes.

'I'm tired Jarrod. I ache. My hands and feet hurt and I'm bruised all over.'

'I know. We will deal with that later, I promise. Sarala, stay awake!' Jarrod pulled a chair from near his grandiose desk and sat in front of the detective. 'I don't know what you will see; it is different for everyone. Some see clouds of colour surrounding a person. For others, shades of light. It could be dots, it could even be purely a sense of a person's nature. Do you understand?'

'I'm going to see colours, yes.' She yawned as she replied, placing a scuffed and swollen hand over her mouth.

'What do you see?'

'I... I see metals of different colours and hues.'

'I suppose my fixation on my low-quality affinity metals transferred through to my inner eye,' Jarrod answered.

'Affinity metals? I don't understand.'

'Doesn't matter. What matters is that everyone sees auras differently. Only good and bad are immovable, light and dark. A person made up of light is a good person; black indicates they have performed great evil in their lives. The blacker it is, the worse the person is. If a person's aura is dominated by the black, it will dominate him or her. It will change their personality. Do you understand?'

'Shhh, just let me sleep.' Detective Widcombe pulled her bare feet onto the stool and hugged her legs and rested her head on her knees.

'Hold this crystal between the palms of both your hands and allow a little light to shine out upon your face.' Jarrod placed the glowing gem in one of her hands, clasping the other around it. Moving her thumbs apart, he allowed a shaft of gentle light to illuminate her face.

'It's pretty.' The detective's eyelids drooped as she fought to remain awake.

Shaking her shoulder, Jarrod prompted, 'I want you to turn your head and look at Xiu on your right. I want you to feel a third eye in your mind and look at Xiu. Your third eye is not a physical object, it's an esoteric concept. You are looking with your soul, not your body.'

'I don't...'

'You are going to feel my mind enter yours now,' Jarrod interrupted. 'I will show you the way, Sarala. I want you to ask me in and for your thoughts to welcome me when you feel my presence. Okay?'

'Yes.' She yawned, tilting on the stool until Jarrod held her steady.

Jarrod clasped his free hand around hers, ensuring not to block the delicate beam of light emanating from within her cupped hands.

'I can taste metal. Iron.'

'That's fine, Sarala. Think about my mind entering yours.'

'I think I'm tripping... I can feel your words. They're solid, gun metal grey. I can *feel* them.'

'It's okay, relax. Concentrate on Xiu. What do you feel?'

'My mind, it's... it's like I can see her with my thoughts. It's like I have pushed my consciousness out of my head. Oh, Jarrod, I can see her. I can feel my mind outside of my head. Xiu, you're even more beautiful than before. So much light.'

'Ask for the light to dim, Sarala, so you can see her colours.'

'Please can you...'

'In your mind, ask your spiritual self to reduce the light slightly so you can perceive Xiu's colours,' Jarrod interrupted.

'So many pretty colours. She's made of white with coloured silk fabrics slowly swirling and floating through her radiance. She's beautiful, Jarrod. She's so beautiful.' Detective Widcombe had tears running down her face, unnoticed in the moment.

'Xiu is one of the few I know with little sin. She harbours no ill thoughts, has performed no deeds of destruction, has never tasted meat,' Jarrod said. 'Now look at me.'

'Jarrod!' Sarala exclaimed in shock, almost falling backwards as she turned away from the vision of Jarrod's aura.

'It's okay. I told you about my past, my history and the darkness that I carry.'

'Jarrod, there's so much black.'

'Less than half, Sarala. Which is why Xiu is here to watch over me. Her father fears I may yet turn.'

'No. I can feel the good in you, Jarrod. An iron will to do better. I feel safe.' Detective Widcombe's expression changed to one of pity. 'Your colours are changing. There are more reds and greens. What does that mean?'

'Only you can figure that out Sarala. The colour interpretation is a personal thing based on your life experiences. I feel tired, concerned and happy that you have accomplished so much on your first attempt.'

'Indian colours, they're all traditional Indian colours. I can see and feel your fatigue, your happiness. That's the blue.'

'Sarala, I need you to remember the feeling you have now. You will need to recall these feelings later when you try to see an aura on our own. Do you understand?'

Detective Widcombe nodded, overwhelmed once again by the experience.

'I want you to sleep now,' Jarrod said, using his magic to induce a healing slumber. 'Sleep.' Still supporting the detective on the stool, Jarrod felt her body shiver as he performed his spell.

Xiu moved behind Detective Widcombe, preventing her from falling backwards.

'She did well, Jarrod.' Xiu's face lit up when she smiled. 'You have chosen well. She will be a great asset in our fight against evil.'

'You will take care of her when I'm gone?' It was more of a command than a question.

'We will ensure she rises in the police ranks and she, in turn, will look after us.'

'You know what I mean?' Jarrod asked.

'I, or one of my sisters will be nearby at all times. We will continue to train her even after you leave.' Xiu lifted the taller woman off the stool as if she were a mere child. 'It has been a long time since we found a new apostle. Modern society does not encourage ethics and purity of thought.'

Chapter 20

'Xiu, did you put me to bed last night?' Detective Widcombe asked entering the large kitchen, settling by the breakfast bar.

'I assisted you Sarala, yes. You would have slept in your jeans otherwise,' Xiu answered offering a glass of light green liquid. 'How do you feel?'

'Tired — a good tired.' She flexed her arms. 'Like after a good workout.'

'Jarrod has asked me to continue to train you.'

'Last night... did that really happen?' the detective asked hesitantly, afraid to speak the words aloud lest she make a fool of herself.

'Open your mind and look for yourself.'

After a moment's silence, Xiu prompted the detective: 'Remember what it felt like when Jarrod was in your mind, the shape and texture of your thoughts. Feel your energy flow.'

Xiu watched the energy in Sarala's aura shift and change as she struggled to free her mind's eye. All of a sudden, the detective's energy burst forth, enhancing the glow of her normal aura.

'Xiu!' Detective Widcombe cried, 'I see you.'

'Congratulations. You have taken a small step on a journey that will change you forever.'

'Change?'

'You will see people for who they are. Once you have mastered reading an aura, you will know when someone is lying, who is corrupt and most importantly, who is under the influence of evil.'

'I don't understand.'

'Evil is everywhere, Sarala. It consumes the weak, corrupts the impressionable. Rarely does evil show itself as an entity. The Order of Light enters the shadows to cast evil from our world.'

'You're talking about the devil?'

'No. There are many forms of evil. We leave the devil for your western churches to deal with, it has become their speciality. You do know that Jarrod is from another dimension? You Stepped with him to the space between worlds.'

'Nowhere? Oh God! I can talk about it with you…how? Jarrod stopped me mentioning anything about...' Sarala paused as if the word refused to exit her mouth, 'magic...'

Xiu smiled, ignoring Sarala's question. 'Nowhere is Jarrod's term for it, yes. Some dimensions are more magical than others — from these we suffer the most powerful denizens.'

'Jarrod mentioned this. He said they cannot stay on Earth for long.'

'Long enough to twist the minds of those around them. Deviants abound nowadays. Murderers, child molesters, rapists — all of these would have been slain in times past. This was not just to prevent them from repeating their heinous crimes. It was to limit the volume of unwitting recruits the demons could enslave for their machinations.

The more abhorrent the crime, the easier the person is for the demons to twist and manipulate.'

'I'm sorry, you can't expect me to take all of this seriously. It sounds like a plot for a horror movie.'

Xiu smiled. She had said too much, too soon. Western civilisation bred cynics. 'When do you go back to work?'

'Monday,' the detective replied looking at the clock that stated that it was eleven minutes past ten. 'What day is it?' Suddenly she was unsure how long she had been in Jarrod's apartment.

'Friday. You slept through Thursday.' Xiu did not add that she and Jarrod had healed the woman's body from the rigours of training and worked on her soul, prompting the detective's higher-self onto a course of discovery while her consciousness slept unaware.

'Shit! My cat!' The detective shot off her stool, looking for the rest of her belongings.

'Jarrod is there now, he likes animals,' Xiu assured.

'In my flat? What?' Detective Widcombe gasped, her keys and purse in her hand.

'Someone had to feed your cat.' Xiu smiled once more. 'Jarrod is protecting your property. Johnson Security installed an alarm and cameras for you yesterday and Jarrod is there now casting protection spells. I told you, he likes you.'

'Bloody hell, Xiu! The place is a mess! I left my... oh, shit! He had no right!'

Laughing, Xiu placed a soothing hand on the detective's shoulder. 'Relax. Jarrod asked if I would enter first to maintain your dignity. Although between the two of us, I think it was to maintain his own. I don't think he could have coped with your underwear drying in the bathroom. He's very old fashioned, you know.'

'But...'

Xiu moved her hand to one side, dismissing the detective's concern. 'Don't worry. I put your dirty washing in the basket.'

Detective Widcombe sat back down. 'What kind of spells is he casting?'

'The usual: general protection from evil, wards to prevent spells entering your premise, a confusion spell for would-be intruders. They'll either see a house full of people or no one at all, depending on their intent, and a healing spell for when you are home. You're very lucky. Jarrod is better than my father at such things.'

'Do you...?'

'No, my sisters and I use the tools my father provides to fight the dark side. Jarrod joined our cause eight years ago, when he met my father. His quest for knowledge aligned itself quite well with our quest to eradicate evil.'

'And yet you are here spying on him?'

'Spying? No. Jarrod knows I am here to watch the darkness in his aura. He takes no umbrage over the fact.'

'What...' Detective Widcombe hesitated to ask. 'What happened to his wife?'

'He doesn't talk about her much. I know it broke him though. He carried her death around with him every day and it weighs him down. She died in some sort of accident.'

'Broke?'

'He believes that if he learns everything he can and becomes the greatest wizard ever known, that he will not have to be reincarnated. No soul has to be reincarnated, Sarala; once we have passed over to the other side, we choose to come back, we are not forced. This side of death is a mere stage and we are ad-libbing actors playing a role. We are here to learn, to be good or evil, compassionate or vindictive. Once we step off the stage, the woes of the play become irrelevant — only how well we performed and what we learnt matters.'

'A play?' Detective Widcombe asked with incredulity. 'I am an actor in a play?'

'A metaphor Sarala. Your existence here only matters while you are here; afterwards, it's about what you learnt while doing so. I'm sorry,' Xiu apologised. 'You need to find your own way, your own interpretation. Man has always imprinted his own culture and beliefs on who he chooses as a deity, shapes his God to resemble himself. You must think past this, Sarala. The next time you see someone die, it will all change for you.'

'What? Why?' she asked. 'I don't want to see anyone die.'

'You will see their soul depart, it is a thing of beauty and yet a thing of great sadness.' Xiu passed a plate of prepared fruits towards the detective. 'Seeing is believing, and you need to start believing.'

The copper leaves chimed, starting in the master lounge, the sound flowing around the apartment. A non-harmonious melody alerted the women to an unsavoury visitor.

'Someone has entered the hallway,' Xiu announced as she sprang off her seat to head for the door. 'Jarrod does not attract visitors as there is a spell of hesitation and repulsion in the hall and corridor.'

'I went back to the elevator,' Sarala said.

'Sorry?'

'When I first came here, I felt compelled to check for another doorway even though I knew I hadn't seen one. I walked back to the elevator.'

'Yes, doubt was put into your mind,' Xiu explained.

'Jarrod could stop the elevator from coming up this far,

that would be more efficient.'

'But then he would not see those who seek him out. Wizards are paranoid on Prushal, there is always someone who wants to prove they are better than you. Think of the American gunslinger: once they had a reputation of having a quick draw, life was a series of duels until death. That's why Jarrod remains a university professor. He is protected on the campus.'

'Is he scared?'

'Only of killing the innocent and dying before he learns enough not to come back.'

The women walked to the copper clad front door and Xiu slid a cover in the wall to reveal an embedded flat screen.

'Not very magical,' Sarala observed.

'Magic is a tool, there is a time and a place to use it. Do you know who she is?' Xiu asked, looking at a scruffy teenager with a small rucksack over her shoulder.

Shaking her head, Detective Widcombe replied, 'No. Never seen her before.'

The girl hesitated halfway along the corridor, just as Detective Widcombe had done a week earlier. Nervous, she chewed on the ends of her mousy hair and turned to leave but paused when she heard movement behind the lift doors.

Eventually the elevator doors opened and three men walked out. The first produced a sawn-off shot gun from the hold-all that he carried and passed it to one of his comrades. He then removed a crude looking door ram, similar to those used by police to force entry into houses. The heavy bag was dropped in the elevator doorway to prevent the lift being called downwards. Upon seeing the men, the unknown girl ran towards the copper door.

'Shit!' Detective Widcombe shouted, holding her phone

in the air attempting to find a signal. 'Let her in!'

'I can't.'

The young girl's fists pounded on the door, she screamed and begged to be let in.

'Xiu, let her in!' Detective Widcombe pushed the Chinese woman to one side and attempted to open Jarrod's front door. 'Where's the fucking handle?' she screamed.

'Only Jarrod can open this door. The palm reader on the other side is for show. This is a magical door.'

'We're trapped?' Sarala exclaimed.

'We can leave via one of Jarrod's escape routes.' Xiu pulled the detective away from the door just in time for a pair of manly arms to open it and heave the young girl inside.

'Jarrod!' the detective said. 'Where did you come from?' She felt foolish the instant the words passed her lips.

The girl landed softly on the sofa, slightly dazed by the Herculean throw. The men in the corridor rushed the door, the twin barrels of the shotguns pointing at Jarrod.

There was no warning, no motion from Jarrod, no hand waving or audible incantations. The two men nearest toppled over, their feet stopped running and their momentum carried them forwards in a downward arc. They were dead before they hit the floor. The third man at the lift door screamed in pain, howls of rage and frustration filled the hallway as he clawed at his clothing, blood seeping through his white shirt, visible through the open front of his leather jacket. The man tore the front of his shirt off and clawed at a medallion on his chest, the molten metal burning its way through his skin and resting on his sternum. The medallion fell to the floor covered in burnt flesh and blood. Jarrod and the three females saw runes carved into the man's flesh bleeding profusely as the protective wards etched into his skin strained against

Jarrod's spell. The man stumbled into the elevator, fumbling with the buttons, kicking the bag out of the door's way. He stared at Jarrod as the door closed. Hatred burned in the man's eyes.

Jarrod stepped back into the room and commanded, 'Shut the door!' before he collapsed.

Xiu slammed the door closed and rushed to the kitchen, quickly returning with a glass of herb-laden fluid.

'Drink this, it will be better than that sugar cake you use.'

'Jarrod?' Detective Widcombe asked concerned.

'I'm OK, just the Wayfarer's Step taking its toll.'

'What the fuck!' Three heads turned to see a scared young girl, clasping her daypack to her chest. She stumbled, giddy, tired, suddenly heavy and collapsed on the settee, the bag falling from her hands onto the floor.

'You put her to sleep? I felt your spell this time. Just like I felt.' Detective Widcombe turned towards the door, remembering the feeling as Jarrod cast his spell of death. 'You did something to their hearts... I could see their hearts.' She shuddered as her mind replayed the sensation. 'You killed them.'

'It was you or them, Sarala. I will not mourn the loss of a murderer.'

'Your aura?' Detective Widcombe strained to see Jarrod's life energy. 'It hasn't changed?'

'Protecting me and mine is not evil, it does not leave a mark,' Jarrod said wearily between sips.

'You could have stopped him at Caster and Randle?'

'Yes and no,' Xiu answered for Jarrod as he closed his eyes to rest. 'Jarrod cannot overtly use his magic in public, especially where there are cameras. It would generate too many questions.'

'And two dead bodies,' Detective Widcombe pointed at the front door, 'I need to call the police. Jarrod open the door.'

'No police,' Jarrod said firmly. 'I'll deal with the bodies.'

'What? No, you can't. A crime has been committed.'

'Sarala, both their hearts stopped at the same time for the same reason. It will cause questions. I cannot risk an investigation.' Jarrod stood up, holding the wall for support. 'Just give me ten minutes to recover.'

'What happened to the man by the lift?' the detective asked.

Jarrod waved for Xiu to answer as he made his way to the settee.

'He had an amulet to protect him and runes etched into his skin. The amulet took the brunt of Jarrod's spell, which is why it burnt up. His scarifications took the rest. Something powerful engraved them,' Xiu said. She looked at Jarrod, her face creased with worry. 'Possibly something more powerful than you, Jarrod.'

'Selgroch, the Demon. I felt the resonance as my magic struck. The image of the idol flashed into my mind.'

'She's real then?' Detective Widcombe asked, worried.

'Very real and very dangerous.' Jarrod's voice faded with exhaustion.

'Jarrod, open the door,' Xiu asked, 'the man dropped his amulet.'

Following Xiu out of the apartment, Detective Widcombe examined the bodies on the floor. 'Dead,' she proclaimed.

Xiu walked further along the corridor to the lift doors.

Unsure what to do, Detective Widcombe returned to the lounge and asked, 'Jarrod, why does the Wayfarer's Step take so much out of you?'

Jarrod sighed, too tired for such questions. 'The power of the universe is all around us, and we can tap into it at any time and if you know how, you can store some for use later on.'

Jarrod flicked two of his coins towards the detective. She felt them for a second, holding them out in separate hands as if weighing them.

'You've used the energy from this one, it's lost its warmth.' Focusing her mind's eye, she proclaimed, 'This one is glowing.'

'Good. You're learning to use your gift.' Jarrod tried to smile, his eyes tired. 'I can gather magic from the surrounding area. Once I have absorbed it, it takes a short while for more to flow into the void that I just created. If I need more magic, I have to use the universe's energy that naturally resides within me, which leaves me weak. This is why I imbue my coins while on my travels. They are magic batteries, for want of a better analogy.'

'So why does the Step tire you if you have your batteries, your coins?'

'There's no ambient magic in Nowhere and time is different. Remember what I said about the sugar cake remaining undigested until we Stepped out?' Noticing the detective's nod, he continued. 'As the calories in the sugar are inaccessible, so is the magic stored in the coins. I use a coin to Step into Nowhere and energy within me to Step out.' He waved his arms to indicate the exhausted condition it had left him in.

'Sorry.'

'For what?'

'You came back to save me, again.' Detective Widcombe said apologetically. 'How did you know?'

'The leaves. If they detect a presence of malcontent, they alert me, wherever I am.' Jarrod lay his head on a cushion and fell asleep.

Detective Widcombe jumped as Xiu dropped the remains of the metal amulet onto the coffee table. She unloaded the shotgun and lay it and the hold-all on the floor.

'Slugs,' the Chinese woman said, passing a cartridge to the detective. 'Single projectiles, probably to shoot the hinges if the door-ram failed.'

'What's in the bag?'

Xiu knelt down and opened the top of the large bag. Rolls of picture wire fell to one side to reveal an assortment of blades and medical instruments. A tatty label on a brown bottle of liquid declared it to be some form of acid.

Detective Widcombe shivered at the thought. Nodding towards Jarrod she asked, 'How long will it take him to recover?'

'Usually ten to twenty minutes. Using magic as soon as he returned didn't help. Every spell exacts a small price from the user's body. It takes time to replenish the natural energy.'

'Yes. He said something about it when you...' The detective used a hand to indicate while Xiu was in the corridor.

'We will find him, Sarala.'

'But how many will die in the meantime?' Turning towards the girl sleeping on the other end of Jarrod's large settee, she asked, 'Do you know who she is?'

'No. Do you?'

'No. She's young, mid-teens.' Detective Widcombe rolled the girl's sleeves up to check her arms. 'No needle marks, that's something. Will she wake up if I search her?'

'No, she'll be out for half an hour or so, more if she was tired already.' Both women looked at the bags under the young girl's eyes. It looked as if she hadn't slept properly for weeks.

Searching the pockets of her jacket and jeans first, Detective Widcombe then continued to perform a full pat down and examination. The coffee table soon filled up with an array of paraphernalia. 'She's no sweet sixteen,' she admitted as she finished.

Among the contraband was several bags of powder of an unknown substance, two flick knives (one removed from the lining of the girl's left boot), a fake identification card proclaiming her to be an eighteen-year-old called Samantha, a Nokia phone similar to Jarrod's and a wad of twenty-pound notes.

Xiu opened the girl's backpack and produced a loaded Eastern European nine-millimetre pistol, another knife and an item rolled up in a t-shirt. 'Oh!' she said as she placed the missing idol of Selgroch on the table.

'She is beautiful, in a menacing way,' Detective Widcombe proclaimed.

'I can feel why the girl took it,' Xiu said, looking at the detective for confirmation.

'I...' she focused her thoughts on the idol. Slowly and with difficulty her mind's eye opened once more. 'It's harder this time.'

'You acted on instinct when you examined me before, now you are consciously trying. Your own inhibitions are blocking you. You know you can do it. Accept the truth, free your mind.'

'It's glowing... it's like it's whispering, promising me the things I desire.' Detective Widcombe turned her mind's eye away quickly. 'Jesus Christ! Xiu, It's evil!'

'Look at the girl's aura, Sarala.'

'Oh, Xiu. She's so young. How?' Tears streamed down Detective Widcombe's face.

'You know as well as I that the gangs in the city have initiation ceremonies — a random shooting, or a stabbing. You can see she has been abused — a lot — that always leaves a mark. Can you see her addiction?'

'Yes.' The detective's hand rose as if to point at part of the girl's aura. 'She's so young.' Sarala closed her inner eye, unable to look at the girl's grotesque aura any longer.

Chapter 21

Jarrod roused on the settee and sprang up. 'I need to get rid of the bodies,' he proclaimed, sitting back down equally as quick. 'Oh,' he gasped.

'You're not strong enough. They can wait another half an hour,' Xiu insisted.

'What will you do with them?' Detective Widcombe asked, the discomfort at being party to a murder evident on her face.

'Nowhere.' Jarrod nodded at Xiu in gratitude for the mug of herbal tea she placed in his hand. 'The tide will take the bodies — eventually they will fall through a weak spot into another dimension. Seeing a question form on the detective's face, he elaborated. 'I don't know where they'll go. It's like ocean currents; your starting point dictates which currents grab hold of you. I found a lost friend once that way. I sat down where he went missing, cleared my mind and waited. It's conscious thought that protects you while you are in Nowhere. The bodies, inanimate objects or anyone foolish enough to fall asleep, will eventually be expelled.' Jarrod stood, drained the contents of his mug and declared, 'We really need to get rid of those bodies and

I need to check in with security downstairs. If they've hurt my doorman...'

'I'd better check the men for ID before you dispose of them,' Detective Widcombe said. 'There might be clues as to where they came from.'

'Hired muscle, Sarala. Be my guest, but we can't go around asking their colleagues who hired them, can we?'

Opening the front door, Jarrod staggered into the long corridor and rolled the first man over. Ripping open the man's shirt, Jarrod examined his chest. 'There are no runes engraved on this one.' He emptied the man's pockets and handed the contents to the detective.

'Fresh blood,' Xiu said, looking at the knuckle duster Jarrod dropped into the detective's hands.

'Go and check downstairs, make sure everyone is OK,' Jarrod instructed Xiu. Jarrod picked up one of the dead men as if he were nothing more than a sack of potatoes. Focusing his mind, Jarrod opened up the pathway between himself and Nowhere and pushed the man's body through.

'Oh!' Detective Widcombe exclaimed, 'I didn't know you could do that.'

'I don't have enough energy to Step through and return.' He flicked another expended coin towards the detective. 'Each holds enough magic to open the way to Nowhere or assist me in a dozen spells. It takes me half a day to recharge a coin with energy, a full day if I perform the incantations while I go about my usual business.'

The detective rolled the other man over and examined the contents of his pockets. Each man carried an assortment of weapons, a cheap phone and an envelope full of fifty-pound notes. 'Payment?' she asked, holding it open for Jarrod to see.

Saying nothing, Jarrod pushed the man's body through to Nowhere. He flicked another coin towards the detective, the polished surface glinting in the light as it spun. With his shoulders slumped, Jarrod turned and retreated to his apartment, leaving Detective Widcombe kneeling on the floor. She looked along the corridor at the empty space where the man had just vanished. Hanging her head low, she muttered, 'Oh fuck! What have I gotten myself into?'

In a hidden room at the centre of Jarrod's apartment, Detective Widcombe brushed her hand along the fabric of Jarrod's cloak. The copper woven into the material warmed her hands. 'This feels more powerful,' she said, comparing the wizard's garment to the coins lined up on the shelves.

'I have spent a lifetime imbuing protective wards into the fabric. Life on Prushal has its dangers, especially when you have crossed three of the major families,' Jarrod explained. 'Unfortunately, the garment is out of fashion on Earth.'

'May I?' the detective asked, pointing at Jarrod's staff.

Jarrod nodded consent as he returned the spent coins to the racks and retrieved magically imbued replacements. 'I crafted the sphere on the end from olivine crystals, the ones found in meteorites. It acts as a spell amplifier.'

'How many coins do you have?' she asked, picking up a handful from a nearby tray.

'Barry's created thousands for me. He even bought a coin press to speed up production.'

'The guard, Barry?' Detective Widcombe asked. 'That's why you've been paying him, of course.'

'He is skilled with his hands.'

'What does he think you do with them? Surely he's curious.'

'Marketing tokens for my clients — more memorable than a business card. I don't know if he believed it or not... he never asked again.'

They both turned at the sound of the lounge coffee table smashing against the floor.

'The girl?' Detective Widcombe questioned to an empty room. Jarrod had already left to investigate. Sarala ran after him.

'You!' A deep feminine voice boomed throughout the apartment. 'It was you!'

As Detective Widcombe entered the lounge both she and Jarrod were flung from across the room. Selgroch floated near the shattered table, directly above her stone idol. The demon woman appeared semi-naked, shrouded in wisps of red and black vapour. The smell of sulphur filled the lounge.

'I think you need to hold back on the Kala Namak salt, Jarrod. It's smelling the house out,' the detective joked, using humour to mask her fear.

'Bring me my staff!' Jarrod boomed, his face taut with unseen effort.

Detective Widcombe picked herself up and ran. As she moved across the lounge the air surrounding her heated up. Using her inner eye, she saw a layer of Jarrod's magic protecting her from a barrage of black spells. Like a swarm of bees, they rushed at her, only to crash and burn on Jarrod's protection. Detective Widcombe risked a quick look at the demon and tripped with the horror that she saw. Gone was the voluptuous feminine figure; in its place stood a heinous dribbling beast of leather and fur, behind it a burgeoning hole to another place. The smell of burning and screaming filled the air. Except for a minuscule pin prick of light almost buried in the sheer volume of evil, the beast's aura was pure black. A remnant from birth, for every baby is born innocent. Detective Widcombe pulled her right shoulder in tight and using a judo roll to break her fall, she leapt through the door and ran towards the secret room. The room glowed brightly, as she had entered with her mind's eye still open, the trays of coins throbbed as if they contained a heartbeat; somehow she knew they were in tune with the universe. One by one the magic in the coins was dissipating as Jarrod drew on the magic from the other room. A tenth of the trays lay inert, their energy already spent.

'Oh, shit!' Fear pierced the detective's heart. Jarrod was losing. His magic was being used up at an incredible rate. Grabbing the wizard's staff, she closed her inner eye in order to see past the globe's illumination. She ran back into the lounge; the air was thick, physically slowing her down. She fought against an unseen force that attempted to prevent her from returning.

Jarrod had moved closer to the demoness, who had dropped her illusion of beauty. He was on one knee with both arms outstretched, as if directing unseen forces at the hideous creature. The detective dared not use her inner eye again, else she lost her nerve.

'The staff!' Jarrod shouted, pain filling his voice. 'Pass me the staff!'

Selgroch moved a hand in the detective's direction, making furniture fly and rebound off an invisible barrier before her. Although Jarrod's barrier was waning, shrinking as he preserved his energy. Without thinking, Detective Widcombe viewed the scene with her inner eye; she regretted the action immediately. Darkness covered the protective bubble around her, evil incantations oozing over the surface trying to find a way past the barrier.

Straining to stand upright, resembling a person in a hurricane the detective cried, 'I can't move forwards!'

'Crawl if you have to!' Jarrod shouted between gritted teeth. His beard turned red as blood seeped from his eyes, nose and ears.

On the settee, behind the repulsive figure of Selgroch lay the girl, either forgotten or ignored. Without warning, she sprang up and landed on the demon's back. Wrapping her legs around the beast-woman's naked waist, the girl plunged the knife into the demon's neck and shoulder. Screaming, wild with fear, she repeatedly stabbed the four-inch blade deeper and deeper; black vitriolic liquid oozed out, the light in the room reflecting off the metal blade as if it was covered in oil.

The demon grabbed at the wild girl and pulled her over her head, receiving deep knife slashes to her face and breasts in the process. 'You could have served me, you fool. You are ripe and ready for servitude.'

'Selgroch!' Jarrod shouted raising his staff at the demon. Visible energy leapt from the orb end of the staff and struck the demon in the chest.

A barrage of twirling, coloured magic arched from the staff's globe — it scorched, tore and shredded at the flesh of the demon. Detective Widcombe saw brief flashes of Jarrod's intent, hundreds of spells swarmed towards the demon, simultaneously attacking from all directions. The furniture around Selgroch caught fire. The demoness threw the girl at Jarrod and countered with her own magic, but she was not strong enough to defeat the wizard with his staff.

'How long can you keep this up, Wizard? I have the power of millions of souls at my disposal, I can hold you here for days if need be.' Selgroch laughed, blood gurgled in her slashed throat, the wounds in her neck had begun to heal.

Jarrod stood, reinvigorated by the magic in his staff and

smiled. Delicate hands pulled his robe around his shoulders.

'I leave for five minutes and you throw a party,' Xiu said from behind him.

'Took your time, Xiu,' Jarrod said with added strength in his voice.

The light behind Selgroch flickered and ghostly apparitions of two abhorrent and vile demons appeared beside her.

'No!' Jarrod screamed as the beasts attempted to physically manifest in Jarrod's front room.

Xiu held an amulet close to her mouth and said, 'Father we need your magic.' Placing her hand on Jarrod's shoulder, the Chinese woman went rigid as she acted as a magical conduit. Her eyes turned white, hair electrified, the strain of the energy coursed through her arching her back.

More apparitions appeared behind Selgroch and the demoness smiled, blood smeared across her perfect teeth. 'Oh, I have armies, Wizard. And you brought my likeness into your home, past your defences.'

Jarrod's eyes flicked to the idol under the floating demon. 'Xiu? Sarala?' He pleaded for help, unable to lessen his onslaught against the demons, lest they enter the humans' dimension.

Detective Widcombe lay still at his feet. He was unsure if she was alive or dead. Xiu was still fused to his shoulder, agony turning her sweet face into a contorted skeletal horror. Jarrod attempted to move closer to the demons but something unseen, stopped him from doing so.

Loud cracks of a weapon filled the air. Selgroch and her fellow demons were sucked out of this reality, their screams of frustration fading away. With the weight of the demons' onslaught gone, Jarrod fell forwards. Taking Xiu with him, they fell to the ground exhausted.

Hellcat sat on the floor with terror-filled eyes. With her arms pointing forwards, resting on her knees, her finger continued to pull on the empty pistol's trigger. Her t-shirt was torn open where the demon's taloned hand had grasped her, deep gouges on the girl's chest were bleeding profusely. The cups of her white bra, now scarlet.

Jarrod dragged himself next to the girl and placed his hand over the pistol, taking it away from her. 'You did well, kid.'

'What *was* that?' Tears streamed down Hellcat's face, her body shaking against Jarrod's as he pulled her close.

'Evil. Pure evil.'

'The statue, it looked like her,' Hellcat cried. 'I heard her voice in my head when I held the idol, tempting me. What was it?' She looked at Jarrod not as Hellcat, a member of the Razor Crew, but as a scared, teenage girl.

'Selgroch wanted you to turn yourself into her slave. She needed the idol and she saw the bad things you have done in the past.' Jarrod held her close. Her instinctive, unthinking intervention, risking her own life had saved them all. And, just like his heroic moment years earlier had done, her actions added a portion of pure white to her aura. Jarrod held her close, his bloodied chin on the top of her head, a tear of weary joy crept down his cheek. She too could be saved.

'Jarrod?' Xiu asked from the floor, too tired to move.

'We're okay, Xiu. The idol has been destroyed, their gateway to our world is gone.'

'Will she come back?' the girl groaned as she tried to move.

'Yes, there are other idols. They give her strength when

she Steps through. Without one she is much weaker. I doubt her followers will risk using them to confront us again, they're too precious. Irreplaceable in this modern age.'

Stretching, Xiu placed two fingers onto the detective's neck and nodded to Jarrod, confirming that she was alive. Xiu said, 'Jarrod, Selgroch Stepped directly from her dimension to ours, she didn't use Nowhere.'

Jarrod nodded, tiredness and worry filling his eyes. 'The guard downstairs?'

'Unconscious, he has a broken jaw and judging by the footprints on his jacket, they stamped on his chest, breaking several ribs. He's being taken to a private hospital. Members of the Order are down there. I left them to sort things out when I felt the overpowering presence of evil.'

Jarrod's copper leaves chimed at the door — someone had arrived in the lift's lobby. The melody was harmonious, celebrating the pureness of the individual. Jarrod waved a finger in a circular motion, releasing the door, fatigue regressing him once again to using gestures and symbols. A pretty Chinese woman stared into the room. She was aghast at the carnage and destruction that befell her gaze.

'Hello sister.' Xiu managed to lift a hand in greeting. 'Did you bring a broom?' Xiu's chin sagged as she slipped into unconsciousness.

Chapter 22

'What happened?' Detective Widcombe croaked as Xiu's sister gently roused her awake.

'I was hoping you could tell me?'

At the sound of a strange voice, the detective woke with a start. Her hands rose to fend off any incoming attack.

'Relax, Detective. I am on your side,' Xiu's sister reassured her. 'My name is Li Na. I am Xiu's sister.' Offering a hand to assist Detective Widcombe off the floor, she said, 'Call me Li. Everyone does.'

'Sarala,' Detective Widcombe replied. The resemblance between the two Chinese women was uncanny and both were startlingly beautiful. 'The demon?'

'Gone. It put up a fight. Xiu and the girl are unconscious.'

'I couldn't move; Jarrod needed his staff.' The detective looked across at the wizard; he had fallen asleep with his head on top of Hellcat's. 'She,' the detective indicated the slumbering girl, 'she attacked the woman, demon, whatever she was. I thought she would have surely died. I managed to crawl to Jarrod in the confusion. She was so brave. I don't remember anything after passing him the staff.'

'Are you strong enough to help me get these two on the couches?'

The detective winced as she moved, a hand darting to the back of her head. 'Ow! Sure.' Looking at the remains of the scorched furniture, she commented, 'What's left of the couch. Jesus, this place is a mess.' Lifting Xiu's legs, she assisted Li to place her sister on a disturbingly warm section of the settee. 'How did you get in here?' Her eyes darting to Li, suspicion replacing her weariness.

'Jarrod let me in. Otherwise I would have had to use the stairs from Xiu's apartment.'

'Xiu lives here? Stairs?'

'On the floor below this one. Jarrod had a secret staircase installed. He owns the building.'

'Yeah, I know,' the detective said, frowning.

'Jarrod supports my father's cause and we lease the two floors below. Xiu and a few others are stationed here.'

'Lease? Not free?'

'An accountant would ask questions if there was something amiss; we must remain invisible to the public. Money is of little importance.'

Jarrod stirred as the girl was manoeuvred from beneath his chin. 'Li, you missed the party,' he smiled.

'You need to sleep Jarrod,' Li ordered as she pushed his rising body onto the sofa. 'Rest a while. I'll be here when you wake.'

'They're all empty!' Detective Widcombe gasped as they entered Jarrod's secret room. Row upon row of once glowing coins sat inert in their trays. 'How close were we to losing?'

'There are other stores of energy that you are unaware

of. Huge reserves, so large that I daren't tap into them without my staff. Even so, without Xiu's father, all would have been lost. He has more experience fighting evil than I.'

'Xiu's father?'

Jarrod smiled. There was so much for the detective to learn. 'She channelled his energy and thoughts into me. Ultimately, it is he who held the demons at bay. If it wasn't for the girl shooting the idol...' He shrugged.

'I thought you had protection here... Your trees?' Sarala asked with alarm in her voice.

'The girl brought Selgroch's idol in. Once inside, the demon had unhindered passage into my home. Selgroch won't be happy the girl destroyed it. The power the idol contained was immense.'

Jarrod placed his wizard staff back on its stand and brushed his cloak before placing it reverently back on the mannequin.

'Is it over? Is she dead?' Sarala asked.

'No, we only banished her from here. Once the girl destroyed Selgroch's idol, she had no hold on this dimension. They are weaker on this planet than in their own dimension. The demons we normally face are much weaker than Selgroch and are easier to kill because of this. The Order of Light has slain thousands of demons, most of which have stumbled upon Earth for the first time. If they encounter an established demon, they usually eradicate the demon's followers first.' Seeing the detective's anger flaring, he elaborated,' You have to remove the demon's followers to weaken it. This is why your churches historically burnt anyone they thought was in league with a demon.'

'So, she's gone, right? She can't come back?'

Jarrod shook his head, 'There are other idols Sarala, I

am certain of it. She has followers, the man at the lift for example, the murderer.'

'Why did you bring me into this nightmare?' The detective's eyes were wide, glistening with unspilled tears.

'You felt my magic, you are sensitive. Xiu and her father need soldiers — fewer are born with the ability every year. Fewer still are willing to stand up for the weak. People such as you, Detective Constable.' Jarrod held her hand for a second before becoming uncomfortable with the intimate contact. 'Besides, you're relentless and you wouldn't have stopped asking questions,' Jarrod teased.

'There's no going back, is there?'

'You can't un-know something, Sarala.'

'You could make me forget.'

'No. You would still feel something was wrong and come back asking questions. Would you want to go back to not knowing the truth? You strike me as a person who needs to be in the thick of it.'

'Not my best trait, apparently,' the detective huffed.

Chapter 23

Loukas woke covered in sweat. He'd had the nightmare again. It was always the same dream and he always awoke at the same memory. The dream started when he was a young man and loyal to the crown when he and thousands of others were fighting in the Great Turkish War. He fought bravely, his innate savagery served him well on the battlefront and missions behind enemy lines. He was not afraid of killing or dying; he believed in the Church and what the clergy instilled upon the masses. Loukas was a soldier in the Holy League. He had been blessed by Pope Innocent XI.

He was unaware, while he was away fighting the Turks in a savage and dirty war, that his wife and daughter were being tortured to confess to the heinous crime of witchcraft. All who were questioned in the seventeenth century confessed, preferring the tranquillity of the gallows to the torturer's chambers. Loukas watched a vision of his family dangling on the noose; not the quick snap of the neck proffered by the inquisitor but the choking, struggling, gasping death as the hemp rope slowly strangled the life out of his family. Loukas watched as the crowds cheered when his eight-year-old soiled herself as she wriggled at the end of the rope.

The woman before his bloodied blade showed him this in a vision and he knew it was true. The hag handed him a scroll with symbols and told him to bloody it in revenge and burn it over a black candle to summon her. Loukas deserted his position and returned home. After weeks of travel he arrived at his house only to find it had been burned, and his family buried in unconsecrated graves. His wife and children had been abandoned and shunned by the church, family and friends. He slaughtered those in his village: man, woman and child and soaked the scroll with their blood. Thus was his pledge to Selgroch sealed. He soon rose in rank. From a simple servant he became a foot soldier in her army and eventually an errant Knight, going where she directed, killing those who slighted Selgroch in any way. The dream always ended with one last glimpse of his crying family and his wife shielding the children from the violent crowds as they were led to the gallows.

Sitting up in bed, Loukas wiped the sweat from his forehead, wincing as pain lanced across his chest. He lay there for a second, recalling the previous day's events. With two hired lackeys in tow, Loukas couldn't believe his luck when the young girl called Hellcat had turned up at the antiquity collector's apartment. *Two for the price of one*, or so he'd thought. He moved his hand from under the twee quilt cover to examine the wound on his chest. Selgroch's amulet had turned to molten metal and burnt through to the bone. His scarifications opened as the runes shielded him from magic. Jarrod — the purveyor of relics — was a mage, a wizard.

Loukas had not fled the building as the enemy would have assumed. With the security system down and the doorman dying, no one would know that he chose a random apartment to recover in. Sacrificing the young couple and their child to Selgroch, he reported his findings and prayed for assistance and aid. Selgroch had partially healed his wounds, turning the lethal burn into a badge of suffering. He knew it would hurt for evermore; it was to be a constant reminder of his failure. Before being pushed back into his own dimension, he'd heard her mutter, 'A wizard and the girl.' He had barely made it onto the bed before passing out into a pain-filled healing sleep.

Something jumped on the bed, startling Loukas. It was a large, ginger feline. Cats liked Loukas. They could sense the veil of magic around him. As a Knight of Selgroch, Loukas did not hate animals — they were innocent. He took no delight in killing or torturing them. On occasion, he even went out of his way to protect animals from negligent owners. Picking up the feline, Loukas took it to the kitchen. He felt like company while he ate breakfast.

Chapter 24

'Jarrod, where are you?' Detective Widcombe asked over the phone.

'At Caster and Randle's. How's your first day back at the office?'

'It's shit! I can't talk to anyone about what's going on and having seen their auras, I trust fewer than I used to.'

'Sorry.'

'It's not your fault. I just need to get to grips with it all. I have figured out when people are lying by the colour, but the rest is still a mystery.' She whispered into the phone. 'That's not important at the moment. Bert was attacked last night. He's in A&E now, he took a blow to the head. Wily old devil kept a pot of powdered chilli pepper in his car, the super-hot kind. Says he bought it to make a curry. It's an old cabbie trick, non-lethal self-defence. The investigating constable let it pass. Anyway, he threw the contents into the eyes of the attackers and they fled.'

'Is Bert okay?'

'He will be. I'm only mentioning this because two men were found with their eyes gouged out and their throats cut. Both had a residue of chilli powder on their clothes.'

'You're thinking this is related to the other night?' Jarrod asked.

'We're in Manchester for God's sake, we don't normally find thugs minus their eyeballs. I think the man in the lift is going after your friends and he got pissed when his goons failed their task. I thought I should warn you.'

'Thank you, Sarala,' Jarrod said slowly, his mind elsewhere. 'I'll take precautions this end.' Pausing for a second he added, 'I think it might be an idea if you slept at my apartment tonight.'

'I'll swing by my place and grab my things after my shift.'

'No, I'll send Xiu and Li. There may be people there waiting for you.'

'Good. I'll be the cheese.'

'I'm not comfortable using you as bait, Sarala. The risks are too great if we should fail.'

'I'll be home at seven. I'll get one of the uniforms to give me a lift. You set the trap,' she instructed. 'I've got to go. The Super is calling us all in for a meeting.'

✶ ❍•❍ •❍ ❍• ❍• ❍• ❍• ◯ ❍• ❍• ❍• ❍• ❍• ❍• ✶

Detective Widcombe felt guilty asking Bob to give her a lift home. She feigned feeling ill after her first day back at work, blaming the knock to her head and fumes from the fire. Constable Dowery was more than eager to assist her, hoping to get into her good books and maybe into something else. She could see his desires in his aura as they drove through town. He wasn't tainted like some of her colleagues, the ones she'd always felt uncomfortable with. Three of the men in her station were corrupt, she now knew that for certain and she swore to herself that she would deal with them once this was all over. Bob on the other hand was a simple opportunist that let his sexual desires rule his life. He was also a liar. The delicate aura surrounding him was predominantly brightly coloured. She could see that Bob had a health issue that he didn't talk about, but she was inexperienced in reading auras to ascertain what it might be. The wisps of dyed silk, which is how she visualised auras, floated freely around her suitor. It was unfortunate that muddled knots of mixed colours appeared when he discussed his personal life and his single status.

'Thanks, Bob.' Detective Widcombe patted the man's arm. 'See you tomorrow?'

Disappointment clouded the man's face. His aura changed, lust faded and frustration and anger briefly flared. 'Yeah, see you in the morning, Sarala,' he replied, accepting his failure with bitterness.

Closing the car door, Detective Widcombe accepted an incoming call on her hands-free, masking the gesture by straightening her hair. 'Jarrod?' she whispered, covering her mouth with a hand, pretending to yawn.

'Don't speak, do your normal routine. Xiu and Li are in the house. I am close by.'

As Detective Widcombe neared the tower block, a pizza delivery moped pulled up by the front door and a Chinese man removed several flat boxes from the bike's rear box. He pressed the door buzzer as Sarala walked towards him. The intercom sounded tinny as the resident complained about how long the pizza had taken.

'Walk in with the pizza man, he's one of Xiu's men. He'll accompany you in the lift,' Jarrod's voice said through her earpiece.

Detective Widcombe thanked the man for holding open the door for her, and they fell into an awkward silence in the lift. He remained in the elevator when she exited at floor six. Detective Widcombe was unaware that he exited on floor seven to walk down the flight of stairs in preparation.

The lights in the hallway seemed brighter, until Detective Widcombe realised she had turned her inner eye on again. A black shadow appeared at the far end of the hallway, *not a shadow*, she thought, *a man, a man with a black aura.*

Turning the key in her door, Detective Widcombe watched for the man, the door's recess blocking her view slightly. She didn't hear his accomplice approach from behind. Rough hands grabbed her — one around her waist, lifting her, pushing her through the unlocked door — and the other smothering her mouth and nose, preventing her from shouting, from breathing. She squirmed, pretending to be the helpless victim, allowing him to enter the trap. She may be the cheese, but Xiu and Li were spiders and he the fly. She managed to smile beneath the man's calloused hand.

The door shut behind them. Her attacker didn't look back in expectation of his cohort. The hands fell from Detective Widcombe and as her assailant dropped her, he screamed. Her attacker's knees buckled involuntarily and he fell forwards, confusion on his face. With frantic movements, he checked and double-checked the backs of his legs. His hands returned, covered in blood each time.

Having severed his hamstrings, Li moved closer behind the man. At the same time Detective Widcombe forced Mr Wiggums — her cat's toy — into the man's gawping mouth. Li held the bloodied blade to his throat and whispered, 'Don't move!'

Xiu placed a large cable tie over the man's hands and cuffed them together. 'We need to talk. Your friend outside will not be joining us. Lie to me and my sister removes parts of your body. Do you understand?'

The blade on his throat moved to his left ear. The man's eyes widened in fright and he nodded carefully so as not to sever his ear.

'The man who hired you, who is he?'

'Lucas,' the man attempted to say, spitting Mr Wiggums from his mouth. 'Lucas, that's all I know. He paid us cash to rape... to hurt her.' His eyes darted momentarily to Detective Widcombe.

'Hurt? Only hurt?' Detective Widcombe kicked the man between the legs. Li placed a strong arm around his throat preventing him from doubling over.

'Do you mean Loukas?' Li asked once the man had recovered enough to talk.

'Lucas, Loukas. He was foreign, who can tell,' the man gasped with tears running down his cheek. Seeing the detective move her foot for another savage kick, he added, 'We had instructions to leave you blind and disabled. Lucas... Loukas said it was a message.'

'Where is he now?' Li demanded, the blade slicing into the man's flesh, partially severing the ear.

'I don't know, I don't know, honest.'

'Xiu, take Sarala to Jarrod's while I have a conversation with our friend here,' Li instructed her sister.

'What will you do with him?' the detective asked, afraid of the answer.

'He came here to hurt you, Sarala — what do you think I'm going to do?'

'Let me call this in. The police can deal with him,' Sarala asserted.

'You know we can't do that! He's seen us, I've cut him. We cannot have the police asking questions... Jarrod will... you know...' Li performed a push gesture.

'I can't Li. I'm a police officer. I can't be party to murder.' Remembering that Jarrod was still on the phone with her, she said, 'Jarrod, we can't kill these men.'

'Man, Sarala. It's a little late for the other fellow. He attacked me with a knife.'

'Jarrod!' the detective's hand flew to her mouth in shock. 'We are meant to be the good guys!'

'You are now part of an ageless war, Detective. You do not hand the enemy their pawns back after removing them from the board. These are bad men.'

Detective Widcombe felt Jarrod's magic. He was nearby. 'You just pushed his body into Nowhere, didn't you?'

'It had to be done,' Jarrod said; disconnecting the phone, he walked through the detective's front door. The pizza man followed, handing the detective his pizza boxes. They were still warm and smelt divine.

'Take the pizzas and go home. Xiu can wake up the girl. I had to force her to sleep. She... I don't trust her to be on her own in my apartment,' Jarrod stated.

'I thought she'd have gone by now,' Sarala murmured, staring at the blood pooling below the man's knees. 'I didn't think.'

'She too has seen too much. She has decisions to make, habits to kick, and she needs to choose a side.'

'Jarrod! She's a child!'

'She has performed heinous acts whilst a member of the Razor Crew, Sarala! She is no longer a child! We talked about it the other night. I promised to ease her withdrawal on the condition she tells me everything.'

'What will you do with her?'

'Foot Soldiers in the Order of Light are usually converts, Sarala. She will be asked to join,' Li answered for Jarrod. Seeing the detective's disapproval, Li added, 'It takes people of action to fight evil, Detective. Not pure and gentle souls. Those who faint at the first sight of blood are no use to us. The girl saw evil and chose to fight — she can redeem herself with us.'

'The wound she endured to her chest will never heal properly. The imprint of the demon's hand will ache in the presence of evil. She has also been given an advantage in the coming battles. Li will take her back to China, where she will be trained.' Xiu held the detective's hands and looking at the pizza boxes they both held, she added, 'I think she will appreciate some pizza when she wakes up.'

Letting go of the door handle, Detective Widcombe turned back to the group. The man on the floor looked at her, mouth covered by Li's hand, eyes pleading. 'I can't let you kill him, I'm sorry.' She stood poised for an argument.

'Oh, for God's sake, Detective! This man is only on the streets because your judicial system refuses to properly punish criminals. He should have been executed years ago,' Li argued.

'Unlike your Chinese justice?' Detective Widcombe asked. 'I watch the global news. You're not exactly a democratic society with equal rights, are you?'

'I was referring to your ancestral justice system, the one that recognised the presence of evil and removed vermin such as he.' Li huffed, angry at being questioned.

'Ladies, we can debate this at another time. Sarala, please believe me when I say I will deliver the man alive to Xiu and Li's father. He will have to work to remain alive.' Jarrod turned to their prisoner. 'If you commit a crime once you are there, they will leave you in the desert to die. Do you understand?'

The man nodded gently, Li's knife threatening to slice his throat as his head moved.

'Promise?' Detective Widcombe asked Jarrod.

'You have my word,' Jarrod said, pushing the detective out of the front door. *If he survives Li's interrogation.*

Chapter 25

Li returned with Jarrod to his apartment building only to be greeted by a throng of uniformed police manning a makeshift cordon around the front of the building. Two medical crews exited the building and returned their trolleys and equipment to their ambulances — parked alongside them was a white van with no livery. The paramedics and the men from the van talked, their body language suggested that they were familiar and comfortable in each other's presence.

'They're from the morgue, Mr Wentworth,' a voice spoke from behind the flashing blue lights. Constable Robert Dowery stepped between the lights and Jarrod.

'Constable, nice to see you again,' Jarrod offered his hand. 'May I ask what is happening?'

'I'm not at liberty to say, Mr Wentworth. I'm sure you'll read all about it in the morning papers.' The constable removed a notepad from his pocket. 'May I ask why you are here, sir?'

'I live here, Constable, the penthouse.'

Constable Dowery turned to Li. 'May I have your

name?' he asked.

'No, you may not!' Jarrod answered. 'And nor does she have to provide it.'

'Only following procedure, Mr Wentworth. If you have nothing to hide...' the constable left the comment unfinished.

'Are we able to enter the building, Constable?' Jarrod queried.

'Stay off the second floor, Mr Wentworth. You may receive a visit in the morning to answer a few questions.'

Another uniformed officer stopped them before they reached the main doors and Jarrod's identification was requested before she would allow him to enter. The building's doorman directed a grim smile towards Jarrod.

'A couple on floor two, sir. Murdered. The husband's daughter, from his first marriage, let herself in and found them. She had enough sense to get out of the apartment. Her screaming brought the neighbours out and probably saved her life.' The doorman produced a printout from the surveillance system. 'This man left the scene pretty sharply, punched one of the male neighbours as he made his way past and as you can see from the photo, left by the stairway.'

Jarrod stared at the man in the photo... it was the man from the lift. He hadn't left the building.

'Sir, the police aren't happy that you didn't inform them about the attack the other night,' the doorman said. Seeing Jarrod's querying eyes, he added, 'They noticed the gap in the CCTV. The system recorded the attack on Josh before they broke into the server room and disabled everything. Sir, the boss also wants a word with you.'

Jarrod thanked the doorman. Like Josh, he was ex-military and an employee of Johnson Security.

Opening the lift door, Jarrod wasn't surprised to find a police officer present. She asked for Jarrod's floor and pushed the button, explaining she was there to prevent unauthorised access to floor two.

'Have you seen the police below?' Jarrod asked as he entered his apartment.

'Police?' Xiu and Detective Widcombe asked in unison.

'Lucas — or Loukas as he prefers to be called — didn't leave the building after the attack. He killed a family on the second floor.' Jarrod rubbed his forehead in frustration. 'I should have killed him when I had the chance.'

'You tried,' Xiu reminded him.

'I meant when he first attacked Sarala.'

'You know, you can't act in public.'

'He's killing people, Xiu and he isn't going to stop.'

'He's just a man. The police will catch him, won't they, Sarala?'

'Is he a man? He survived Jarrod's spell...' the detective replied, unsure.

'He had protective wards from Selgroch. We couldn't have known that at the time. Up until that point, he was just a thief and a murderer.' Xiu handed Jarrod a herbal tea. 'How did you get on with...'

'He talked. Li poked him a little with her knife once you left. With Sarala gone, he realised, if he wanted to live, then he had no choice but to talk. He and his cohort received a list of names over the phone, payment arrived shortly after by courier. It must have been shortly after Loukas escaped; our friend said Loukas was breathing heavily on the phone, as if he were in pain. Li's arranged for the Order of Light to keep an eye on my colleagues and friends.'

'Who?' Detective Widcombe asked, concerned. 'Who's on the list?'

'Barry, Johnathan Caster, Archie Randle, Bert and others you don't know. People I associate with. His orders were quite explicit; they were to be disabled and disfigured.' Jarrod looked at Detective Widcombe with worry in his eyes. 'I'm glad you left when you did.'

'Jarrod?' Sarala enquired, concern in her voice.

'Loukas gave special instructions for you.' Jarrod's face blushed in shame as he spoke. 'I think you need to phone in sick, Detective. It's not safe at the moment.'

Chapter 26

'Any trouble from work?' Jarrod asked the detective, as he passed her a plate of breakfast pancakes.

'They're not happy but considering everything I have been through, they understand. I could have used the knock-on-the- head for months, I've seen others remain off work for less.'

'Pancakes!' the Chinese sisters chimed as they walked in.

'You're such a gentleman, Jarrod,' Li said.

'Do we have a plan?' the detective asked, slapping Li's hand from her plate.

'Ah, I have fallen behind on my usual schedule, I have... I have a duty I need to attend to,' Jarrod said apologetically. 'You'll have to stay here.'

'Swalon?' Xiu asked, accepting a fresh plate of steaming pancakes.

Jarrod nodded, in silent acknowledgement.

'Take Sarala, it will do her good.'

Jarrod paused at the cooker, thinking. He flipped the next batch of overcooked pancakes at the sink with a scowl, annoyed at himself for getting distracted. 'I was up all night thinking about Selgroch, how she Stepped here from her dimension and not from Nowhere.' He turned and offered an expectant Li her breakfast. His speech slowed as he thought through the permutations. 'I should be able to replicate the process.'

'Does it matter?' Li asked.

'Stepping out of Nowhere uses all of my personal energy. If I could Step directly, I would arrive at the destination fit to fight,'

'What's a Swalon?' the detective asked.

'Who,' Li corrected.

'Who's Swalon?' Sarala tried again.

'He is the most feared man on Prushal,' Jarrod answered, slightly embarrassed. 'He's my mentor's son and a good friend.'

Sitting at the breakfast bar in Jarrod's kitchen, Detective Widcombe opened her hands, palms upwards as if to question, "And?".

'For centuries my people lost the ability to perform the Wayfarer's Step. Swalon rediscovered it. A few years later he went missing, presumed dead. Research into the Wayfarer's Step was forbidden, deemed too dangerous. Fifteen years ago, he re-appeared a changed man, both mentally and physically. He was incoherent at first, quite mad. Over weeks of nursing, it transpired that he had Stepped into a demon's dimension where he was tortured and kept for sport and pleasure. Somehow, he escaped and returned home... but his aura was black and his personality was as twisted and deformed as his body. He turned on his father and Prushal. What the Wizards' Council won't acknowledge is that Swalon could have killed dozens of them, as they attempted to subdue him. Instead he Stepped out of their trap into Nowhere and was never seen again.'

'But *you* know where he is?' Detective Widcombe asked in a hushed voice.

'Yes, I found him. He's the friend I told you about, the one who I found by sitting in Nowhere to see where the tides would take me.'

The leaves around Jarrod's apartment chimed — neither a symphony of pure melody nor a composition of chaos to indicate evil. Li left the kitchen area to investigate.

'Two police detectives are in the lobby. Your spell of doubt is causing them to pause by the elevator.'

'We must go,' Jarrod said. 'Xiu, do you still have your emergency bug-out bags?'

'Of course, packed and ready to go,' Xiu answered, unsure of where Jarrod was going with the conversation.

'Get them. You and Sarala are staying with Swalon for a while.' Jarrod man-handled the detective off her breakfast stool. 'Li, deal with the police and see if you can find any leads to Loukas while I'm gone.' He handed her one of his coins. 'This will allow you to open the front door.'

Li and Xiu nodded in confirmation of Jarrod's plan. Xiu left the room, darting into the detective's bedroom while Jarrod took Sarala down the corridor.

Xiu's apartment was accessed by a hidden stairway in one of the guest rooms. Detective Widcombe noted that the bed Xiu should have slept in was pristine and unused. *Why should she when she can walk down to her own bed*, she thought to herself.

As they exited through a sliding wall panel in the apartment below, they were greeted by the pizza man from the other night, now clad in nondescript clothing. The apartment itself was decorated Chinese style: majestic, calming and somehow ancient. Detective Widcombe knew without asking that all the ornaments were genuine relics.

Jarrod said something in Mandarin that the detective did not understand and the man left, returning shortly with two packed sports bags.

Xiu appeared from behind Jarrod and took the bags, proceeding to dump clothing from one of the holdalls onto the floor. Stuffing a handful of the detective's clothes in, she explained, 'Sorry Sarala. I didn't think you'd fit into Li's clothes. There's food, weapons and tools.' Xiu smiled at Jarrod in confirmation. 'We're ready to go.'

'Where are we going?' Before the last word left her lips, Detective Widcombe found herself at the top of a huge fertile valley full of trees and lush vegetation. The sky was orange and the grass red. 'Jarrod?'

'It worked,' Xiu breathed out with relief. 'Did you at least practice before taking us with you?'

'There was no time,' Jarrod admitted with a cheeky smile. 'Once I figured it out, it was easy to Step without entering Nowhere. Although, I haven't figured out how Selgroch managed to open and maintain a portal for her minions to walk through...'

The plateau above the valley was a stark contrast to the lush, vibrant valley; orange soil sprouted small withering plants and cracks from prolonged droughts marbled the surface.

'This way.' Jarrod and Xiu trekked off along a frequently trodden path leaving the detective gawking at the scenery. Birds chirped and warbled in the distance, nearby bushes moved as animals scurried away, spooked by their presence.

Realising she was standing alone in a strange place, Detective Widcombe shouted, 'Jarrod! Wait!' Her head pivoted around like an inquisitive tourist as she ran to catch up.

At the bottom of the valley, a stream trickled at the middle of a large riverbed. Once, long ago, a large river must have raged but no longer. Now small saplings grew amongst the rounded pebbles, nature had begun to reclaim the rock-covered ground.

'All this is because of Swalon,' Jarrod informed the detective.

'What is?'

'All this.' Jarrod spun around as he walked waving his arms at the trees. 'Shortly after Swalon arrived here, an earthquake diverted the springs in the far mountains. This valley began to die; without water the plants and trees started to wither, no plants means no insects, so no birds. You know how it goes. Swalon saved the valley.'

'I don't understand, you said he was evil...'

'No. I said he had a black aura that affected his personality,' Jarrod corrected her. 'When Swalon escaped the Wizard's Council, he entered Nowhere with no reserves of magic, he couldn't exit there. Eventually, after weeks in Nowhere, he fell asleep. Remember, I said time moves differently there so you tire more slowly. The currents brought him here. He woke, or so he tells me, with tree dogs protecting him from predators. They brought him nuts and berries.'

'Tree dogs?'

'That's what Swalon calls them. They are... a bit like a poodle, a monkey and a sloth mixed together. Friendly little things, intelligent too.'

'He saved the valley? I don't understand.'

'At the moment, most of the indigenous life on this planet live in valleys, where there's shade. The planet's in its summer phase, it gets very hot at midday with little precipitation.'

'You're not making sense. You said he was bad, but he saved a valley... What? Why?'

'Because it saved me, or the tree dogs did,' a booming voice shouted from the trees.

A hooded man taller than Jarrod emerged from the trees. A large staff in one hand and a rudimentary crossbow in the other.

'Swalon,' Jarrod cried in greeting.

'Jarrod,' Swalon replied, more cautious. 'You bring strangers!'

'Friends, Swalon. These are my friends: Xiu and Sarala. You've met Xiu before, remember?'

'I must continue with my routine. Follow,' he replied brusquely before retreating back into the trees.

'Friendly fellow,' Detective Widcombe whispered with sarcasm dripping from her voice.

'He's unaccustomed to guests and we are disturbing him during his routine. He is weary of you because he's used up most of his energy,' Jarrod replied.

'You're not helping,' the detective said, moments before she shivered. 'Jarrod, he's casting magic, I can feel it.'

'Good, tell me what you feel,' Jarrod replied as he prodded her to continue walking.

'I feel... I feel rock, pressure, water. He's forcing the water underground to rise, he's... he's altering the water table, he's moving water.' She looked at Jarrod bewildered.

'He's saving the valley and all the animals within. This is his duty, now. He feels beholden to them.'

When they caught up with Swalon, he was sat on a rock, exhaustion causing him to lean against his staff for support.

'There is little magic in this place. The universal energy that we utilise is in short supply here. It took Swalon over a year to prepare to Step away from this place. As he was about to leave, disaster struck the valley.'

'How could I leave my friends to die?' Swalon asked from the shadow of his cloak. 'They who had fed me, taught me to live and showed me nothing but compassion. The tree dogs adopted me, asked for nothing in return. Their loving nature nurtured me, brought me back from the brink of madness. I think they mistook me for one of their own.' Swalon removed his hood, his bearded face a mass of scars, his features distorted - no natural affliction could have caused such wounds. Standing, he shed his cloak and stood before them in shabby rags. His arms and legs were bare, disjointed, skin twisted, fur and scale intermixed with his skin. 'Do I offend you?' He looked directly at Sarala and Xiu.

Holding back the bile in her throat, Detective Widcombe answered, 'Nothing a bath wouldn't cure. You should use some of that water for yourself.'

Pointing his staff directly at the detective, Swalon shrieked with laughter. 'I like her Jarrod. I can see why you keep her.' The fire died in the man's eyes as quickly as it came, his reserve of energy spent. 'I have one more spring to invigorate,' he informed them, stumbling off once more.

'Swalon, allow me this time please,' Jarrod pleaded.

'Jarrod, you know I must do this alone. I must repay my debt.'

'And I need you awake when we get you back to your home. We need to talk. One of the demons you once told me about is after us.'

Swalon spun round and looked at Detective Widcombe. 'Why?' he asked. 'Why would a demon care about you?' He stepped towards the detective and placed a dirty hand on her head. 'Sensitive, innocent. She has no magic, why would the demon be after her?' Suspicion filled his words.

'Selgroch, Swalon. You mentioned the name a long time

ago when you told me your story.'

Swalon touched his disfigured face, resting his forehead against the staff as he did so. 'Selgroch,' he cried aloud. 'You dare mention her to me, here? Do you know what she did? No, you could never understand.'

Jarrod stood still as Swalon grabbed the lapels of his jacket, the man's spittle flying into his face.

'Why do you mention her? Why?'

'She attacked us in my home, Swalon. Her Knight has been killing people.'

'Why? Why would she? You are nothing to her!'

'I found her idol, but it was stolen before I took possession and her Knight has been hunting for it ever since.'

'Why would you go looking for her? I told you how powerful she is! I told you what she had done! Why? For all that is pure, why?' Swalon was ranting now, tears of remembrance running down his face, anguish at what once was and what was to come, exhausting him. 'Why? Jarrod, why?' he cried, slumping at Jarrod's feet, exhausted. 'Why?' he pleaded.

'Jarrod?' Detective Widcombe asked, moving to comfort the man on the floor.

'Selgroch captured Swalon. She tortured him until she became bored with her magical toy. He was traded to a less powerful creature, which is how Swalon managed to escape. His new owner took him to Earth, believing Swalon would be his Knight. Swalon fled home, a broken and twisted remnant of a man, his loyalties torn, the demon's conditioning tearing at his sanity.'

'So, you knew of Selgroch?' the detective questioned, anger rising in her voice. 'You knew who she was when you bought the idol?'

'Yes. I came across her name while performing my own

research on Earth. When I first stumbled upon Swalon here and we talked, I realised she was a danger to your society.'

'Talked?' Swalon laughed weakly. 'I tried to kill you.'

Jarrod shrugged. 'He managed to shoot me with his bow while I was recovering from being ejected from Nowhere. It wasn't a pleasant experience. Thankfully he had little magic to fight with, so, injured as I was, I managed to overpower him.' Lifting Swalon to his feet, Jarrod swung the man's arm over his shoulder and helped him remain upright. 'Eventually he remembered who I was. So, once a month I bring supplies and we talk. I want him to train you. He was always better at empathic abilities than I.'

'She can't stay here Jarrod. I can't protect her, not here.' Worry filled Swalon's eyes as he looked at his guests.

'There are no idols for her here, Swalon. If she finds you here, her power would be limited. Parlour tricks and persuasion is all she'll have.'

'I'm not staying here Jarrod,' Detective Widcombe protested. 'We have to find Loukas and bring him to justice.'

'I will find him,' Jarrod said.

'Who's Loukas?' Swalon asked.

'The Knight of Selgroch. I nearly killed him. I didn't know he had protective wards at the time.'

'She's weaker than she lets on, Jarrod,' Swalon said. 'They all are. The universal energy has been all but used up in their own dimension. It flows in from other realms — flows is the wrong word — it trickles in. There was a cull of lesser creatures, the weaker demons, while I was there. She said it was to preserve what little energy they had left from being used frivolously.'

'They'll be pissed at how much she used up in my

apartment then,' Jarrod said. 'I... I have never fought such a powerful creature,' he confessed.

'Souls, Jarrod, souls. Most demons destroy the soul out of malice. She and a handful of others know how to feed off the energy in a soul. For are we not all created from the energy of the universe?' Swalon coughed, a chest rattling fit that racked his body. 'She won't manifest again, not so soon. If the others of her clan find out she is weakened, they will kill her.'

'Clan?'

'Coven, clan, call it what you will. The creatures of that dimension band together in loose associations based on mutual gain, forever feeding on the weak. They are heinous, Jarrod. I never in my worst nightmares imagined such a place could exist.' Stumbling forwards, Swalon commanded, 'Come. We must continue.'

Looking at Jarrod, Detective Widcombe raised a questioning eyebrow.

'There is one more location for Swalon to raise the water table. It's at his home, as he usually collapses afterwards. Thankfully the tree dogs look after him until he recovers.'

A short walk along the worn path led the group to a crude log cabin. Strange animals lounged on the roof, basking in the sun.

'Swalon, I need you awake. Please, allow me,' Jarrod urged as he prepared for the spell. Taking a coin out of his pocket, Jarrod closed his eyes in concentration. Feeling for the fissures in the rock below, he cast a spell, forcing the underground water upwards. The detective shivered as he did so.

'Thank you,' Swalon whispered, collapsing onto a bunk shaded by the cabin's veranda. He fell asleep immediately.

Jarrod pulled a blanket over him and sat in a wooden

seat beside him. Dozens of tree dogs crawled down off the roof. They examined the new-comers hesitantly.

'He'll be ok in the morning. Swalon gathers in the available energy and uses it to bring water to the valley. It is his self-imposed penance and he will remain here until the season changes.'

'Jarrod, you said his aura was black?' Detective Widcombe asked, eyes wide, but not seeing. She was viewing Swalon with her inner eye instead.

'It was,' Jarrod smiled. 'He remains here out of love, for the tree dogs and the other animals. With so little magical energy available, he experiences pain with every spell. To bring up the water from below, he uses a small amount of his own life-force, dying a little every time. He puts these animals before himself. He defends them when predators enter the valley; with no spare magic he has to rely on his bow and knife. Once, I found him torn to shreds, claw marks all over his body. I healed the wounds the best I could and performed his duties for a couple of days.'

'But his body is still deformed?' the detective asked.

'Yes, it's twisted and broken by magic. He's far beyond my healing capabilities. Only healers from Prushal can repair those wounds. He left there before they could finish.'

'He was worse than this?' Detective Widcombe gasped.

'Much, Sarala. His mind was the worst affected. They concentrated there until he could withstand no more, then they worked on his body while he slept. His father — my mentor —grieves for him and I cannot tell him that his son is alive. If the Council found out, they would insist that I bring him to justice. He is not a monster, Sarala. He has never told me how he gained so much black in his soul, the things he had to do to survive. But I know he wants to atone for his sins.'

Sitting next to Swalon, Detective Widcombe asked, 'Jarrod, what happened to George Mannering, the person whose identity you stole?'

'He's doing well,' Jarrod chuckled, 'I promise. When I discovered him, he was about to commit suicide. He was suffering with depression and the stalker we discussed didn't help.' Jarrod took a piece of proffered fruit from a tree dog and sat down next to the detective. 'Seeing the resemblance between George and myself, I saw an opportunity. I had been roaming on your planet for a number of years and longed for a place to settle. I offered George a new life and he is now living on Prushal and doing well.'

'Promise?'

'Once this is over, I will take you to see him, if you like? The Wizards' Council won't be happy about it, but...'. He shrugged in resignation.

'Jarrod, how long have I slept?' Swalon croaked.

'It's morning, Swalon. You slept through the whole of yesterday. I have performed your duties. The water was much deeper than before.'

'It's been receding for a while. I don't know how much longer I can maintain the valley,' Swalon admitted with a guilt-ridden voice.

'I have fractured the bedrock further down, there's a huge reservoir down there. Most of the water on this planet remains locked underground,' Jarrod explained to Xiu and the detective. 'I have a gift for you Swalon.' Producing a ball of polished metal from his pocket, Jarrod handed it over.

Swalon's hand dipped as the weight bore it down.

'Jarrod! How? I've never seen so much in one place.' All trace of fatigue evaporated as Swalon swooned over his gift.

'Rhodium,' Jarrod explained to Xiu and Detective Widcombe. 'It's the rarest non-radioactive metal on the earth — rarer still on Prushal. It's heavier than lead and one of Swalon's affinity metals.'

'I've heard of Rhodium magnets.' Detective Widcombe tilted her head slightly as she studied the reflective ball in Swalon's hand.

'You could buy a house in London with that ball, Sarala. On Prushal, it's so rare, you could buy a whole country.' Jarrod smiled at his friend's reaction.

'Thank you.' Tears ran freely down Swalon's face. 'No one has ever given me such a gift. With this I can focus my energy and I will be able to maintain the flow of water.' Looking at the women, he recognised Xiu for the first time. 'Xiu, I didn't recognise you yesterday, I apologise. I have not been myself.'

'Yes, you have Swalon. You were just as absorbed in saving your valley the last time I came to see you.' The young Chinese women hugged the tattered wizard. 'My father sends his regards and asks when you will be joining us?'

'My friends, Xiu.' Swalon held out his arms and tree dogs flocked to him for cuddles. 'I cannot leave them, not until this summer is over.'

'How long does a summer last?' Detective Widcombe asked, still mesmerised by the rhodium ball in Swalon's hand. Through her inner eye she could see that Jarrod had already imbued it with the universe's energy.

'Autumn will be here in seven months. The plants will flourish on the plains and these,' he held out his animal covered arms, 'will leave the protection of the valley. I will no longer be needed.' Swalon's face grew sad at the thought.

'You have a home with us Swalon, you know this,' Xiu comforted the man.

'To fight, Xiu, in your endless war.' His sad eyes fell upon the Chinese woman.

'You know more about demons than anyone alive. If you choose not to fight, you still have a place with us. Knowledge is power.'

'Talking of which, before you passed out, you said Selgroch was weaker than we thought. What did you mean?' Jarrod butted in.

'It's as I said Jarrod, millennia of frivolous use has expended the energy in their dimension. The universe, space and time are weak there. The demons are feeding off each other. The ancient ones who Step through to other dimensions are bolstered by their followers and sacrifices they offer. Selgroch is one of the most powerful. If her peers discover that she is weakened, they will pounce on her.'

'Why Earth? Why do they come to us?'

'Humans are inherently weak, corruption is rife and so you are easy to enslave. Be thankful that the location of Earth is kept a secret. Those that feed on human souls have no intention of informing the others about their feeding ground. Furgus, the demon I escaped from, was the only demon in twelve generations to discover the Wayfarer's Step and locate earth.'

'How did you escape?'

'I don't want to talk about it,' Swalon snapped. His pupils narrowed, his stare became hard. 'I sent him back, injured. His peers will have devoured him for his weakness.'

'It's okay, Swalon.' Jarrod stepped forward and placed a

calming hand on the man's shoulder. 'Sarala didn't mean anything by it. She is a police officer and it's her nature to pry. Before I go, is there anything else you can tell me about Selgroch?'

'She has six active idols on Earth, Jarrod. Her worshippers create disasters, train derailments, air disasters, huge fires. The souls of the victims are pledged to her. You must destroy the idols if you want to rid Earth of her influence.'

'How?'

'Only one who has been touched by Selgroch can locate her shrines. She blesses each acolyte personally with scarification, symbols of obedience and fealty. Her claws poison their blood. They feel her presence when she is near.'

'The girl?' Detective Widcombe said, looking at Xiu. 'You said she would feel if evil was near.'

'A girl?' Swalon enquired.

'She fought alongside us when Selgroch attacked. She jumped upon the beast and slashed at it with her knife. Her chest holds an imprint of Selgroch's hand.'

Looking at Jarrod, Swalon suggested, 'Find the Knight. I have not met him, but I know he is relentless. She will instruct him to sacrifice you all. Your friends will die first, Jarrod.'

'Exactly why I brought Sarala here.' Jarrod smiled. 'She needs to be trained. Xiu will work on her physical aspects, I want you to enlighten her.'

'Jarrod, I...'

'Swalon, you are in balance and have been for a long time. Your sacrifice here has saved you. Each time I visit you have changed a little more. I am trusting you with the most precious items I possess — my friends — and I do so with no doubt that you will treat them fairly and lay down your life for them if it came to that.' As an afterthought Jarrod asked, 'Do you know how Selgroch keeps a passage open, allowing her soldiers to walk through? I have figured out how to circumvent Nowhere, but not how to keep the passage open?'

'I know what you mean. I saw her move a whole army once.' Swalon entered his log cabin, returning moments later. 'I have written everything down Jarrod, everything I experienced in their dimension, everything I saw and learnt.' He handed a crude leather-bound book to Jarrod. 'It took years for my mind to heal enough to remember it all, writing it down helped me make sense of what happened.' Swalon picked up a tree dog and held it close. 'I cannot imagine what I have put my father through. These tree dogs are the closest I'll ever come to having children. I have lost three to predators and the pain I feel is unbearable.'

'Swalon, you're still young,'

'No, my friend. Selgroch made sure I could never sire offspring. Please give the book to my father when you have finished with it. It is my apology.' With sadness in his voice he instructed, 'Go. I will look after your friends. God knows, I could do with the company.'

The men hugged, Jarrod nodded at the two women and before Detective Widcombe could complain he Stepped out of their dimension.

Chapter 27

Jarrod performed the Wayfarer's Step, re-appearing in his secret room. Pleased how the meeting with Swalon had gone, he was also elated that he had learned how to perform the Wayfarer's Step without leaving himself exhausted and vulnerable. He'd learnt a lot from his brief encounter with Selgroch, although most of his new knowledge was unusable unless he wished to darken his aura again. Returning the spent tokens into their trays, Jarrod then replenished his pockets, carrying double his usual amount. These were extraordinary times after all. Looking at the trays of coins along the shelves, he sighed. It would take him a long time to replenish their energy. More so for the huge blocks of meteoric iron embedded into the walls and floor.

'Jarrod!' Li's gentle voice shouted from the lounge.

Jarrod followed the sound of activity and found Li and the young girl cooking. Li winked at Jarrod to indicate she was making progress, slowly breaking down the girl's years of mistrust.

'Ladies,' Jarrod greeted the pair.

The two females hunkered together and laughed.

'I told you. He's old school,' Li addressed her cohort. Facing Jarrod, she explained. 'Melissa is not used to being addressed in such a formal manner, Jarrod. Your manners amuse her.' Li flashed a smile.

'How are you feeling Melissa?' Jarrod asked, noting the teenager's name and that she was dressed in Xiu's slacks and wrap-around blouse, filling the blouse out more than the Chinese woman did.

'I... if Li hadn't been here to talk to, I would have said I'd had a bad trip. It doesn't seem real.' She moved the top part of her blouse aside to reveal a burn mark in the shape of a clawed hand. The scabs over the deep puncture wounds were stained green from one of Li's medical tinctures. 'This is real though.'

'We talked shortly afterwards... do you remember?'

Melissa shook her head. 'I'm sorry Jarrod, I was...' She hung her head, ashamed to admit she was high on drugs at the time. 'I have flashes of the pretty lady hurting you and the detective. She felt wrong, she kept calling to me inside my head, making promises. Empty words. I have lived my whole life being offered false promises so it wasn't hard to recognise another one. Somehow, I knew that if I went to her, I wouldn't survive. The Razor Crew taught me mistrust, if nothing else. Then, she turned into a monster.' Melissa placed a hand on her chest. It failed to match the size of the ugly scar.

'Do you understand what she was?' Jarrod asked.

The girl nodded, holding back tears, suddenly scared. Li gently guided her to a breakfast bar stool. 'Li has been explaining. You're like Keanu Reeves in Constantine.'

With confusion on his face, Jarrod looked at Li for an explanation.

'You fight evil, Jarrod. Like the character in Constantine.' Li shrugged and mouthed: *It was the only way.*

'Melissa, you have been touched by evil and you will always recognise it when it's near. Even though you were high, you cannot deny what you saw. This ability will be with you for the rest of your life. But you can join us, work with us.'

'Li explained she wants me to go to China and train with her sisters.' Fright filled the girl's eyes, making them wide and as dark as midnight. 'Can't I stay here, with you?'

Jarrod played with the whiskers of his beard as he thought. 'You have been touched by the demon Selgroch, so you are tuned into her presence. You could help me find her nearest coven.'

'Jarrod!' Li protested, 'she is not ready, she has no training.'

'It's OK, Li,' Melissa cried. 'I want to help.'

'No! You don't understand. It takes years of mental training to attempt this. It could rip your mind apart. Jarrod wants you to feel for the idols, for her. If she's on Earth, Selgroch will feel your presence, too. She'll kill you.'

'I will protect her, Li,' Jarrod explained.

'She will not do it, Jarrod. She is still suffering from withdrawal and her chi was fractured before she was flung into this situation. She's only a child.'

'It will be difficult and it could hurt, but she will be safe. I promise,' Jarrod insisted.

'Jarrod's the only man I know who has let me sleep without trying to rape me,' Melissa said, some strength of her former life as Hellcat, a Razor Crew member, glinted in her eyes. 'I... I felt safe in his arms,' She looked at Jarrod and confirmed, 'I would like to try.'

'Inform your father. We may need his assistance again,' Jarrod instructed Li, ignoring the glowering stare.

'You have matters to attend to first, Jarrod. These arrived for you.' Li passed several hand-written notes to him. 'While you were away, the enemy was busy.'

'Shit!' Kneeling in front of Melissa and holding up the notes, he said, 'I need to deal with these, but I will be back as soon as I can. I promise. Li will prepare you for the process.'

Melissa replaced her hand back on to her scar, her teeth biting into her bottom lip.

'Selgroch is the exception, not the norm. After this is over anything else you encounter will be a walk in the park. I promise.'

Before Jarrod could leave, Melissa hugged him. Kissing the top of her head, Jarrod nodded to Li and left the room.

Exiting the apartment, the lift doors opened as Jarrod closed his stout copper front door. Two detectives and Matt Johnson from the Johnson Security company entered the penthouse lobby. Having left the signal-free environment of his apartment, Jarrod's phoned chimed to indicate he'd missed a plethora of texts and calls.

'Mr Wentworth, Detective Jeffers and Harris.' The speaker, a smart looking gentleman proffered his credentials as they drew near the central point of the hallway. 'You're a hard man to find.'

'I'm walking that way gentlemen. If you wish to talk we can do so in the lift.' Jarrod pointed behind them with his umbrella, straining to see the officer's warrant card from this distance. 'Matthew,' he nodded to the head of Johnson Security.

'Mr Wentworth, we need to talk,' Detective Jeffers protested. 'As I understand it, you failed to report an attack on your doorman, which led to the murder on the second floor.'

Jarrod was forced to stop as the officers blocked the passageway. His anger at the delay seething below the surface.

'I believed it to be a random attack, an attempted burglary gone wrong. There was no way I could have known the attacker was targeting one of the residents here.'

'You do own the building, is that right?'

'You already have a comprehensive file on my business portfolio, Detective. Your persistent colleague, Detective Widcombe, was quite thorough in her investigation. She is an interesting person to talk to and attractive to boot. You are neither. This corridor, and the whole floor, is private property. I am asking you to leave. The lift is behind you.'

'Mr Wentworth, I am investigating multiple murders and your name keeps popping up.'

Jarrod remained silent and stared at the detective. After a moment's deliberation, he pulled his retro mobile phone from his pocket and pressed speed dial for his lawyer.

'Did you know the street gang that broke into Caster and Randle are dead, Mr Wentworth? They were tortured and left to suffer. We have recovered twenty-seven bodies so far. Everyone who has come into contact with the stolen idol has died, besides you. Why is that?'

'I have two police officers in my hallway and they are refusing to leave.' Jarrod listened to his lawyer's reply and handed the phone to the detective. 'My lawyer.'

Detective Jeffers waved his hand in refusal. 'We're leaving. But I am going to keep a close eye on you, Mr Wentworth. Sarala was right, there is something amiss with you.'

Jarrod watched the detectives as they waited for the lift to return. He spoke only after they'd entered and the doors had closed behind them. 'Matt, I'm sorry about your man.'

'I appreciate the private medical care. I am sure he does,

too.' Matt surveyed his client, noticing the lack of grooming on the man's usually pristine beard. 'Who are you afraid of, Jarrod?'

'Sorry?'

'You installed the VIP Business package at Caster and Randle after the break-in and this building's security is bespoke. Only this floor is uncovered, which in my business usually means my clients don't want their activities being recorded.'

'I was and am concerned for Caster and Randle, the business, as well as Archie and Johnathan,' Jarrod answered, ushering Matt Johnson towards the lift.

'Three men entered this building, one left days later.' Matt smiled at Jarrod. 'We have surveillance on other premises. I ensure the camera coverage overlaps for occasions such as this.'

'Meaning?'

'Either there are two men still on the premises or they are not. My men have swept the whole of the building, except this floor.'

'I can promise you they are not here,' Jarrod answered tersely, annoyed that a service provider doubted his integrity.

'Are they dead?' Matt stared back at Jarrod, unafraid. He dealt with the rich, the crazy and criminals on a daily basis. An eccentric historian was a breath of fresh air. 'Did you know that there is a back-up server in the basement?'

'No.'

'Three men came up this lift and one left. He was bleeding profusely from wounds all over his body. Then, more bizarrely, an army of Chinese arrive and clean up the mess. They did a professional job, they weren't amateurs.' Matt stopped before he pressed the button to call the lift back up. 'If you had followed protocol, my men would have examined the back-up server and discovered the murderer on the second floor. Do you understand?' Anger flared through Matt Johnson's professional demeanour for the first time. Entering the lift Matt added, 'Jarrod, I'm not paid to care what you are mixed up in. I just need to know the scale of the threat.'

Turning around Matt Johnson found he was talking to an empty corridor. Stepping out of the lift he glanced at the lobby walls for signs of a hidden door and swore.

Chapter 28

Jarrod attempted to enter Caster and Randle from the rear loading bay. His code for the door lock failed and the intercom chimed.

'Mr Wentworth, someone will be down in a second. The entry points have been upgraded. You should have received a phone call to explain the new procedures,' an unknown voice said from the device.

Jarrod pulled out his phone and saw that he had six missed calls and a handful of messages. Huffing at the contrivance, he nestled it back into the depths of his jacket.

A middle-aged woman in Johnson Security livery opened the door and greeted Jarrod with a smile. She held herself with the confidence ingrained by military experience. Her handshake was firm, her arm strong.

'Miss?'

'Katrina. Please, call me Katrina, Mr Wentworth.' She smiled with perfect teeth. 'We have been expecting you, although not at the rear entrance.'

'Why are there scorch marks on the rear walls?' Jarrod asked the guard.

Tilting her head slightly, she studied Jarrod for a second.

Untrimmed beard, traces of orange dust on his shoes, boots, she said to herself. 'Have you been away, Mr Wentworth? Matt left you various messages. It's been a busy forty-eight hours.'

'I had no signal where I was,' Jarrod answered honestly.

'I think you should come to the office. We can brief you properly there.'

'Jarrod, old man. How the devil are you?' Johnathan Caster asked from behind the wooden desk.

Archie stepped from the behind the door and shook Jarrod's hand. 'We thought the blighters had got you,' he said.

'We're under attack, Jarrod. Some fellow tried to bash Archie on the head with a cosh and now they're trying to burn the bloody building down,' Johnathan said, moving his hands beneath the desk to hide their shaking.

'Archie?' Jarrod enquired.

'I'm all right, old boy. Some passing Chinese woman swept the blighter's legs from underneath him, then kicked him in the head. He was still unconscious when the police arrived.' Looking bashful he confessed, 'I kicked the bounder in the family jewels for good measure. Well, he deserved it.'

Patting Archie on the shoulder, Jarrod asked, 'And the woman?'

'Gone, it all happened so fast,' Archie replied. 'Mrs Randle said I should get mugged more often. The excitement raised the libido, if you know what I mean.'

'I am sorry Archie and to you too, Johnathan. This is all my fault.' Jarrod was faced by two uncomprehending stares. 'It's all about the stolen idol.' Jarrod paused to choose his words carefully. 'A group of cultists have been killing anyone involved, and they want the idol.'

'Give it to them. It's not like the damned thing is actually magical or anything,' Johnathan scoffed.

'That might be difficult. I have spoken to the girl who stole it and it was destroyed.'

'Girl? Are you saying one of those rascals who broke in here was a girl?' Archie gasped.

'Can we repair the statue?' Johnathan asked. 'I know a damned fine restorer, old bean. Then we could give it back.'

'She shot it.' Jarrod explained, with a shake of his head.

'Have you told this to the police? Do they know who the cult members are?'

'No, and I don't think they would believe me if I told them.' Jarrod turned to Katrina, who was waiting patiently behind him. 'Can you ask Matt to provide a protective detail for Johnathan and Archie, including their families, please?'

'I can but are you aware how much that will cost?' she replied.

'It's fine.' Jarrod watched her retreat to the security office across the hallway and sit down. 'I am sorry for all of this,' he apologised to his colleagues.

'You weren't to know, old boy. It's not your fault that some crackpot believes in all that hocus pocus malarkey.'

'Archie, did the police say anything about your attacker?'

'They were quite happy in the end. I don't think they believed me about the woman, not until he woke up ranting about *killing the bleeding bitch.*' Archie failed to mimic any recognisable dialect. 'The police said the man was wanted for GBH. He looked the shady type. His eyes were too close together.'

Johnathan laughed. 'Oh, don't get him started, Jarrod. He'd have every teenager in ripped jeans flogged for stupidity,' he guffawed.

'I just can't understand why you would pay for defective clothing. No self-respecting man would ever wear torn clothing. What is wrong with people these days?'

'You make me look downright modern, Archie,' Johnathan smirked, straightening his tweed suit.'

'My taxi driver, Bert, was attacked the other night,' Jarrod informed them. 'They, whoever *they* are, are hurting anyone I come in contact with.'

'Is he OK?' Johnathan asked, his humour sobering up quickly.

'Nasty knock on the head. I called into the hospital before coming here. They're keeping Bert in for observation. I've arranged for him to be moved to a private clinic.'

'Jolly decent of you, old bean.'

'Is Barry working today?'

'Yes. When the new guards arrived, they kept him on as he knows where everything is. He's not overly fond of his new colleagues. This used to be a plod around job, a nothing-to-see kind of establishment. Now it's all Hollywood gung-ho. Have you shaken hands with Katrina? I wouldn't want to arm wrestle with her, old boy.'

'Keep him here tonight,' Jarrod ordered. 'Now, tell me about the fire at the back...' He looked across the hallway. He knew the guards would have informed Matt Johnson of his arrival before he entered the premise. He did not feel like a long conversation with their boss and so needed to make this quick.

'Nothing much to say, Jarrod. Two ruffians with scarves over their faces appeared from the alleys over the back and they pulled bottles filled with sticky petrol from their bags.' Turning his laptop around, Archie said, 'I can bring up the CCTV footage if you like.'

Jarrod dismissed the offer with a gesture of his hand, 'Sticky petrol?'

'Katrina said it was probably a home-made napalm. Apparently, the recipe is on the internet.'

'You really should watch the video Jarrod. It is quite spectacular,' Archie said.

'The fire?' Jarrod asked, ignoring Archie.

'The local youths can thank you for this. Did you know the Johnson Security system you had installed includes foam sprinklers on the outside walls? The whole back end of the building was covered in seconds. It smothered the fire, putting it out immediately. By the time the fire brigade arrived, there were dozens of kids playing in the foam. It was like an impromptu street party.' Archie waved a hand at the recorded footage on the screen.

'What happened to the attackers?' Jarrod asked.

'They threw two bottles of sticky petrol and left once the foam put the fires out,' Johnathan replied.

'Molotov cocktails, Johnathan. They're called Molotovs,' Archie informed him.

Keeping an eye on the security office, Jarrod proclaimed, 'I need to go.'

'Jarrod, what are you going to do?' Archie asked with concern.

'I'm investigating the cult. The police won't take it seriously unless I have some evidence,' Jarrod said as he thought, *I am going to find the cult and end this.* 'Watch your backs and keep safe.' With that Jarrod leapt up and left the office.

'It's all very Sean Connery,' Archie said with a nervous smile.

'Connery? *Connery?*' Johnathan asked. 'When did you last take Mrs Randle to the cinema, Archie?'

Chapter 29

Jarrod swore to himself as he exited the taxi. He missed Bert. On days that Jarrod required transportation, Bert was his private chauffeur. In remuneration, the cab company that Jarrod owned paid the driver a generous day rate. Today's replacement cabbie, whilst being polite, was an aggressive driver.

A fleet of Johnson Securities installation vehicles was parked outside of his apartment building and Jarrod mused that Matt Johnson was performing expensive upgrades as his way of saying, *Don't walk out on me while we are talking.* Jarrod smiled. It was of little consequence. Money held no importance to him here nor at home. Gold was as common as iron on Prushal, which is how he'd managed to fund his property portfolio in Manchester.

Jarrod caught a mug as he walked through his metal clad front door. Saving the flung mug caused the remains of the contents to spill over him. He closed his eyes for a second and calmed his anger. *Solitude,* he prayed, *peace and quiet is all*

I ask for.

'I told you! I can't do it!' The young voice of Melissa, aka Hellcat, broke the silence.

'Yes, you can, you just need patience.' Li sighed, her own patience wearing thin.

'Jarrod, this is useless,' Melissa cried in frustration. 'She keeps saying the same thing. I can't feel anything, I can't feel evil. I told her.'

'I tried! She is untrained, undisciplined and disobedient. I doubt my father's teachers could do anything with her either.' Li's eye's flared at Jarrod, warning him not to provoke her.

'She doesn't truly believe, Li,' Jarrod said handing her the mug. 'She needs unequivocal proof.'

'She fought a demon and carries its mark on her chest. What more proof does she need?'

'She was on drugs at the time, she can deny anything that happened.' Jarrod caught hold of Melissa's hand and instructed, 'Come with me and I will show you something evil.'

'No! You can't! Not that,' Li objected, stepping in-between Jarrod and the girl.

Pulling a paring knife from her trousers, mistrust flashed across Melissa's face as she took a feral stance.

'That's my kitchen knife, give it back!' Jarrod held his other hand out to receive the knife.

'You'll be feeling it if you touch me! You're just the same as the rest.' The harsh Hellcat persona reappeared for the first time in days. She snatched her other hand from Jarrod's grip.

Holding his hands out to calm the girl, Jarrod apologised. 'I'm sorry Melissa, I phrased that badly. What I meant to say is that I have an artefact here that we liberated from a misguided soul. You will feel its presence as soon as I remove it from the container.' Holding a palm up he asked, 'Please may I have my knife back?' After a second of inaction, he added, 'You will have access to a plethora of weapons when your training begins.'

Looking at Li for confirmation, Melissa placed the knife, handle first, into Jarrod's open palm.

'You shouldn't use it Jarrod. It is vile,' Li pleaded. 'She is only a girl.'

'We do not have time, Li. Loukas has been busy. He has tried to burn down Caster and Randle, his men have attacked several of my associates.' Jarrod walked out of the spacious lounge through the equally cavernous kitchen to the inner rooms. The hallway was illuminated with natural light from the skylights that channelled the sun from the roof top.

Stopping at a plain section of an interior wall, Jarrod opened the hidden door to his secret room with a whispered word. A glow emanated from the room and the young girl gasped as she saw Jarrod's cloak and staff.

'You were wearing these the night of the attack. I... I remember it felt warm as you held me afterwards.'

Jarrod nodded with a smile. 'Yes. You can't damage it,' he answered as she gestured towards his staff. Turning to Li, he asked, 'Have you assessed her ability to defend herself yet?'

Li pulled a face. 'She's feral, Jarrod. She's tough, but foolish. She's only survived this long by taking knocks and gutting the men as they tried to molest her. She wouldn't last five seconds in a real fight.'

'I need you to teach her some defensive moves. If this works, we're going after them tonight.'

'And if it doesn't go well tonight? She's not ready.' Li forced a smile at Melissa in apology.

'I have left Barry exposed; they will go after him when

he leaves work in the morning.' Guilt dripped off Jarrod's words. 'If we can get him home without incident, I will Step him out of his house and maybe we can lay a trap.'

'How will that help? The hired goons haven't known anything useful.'

'If she can't find the cult, what else can I do?'

'So where is this mystery item you're going to show me?' Melissa interrupted, annoyed that they were talking about her as if she wasn't there.

Jarrod slid another hidden panel aside and pulled out a shoebox-sized container. It was made from finely grained wood and had Jarrod's leaf design emblazoned all over it.

'Barry made it,' Jarrod smiled. 'He's a talented man.' He placed the box on a nearby table and pushed it towards the centre.

'I don't feel anything. Sorry,' Melissa apologised.

'The box is imbued with restraining spells to prevent the influence of the item from leaching out. Xiu was meant to take it for cremation, but then you came along and stole the idol of Selgroch.'

'Sorry.' Melissa lower her head, ashamed. 'What's inside?'

'Oh... erm... it's...' Jarrod became flustered, embarrassed by the contents of the box.

'For God's sake Jarrod,' Li interrupted. 'It's a severed penis from a Victorian murderer and rapist. It was common in those days for executioners to sell the hangman's rope and parts of the condemned. This item has had a sordid history ever since.'

Melissa sniggered.

Jarrod took hold of the box, unlatched the lock and asked, 'Are you ready?'

Still sniggering, Melissa replied, 'I've never come across a dick that's worth this much of a drum roll.'

Jarrod slowly opened the lid as if by restricting the visibility of the item, he could hold back the flow of malevolence that it emanated.

Melissa's eyes widened with a sharp intake of breath and she thrust a hand on to the scar on her chest. Digging her fingers deep into her flesh she cried, 'No!' Tears rolled down her pale cheeks. The deep gouges from Selgroch's claws throbbed and blood seeped from beneath the herbal dressing.

The withered and desiccated piece of flesh lay on a bed of black velvet. It was not large and was motionless, but it was the most horrific thing the girl had ever seen. Wave after wave of malevolent urges and repugnant feelings towards women seemed to overwhelm the air in the room. Jarrod pushed the lid of the container back down, the solid thud bringing the trio back to their senses.

'That's horrid,' Melissa cried, holding the table to steady herself, still grasping at the wound on her chest.

Jarrod gave her a few minutes to recover before speaking. 'Later I will show you how to tune into the Selgroch's energy.' He pointed at her chest, careful not to touch her scarred breast. 'First, I'm famished. Food?'

Melissa looked ill at the thought of eating, but joked, 'Definitely not hotdogs or sausages rolls.'

✳ ०•• ००• ००• ••० ००• ○ ०•• ••० ००• ••० ✳

Jarrod let Li cook. His gastronomic skills — while impressive — could not match those of the Chinese woman.

'Where's the detective?' Melissa asked.

'I sent her and Xiu to some place safe. She is not ready to fight for the cause and tonight,' Jarrod studied the Melissa for a reaction, 'we may have to kill Selgroch's worshippers.' The girl didn't flinch.

'Do you have any chicken?' she asked. 'I haven't had any meat since I came here. A burger? Bacon?'

'No, sorry.' Jarrod omitted to tell her that he had two cured haunches of Scottish venison in the parlour. Roadkill, sin free and too expensive for a teenager to munch on. 'Li's vegan. I too lean towards that philosophy.'

'Bummer.' The girl pulled a face.

Jarrod swivelled Melissa's stool so the two faced each other by the breakfast bar. 'I need you to trust me,' he told the girl.

'I do.'

'You had doubts before. Such thoughts will hurt both of us.' Jarrod held out a hand and waited.

'What?'

'The knives,' he sighed.

'Oh.' Melissa produced a small collection of Jarrod's cutlery and the flick knives she'd recovered from Jarrod's secret room.

Jarrod collected his property and handed them across the counter to Li. Closing Melissa's hand over the two remaining knives, he proclaimed, 'These are yours. You may need them later. Because you have seen the demon and felt her magic, this is going to be easier than it was with Detective Widcombe.'

'Why?' Melissa asked.

'She did not want to believe. Even though she had experienced my magic first-hand, her upbringing and training would not allow her to believe. You are younger and you have a physical connection to the demon.'

'Is this going to hurt?' Melissa asked, suddenly afraid at

the thought of Selgroch.

'No more than before. The mark will react to the presence of evil.'

'OK, I'm ready.'

'I need...' Jarrod paused, unwilling to place his hand directly on the girl's breasts. 'I need you to put your hand on the mark and I will place mine on top of yours.'

Melissa nodded and placed her right hand at the centre of the disfigured flesh. Jarrod smiled, hoping to assure the girl and placed his much larger hand over hers, his fingertips reaching past hers, falling onto the deep scab-filled impressions from Selgroch's claws. The connection was immediate: Jarrod felt the girl's heart race, her hand tensed under his and she gasped at the painful sensation.

'Can you feel my presence in your mind?'

Melissa placed her other hand over Jarrod's and gave a gentle squeeze. Her eyes were closed and her mouth taut with pain.

'I need you to focus outwards, feel the pain...which direction hurts the most.' Jarrod slowly turned the girl on her stool, walking around with her to maintain his hold on her chest.

'There!' Melissa gasped.

Jarrod stopped turning her and reversed direction.

'Stop!' Melissa moved her hand and pointed across the room. 'There!'

Jarrod smiled. He had felt it through her too. A strong presence, close by.

'I want you to imagine a white wall and each brick is made from the white energy of the universe. You can build this wall quickly: it is strong, it is tall, it is impenetrable. It will shield you from evil.' Jarrod felt for the girl's emotions. As she calmed down, he probed her psychic defence. 'Good. Use this wall whenever you feel threatened by evil.

If you can keep evil out of your mind, you will have a chance to fight it in the real world.'

Melissa placed her hand back over Jarrod's, afraid he may remove it. 'Jarrod, did she feel me? Will she know I was looking for her?'

Jarrod felt the perspiration forming upon Melissa's chest, her fear manifesting as beads of sweat. 'No. No more than the North Pole senses a compass.' He gently removed his hand from between Melissa's. 'Besides, you will have felt the nearest idol. I doubt that Selgroch will have come back so soon.' Smiling at the girl Jarrod suggested, 'Grab a quick shower, then Li will give you a quick lesson in self-defence. For now, I suggest you use the American T-baton, the ones the police use.'

Li nodded her approval. 'I have arranged for an escort for tonight. The Order of Light will provide a back-up squad and an intelligence unit.' Li reached across the countertop and placed a hand on Melissa's arm. 'I will stay with you. You will not be in any danger.'

✳ ∘•∘ •∘ ∘• •∘ ∘• •∘ ∘• •∘ ○ ∘• •∘ ∘• •∘ ∘• •∘ ∘• •∘ ✳

'Why are we going to Rochdale?' Melissa asked, noticing the road sign through the blackened windows of the mini-bus.

'Triangulation,' Jarrod said, ending the brooding silence he had withdrawn into since entering the vehicle. 'I felt the intensity of your connection. Wherever Selgroch's idol and coven are located, it's close. Another twenty minutes and we should be far enough for you to feel for her again.'

Jarrod was dressed in his robe and his staff lay on the floor by his feet. Six Chinese soldiers from the Order of Light accompanied them. They were all dressed in black combat gear.

'I hope we don't get pulled over,' Melissa said, looking at the array of weapons fastened to racks in the rear. What disturbed her the most was the size of a box declaring its contents as body bags.

Li laughed. 'You didn't see the side of the bus, did you? We are a touring theatre company. He's the star of a contemporary Wizard of Oz production.' Li flashed a smile at Jarrod's groan of contempt. 'Besides, any patrol car that enquires about us will be diverted. We have friends. There isn't a cop in the city who hasn't faced a situation involving demons and creatures of such ilk. Many are alive today because we stepped in. Every one of them carries an amulet for protection — it also informs us if they are in the presence of evil.'

'Yeah, you should make a film out of this shit. It would be awesome.' Pointing at the rear storage racks, Melissa asked, 'Can I have a sword?'

Chapter 30

The High Priest dipped the shallow bowl into the vat of sacramental wine. The dish had been crafted by the High Priest years before, from the left parietal bone of his predecessor. Bringing the morbid vessel to the lips of a new believer, the priest held the back of the woman's head as he poured in the concoction of Selgroch's blood, sulphur, and various poisons not from this world. The woman's eyes widened as the liquid seeped past her lips, the vile tasting fluid scorching the woman's gums and shrivelling her tongue into a blackened mass. Only the worthy would survive the ordeal, only those in a position of power or wealth were ever found worthy. His two servants held the woman still as she squirmed, the veins in her neck bulging as they turned black.

Dipping his thumbs into the viscous fluid in the bowl, the dark priest returned it to its stand beside the vat. He wrote two runes of power on the woman's cheeks and pressed the remaining liquid into the corner of her eyes turning them black, shrivelling the organs into a useless pulp. The woman's mouth opened and vented a silent scream, her vocal cords already withered and useless.

The priest looked down at the crumpling form in front of him, the woman's once beautiful body was now black and shrivelled, her hair falling to the floor, her bones stretching her contracting skin. Smiling, he performed his ritual, taking no real pleasure out of the act. This was not a time for self-gratification; this was a time of offering to Selgroch for had he himself not suffered such a fate many years ago? He remembered being taken to Selgroch's domain, his body wracked with pain only to be tormented more. He recalled the ravenous teeth most of all, Selgroch's young offspring nibbling at the extremities of his body. Fingers, toes and his nose had been devoured first, his all but useless eyeballs were sucked out of his skull. He remembered the surreal sensation as something tugged at his optic nerve, the creature's long tongue lapping inside his eye socket, delving deeper and deeper. He had survived the ordeal and his body was restored by Selgroch, transforming him into a true believer. He had shared her table that first night and they dined on her progeny. As they had feasted on him, he now devoured their flesh. Selgroch terminated anyone who may become a threat to her dominance, including her grotesque looking children.

With the ritual performed, the priest nodded to the two bearers beside the gnarled and withered body. Lifting the woman, they turned and placed her on the dais behind them, knelt and bowed their heads. A clawed hand appeared from nowhere and slid the body from the church to Selgroch's dimension, where the woman's real pain and suffering would commence.

Selgroch watched the process from her throne of bones where the Christian lectern once stood. Her stone idol emanated a radiance of anti-light, darkness throbbing all around.

'That is the last of the new converts, my Highness.' The

priest stepped towards the throne and kissed Selgroch's delicate toes. She always remained in her human form for such ceremonies, languishing in the array of human emotions that her earthly body emanated: lust, avarice, carnal desires and perversion were present in her natural body but in human form, they were heightened, the sensations euphoric.

With a wave of her arm the pews in the choir area reappeared, the black veil that hid the members of Selgroch's congregation evaporating. Forty-eight rich members of society sat naked on the laps of Selgroch's kindred. Those that she trusted, those she endured, those of her clan. Each fornicated with the human on their lap, man or woman alike, it mattered not which. Each was filled, ripped and torn by an engorged demon. The human faces contorted between exquisite pain and unimaginable pleasure. Blood stained the pews and dripped freely to the once polished floor. The humans knew their physical injuries would be healed before the night was over. These bastions of human society had nefarious duties to perform in the outside world and in return, they became wealthier and more powerful.

'Bring in the first of my sacrifices,' Selgroch ordered as she induced the shadows once more.

The noise from the debauchery behind Selgroch rose as the demons' sexual frenzy increased, their slaves screamed in a mixture of pleasure and pain. As the shadows coalesced, the sound dimmed, until nothing from the orgy could be seen or heard.

Two hundred dishevelled immigrants from all over the globe were ushered into the congregation area of the church. Relief flooded across their faces as they recognised the building's architecture. A church, a sanctuary. They were safe at last. Their long and arduous journey locked in the freight containers had come to an end. Trolleys of food and beverages were trundled down the aisles. Gracious faces smiled at their benefactors; foreign words of gratitude echoed across the stone walls of the church. From within the darkened end, hidden in the shadows, the demons watched. The sounds of frantic fornication never leaving the area of non-light.

The High Priest watched as relief swept across the immigrants, some started to break into songs of praise, the varying languages making a concerted effort impossible. Cakes laced with psychedelic drugs were being passed along the pews. The elation of the moment would soon come crashing down, the truthful horror about to befall the victims would be magnified by the chemical concoction. Their torment and misery nourishing the demons almost as much as the immigrants' bodies. Only Selgroch had the ability to feed off their souls.

'Jarrod, the intel van has found the church,' Li said as she terminated the connection on her phone.

The second van had headed in the direction Melissa had originally pointed out, settling just outside of Bolton to await further orders.

'And?' Jarrod questioned.

'Patience,' Li replied, her thumbs dancing over the phone's screen. 'Watch,' she instructed as the entertainment screen lowered from the bus's ceiling. As a connection was made, Li briefly spoke into the phone in Chinese. 'This is a live feed from the drone. We have the pilot on the phone, his English isn't very good.'

As the drone rose, the screen showed the roof of a ubiquitous Openreach communications van park alongside a phone exchange. The device changed direction and a chapel could be seen in the distance.

'It's a church,' Melissa said, bewildered.

'Chapel,' Li corrected. 'It was sold ten years ago. It's officially owned by a haulier and used as an office and storage. The demons can't resist old churches or any ground that was once consecrated. They're like moths to a flame.'

The drone flew around the perimeter, the rear storage area that was once the graveyard contained thirteen trucks with large metal freight containers on their trailers. The attached car park contained luxury cars, far more expensive than those the company workers would have owned.

'There's a coven in there now.' Jarrod swore under his breath. He stared at Li, his concern mirrored in her face. 'We can't attack a whole coven, Li. We need more help.'

They watched in silence as the drone flew nearer to the main chapel. The windows contained stained glass, protected by a steel mesh. The drone flew around the building until the operator found a section of yellow glass that had recently been repaired, the newer, cheaper glass didn't distort the view of the interior. Melissa gasped in horror as the yellow monochrome image zoomed to show a healthy man withering before the camera and then disappear completely.

Jarrod spoke in Chinese and the camera zoomed out once more, showing a dark interior with only a small section of the chapel illuminated. Jarrod spoke Chinese once more, and the camera view changed to thermal imagery. The scene changed dramatically. Hot humanoid shapes could be seen at the rear of the chapel fornicating. Sat amidst it all was a solitary figure, a small statue at her feet. No heat emanated from the stone figure — it was as black as night in a heated scene of orange and reds.

'Selgroch!' Jarrod spat. 'Driver, how far?'

'Five minutes,' the man at the front shouted.

All eyes in the rear of the bus remained on the screen.

The bus pulled into a lay-by near the unholy chapel. Melissa was curled in a foetal position on the floor, the pain in her chest unbearable. Jarrod crouched on the floor next to her and cradled her head into his shoulder. No matter what he said, she was unable to take her eyes from the live feed on the screen.

'Pull up to the gate,' Jarrod ordered the driver.

'Jarrod, we cannot attack so many, you said so yourself. There are more demons in there than I have ever seen. We are not strong enough — you're not strong enough.'

'Not directly, no.' Jarrod stood up, releasing Melissa's head, patting it as if to say it would be OK. 'Do you know why my people spend so much time learning self-defence, Li?' He didn't wait for an answer. 'Killing a wizard with magic is too difficult. It has to be performed with an indirect method, a collapsing building, an avalanche, something large and unexpected.' Stooping to retrieve his staff, Jarrod winked at Melissa. 'This won't take long.'

Standing in the centre of the bus, Jarrod's hands articulated in strange gestures, the words from his mouth chilled the bus with every breath. The runes on his staff glowed, the green crystal knob frosted over, ice crystals formed along the length of the wooden staff.

The bus driver looked backward towards Li for assurance. She mouthed: *Be ready to drive!*

Jarrod's movements became more forceful, as if the weight of the world bore down on him. All of a sudden, he thrust his staff towards the church, the bus window in front of him creaked as it froze solid. All eyes moved from Jarrod to the window, to the church and then to the drone's camera feed.

Inside the church the temperature plummeted to absolute zero in a millisecond. Skin, muscle, bone, stone, wood, human and demon crystallised in a fraction of a heartbeat. Shaking with strain, Jarrod flicked the end of his frozen staff, causing the green orb to chime. The crystal sound continued to reverberate around the bus, growing louder until Jarrod pushed the sound's vibrations towards the chapel, amplifying them exponentially. The wooden front doors burst apart first, taking with them the majority of the stone architrave. The footage from the drone showed chaos inside as the interior crumbled into tiny fragments of frozen debris. The creatures that had descended upon the immigrants in a feeding frenzy were frozen, shattered alongside their food. An explosion between Selgroch's feet severed her frozen legs, her immobilised human form crazed over with cracks as she fought with her magic to maintain her body. With the idol in pieces by her shattered feet, the demon reverted back to her normal shape, the unwanted transition stressing her frozen torso, causing it to tear itself apart. In her dying moment, she felt Jarrod's presence outside. With no mouth to scream, Selgroch released a psychic burst of energy — one last order to her Knight.

Chapter 31

Loukas stared at Jarrod's apartment building. He wanted to burn the tower block down, dedicating the souls to his mistress, including that of the magician. His fingers gripped the steering wheel, turning his knuckles white. It had been a long time since Loukas had faced an opponent who possessed magic. The Christian crusade against witches had destroyed the good and the bad. The religious fools could not — or were not — prepared to recognise their allies against evil.

Some people left the building, the movement causing Loukas to hold his breath in anticipation. It wasn't the relic dealer or his police lackey. He sighed in disappointment. The car bomb that he had parked alongside the building's main entrance was unlikely to kill Jarrod, the man would have protective wards just as Loukas did. But it would weaken him, leaving him disorientated and covered in the blood of whomever walked alongside him. Loukas dared not attack the wizard directly, Jarrod was too strong. Loukas would remove his support structure, his friends and strip him of his allies. Loukas never attacked the powerful head on. He preferred a clandestine approach, wearing them down in a secret war of attrition before offering their souls to Selgroch as a sacrifice.

Loukas used a handkerchief to mop up the seepage from his chest wound. The burn was eternal, Selgroch had made sure of that. Two of the remaining idols resided in the UK, the festering modern society of Britain created a corrupt populace — easy prey for Selgroch's recruiters. Only a handful of the thousands survived the ordeal of ordainment each year; those who perished fed Selgroch. The rich and powerful always survived, prospering even more so after Selgroch's heinous blessing, her Dark church influencing the stumbling march of humanity. Her worshippers passed legislation to create strife and misery, others laid the foundations for major disasters in the future, and those in manufacturing produced groceries that were so far removed from the food chain that it failed to nourish those who consumed it.

Selgroch had shown no concern for his wounds when he prostrated himself at her feet. The others in the congregation stepped back believing that he would be consumed in the most unholy manner. Instead, she had taken her frustrations out on the new flock of wannabe accolades. She had physically forced their souls into Loukas's body, giving him their strength so that he may be strong enough to face her new enemy. Loukas could still feel the essence of each wannabe twist and turn in torment as he absorbed their life force. The scarification runes on his body buzzed as the new energy infused with his own. He smiled to himself at the inner screams of the people he possessed.

With his vigour renewed and his protective wards repaired, Selgroch had sent him forth to destroy all that Jarrod held dear, and to bring the wizard's broken body back to the church for her to consume.

Drumming his fingers on the steering wheel in boredom, Loukas doubled over as his protective wards burned in his skin. Taking deep gasps of air, Loukas's grip on the wheel tightened, he focused on his breathing to prevent himself from passing out. His Mistress was calling. She was in pain... she was dying! An image of Jarrod flashed in his mind and Loukas knew that the man was at the chapel.

'Bastard!' Loukas screamed, slamming his hands against the dashboard. He started the vehicle and tore away, the tyres squealing as they fought to gain grip on the tarmac. Without glancing backwards, Selgroch's Knight triggered the detonator for the bomb. His rear view mirror glowed, the interior of his car illuminating as the homemade explosive released a huge fireball, propelling thousands of screws into the surrounding buildings.

Chapter 32

Jarrod slumped against his staff, holding out an arm to keep the others at bay. 'Not yet,' his words creased by the strain. 'I must destroy the chapel completely.'

His arms swirled, his fingers were crooked and Jarrod's eyes bled as he cast the spell. Ancient alien words of destruction were voiced for the first time on Earth. The bus rocked and the driver looked back at Li, eyes wide, waiting for the command to drive. She shook her head, never taking her eyes off Jarrod. She had never witnessed such power; her father's magic was much more sedate in comparison.

Punching the floor of the bus, Jarrod released the accumulation of energy. The ground below them shook and as the bus rocked, Jarrod ordered, 'Drive! Now!'

It started with a vibration, shattering the frozen bus window, frigid air billowing inwards chilling them all to the bone. The ground beneath the vehicle shook some more, the violence gaining exponentially. The quaking sound of the ground moving began to overshadow the revving engine as the driver fought for more speed.

'Jarrod! What have you done?' Li screamed as the bus

215

lurched, a portion of the road sinking beneath its wheels.

'Sinkhole.' Jarrod collapsed on to his seat, fatigue creasing his face, black circles forming under his eyes. 'The area is prone to water erosion. My experience at Swalon's taught me a lot about the movement of water and rock.' His attempt at a smile scared those in the bus.

'Is she dead?' Melissa continued to stare at the drone's footage. The ornate glass in the chapel window had shattered giving them a perfect view of the carnage inside.

'I... I don't know,' Jarrod confessed. 'She should have been sucked back to her own dimension when the idol was destroyed. But she remained. There was so much power in that chapel.'

'How... how did you do that?' Li asked, concerned at the ferocity of Jarrod's power. *Had father been right, when he asked us to watch this man?* she asked herself.

'Swalon's book.' Jarrod produced the crude tome from the folds of his cloak. 'He described how Selgroch opened the way to another dimension and moved her troops through. She moved the passage opening, not the demons. I did the same for the building. Selgroch's protective wards would have thwarted any spells I cast directly at the chapel. The stone walls were covered with her runes. Forces of nature are harder to predict,' he smiled at the shocked group. 'I temporarily moved the chapel into a dimension where there is no heat. It's possible this relocation prevented Selgroch from escaping — I don't know.' Jarrod slipped off his chair, his staff clattering to the floor.

'Jarrod!' Melissa cried, rushing to his side. 'Do something!' she demanded, looking at Li.

Li stood still for a second, torn between duty and her friend. Jarrod was much stronger than he had ever let on. The Order of Light could not have killed so many demons. Previously, covens of such size had been destroyed from afar mortar rounds fired from the back of pickups destroying the buildings, worshipers and unholy relics alike. It was cheap, effective and didn't put the Order of Light at risk. She had just witnessed one man kill dozens of frenzied demons, in their stronghold, with their matriarch and idol. 'Father,' Li cried out, her eyes rolling upwards, showing only the whites to the others in the bus.

'Daughter.'

'What shall I do?'

'What do you feel?'

'He is a good man, father. But his strength, if he turned against us...'

Li felt her father smile at her in the transcendental environment they communicated in.

'Did you know about the immigrants in the shipping containers?'

'Father?' Li gasped thinking of the lorries at the rear of the chapel and the maze of containers.

'Jarrod did, he protected them. Had he not, I would not aid you in healing him. But he knew I would say this. Is he a devious mastermind or a brave fool?'

'Father?'

'Neither Li. He is a good man.'

Li's eyes returned to normal and she stepped forwards to place her hands on Jarrod. Her father's energy flowed through her, healing Jarrod, bringing his exhausted body back from the brink of death.

Jarrod's eyes opened slightly. He looked at Li and smiled. 'He still trusts me, then?'

'Sleep Jarrod,' Li instructed.

'Send your men. Two guards survived... they may harm the people in the containers.' Jarrod's words slurred as he fell unconscious once more.

Chapter 33

The bus driver drove past the turning for Jarrod's apartment building. Fire engines and police vehicles blocked the view of the reception area, the floors above were devoid of glass, shredded curtains and blinds flapped outwards in the breeze.

'What the hell?' Melissa gasped, suddenly awakened by flashing lights.

'Car bomb,' Li answered in a low voice, cradling Jarrod's head in her lap, his unconscious body covered by a blanket on the floor. 'It happened while we were at the chapel.'

'Jesus!'

'No. Loukas,' Li corrected the girl. 'Or one of his henchmen.'

'Where to, Li?' the driver shouted from the front.

'Back to the garage.' Li looked out of the windows at the receding emergency lights. 'We need somewhere Loukas doesn't know about.'

The old factory unit looked scruffy but was in fact meticulously clean inside. Rows of vehicles owned by the Order of Light were lined up in the loading bays. The bus reversed in through a double set of doors, which opened on their approach.

'Bat cave!' Melissa squealed. 'Told you. You should make a movie.'

'Jarrod, wake up.' Li tapped her fingers on the wizard's face.

'Oh, my head!' Jarrod groaned, lifting himself off Li's legs. 'I've drooled on you, Li. I'm sorry,' Jarrod apologised as he sat up, holding his head in both hands. 'Where are we?'

'An old unit by the river. We used to run operations from here before you provided rooms in your building. It's not glamorous, but it is clean.'

'Why here?' Jarrod stood up with the aid of his staff, swaying as he surveyed the mixture of vehicles.

'Loukas set off a bomb outside your apartment.' Seeing the worry in Jarrod's face, she added, 'Luckily no one was seriously hurt. If you remember, when the Order of Light moved in, we replaced the ground floor windows and entrance with blast-proof glass.'

'So why here?' Jarrod coughed. His chest hurt. Small specks of blood coated the hand he had coughed into.

'Because you need to rest, and the apartment is surrounded by the press and police.'

'Loukas... He will go after the others if he can't find us.' Jarrod's strength gave out and he crumpled into the nearest seat. 'Barry!' he cried, remembering that he had left the man unprotected.

Chapter 34

Loukas watched the rear bays of Caster and Randle from the safety of a neighbouring building. His mind seethed in anger; rage had almost caused him to lose control upon seeing the destruction at the coven's unholy chapel. Using the pretext of being a reporter and armed with stolen credentials, Loukas had forced his way through the crowd to the police cordon. Using the high-powered lens of his camera, he examined the area. The chapel, front garden and road were missing, only a gaping maw of a sink hole remained. The old cemetery full of containers and lorries remained intact; police, medics, firemen and people in day-glow jackets that declared themselves as Border Agency assisted the sacrificial immigrants from the containers.

Loukas had no idea where Jarrod was and on top of that, he had lost all of his paid henchmen, the imbeciles having been caught by the police. Jarrod and the detective had disappeared and Jarrod's colleagues and friends were guarded by a private security company. Loukas could wait. The cost of such protection was astronomically prohibitive so Loukas was sure Jarrod couldn't maintain such measures for longer than a week or two.

Staring at the rear doors through his binoculars, Loukas smiled to himself. The night shift staff were exiting the building. Most of the guards were new — burly ex-military personnel, all bar one — Barry — one of the two original guards that had patrolled the building the night of the break-in. The muscle-bound guards nodded to Barry before they entered a large SUV. Loukas had thought to place a bomb underneath the guard's vehicle — a quick dash across the loading bay by a radio-controlled toy, a small explosive placed under the petrol tank... They weren't the target though. The wizard cared little for the newly hired help. Barry on the other hand was a different matter.

Preparation had always been the key to Loukas's survival and so he had already been in Barry's house — an early reconnaissance shortly after Loukas had killed the other guard. He had scouted out Barry's twee little domicile just in case. He had scrawled Selgroch's sacrificial runes all over the walls, written in the urine of his last sacrifice; they were invisible to the naked eye. No one was protecting the guard... why would they? He was nothing but hired help. Loukas smiled. He would be much more soon. He would be a message.

Watching Barry drive away, Loukas sneered at the decrepit car gushing blue smoke as Barry changed gear. 'You die tonight, little man,' Loukas promised as the car turned out of sight. He despised the guard. The man clung to the memories of his deceased wife, unwilling to move on. 'You should have butchered the man who killed your wife, you fool! You would have had your revenge and been reborn.'

Loukas peered from behind a set of net curtains as Barry pulled the car onto his driveway. The owners of the house opposite lay dead on the floor, their blood pooled together as if they were embracing for one last time. It was a quick death, not a pain filled sacrifice. Loukas knew that Selgroch was dead, her hold on his mind was gone. He would serve Jarrod's head to one of her competitors as they often sought Loukas out, trying to turn his allegiance. He didn't crave money and fame as most devotees do. Loukas asked only for longevity and the chance to eliminate the family lines of those who tortured his wife and daughter. For over three hundred years he traced ancestral lineages, pruning whole branches until only one member remained. These he sterilised and disfigured, informing them they were the end of a corrupt family. Selgroch attended his private ceremony to claim the victim's soul, informing them that when they died, she would torment them forever. Loukas always left their maimed and broken bodies near a hospital — he relished the anguish he left his victims in. Having seen a demon for themselves, none chose to end their own lives, not even to end their constant pain.

Loukas smiled as Barry alighted from his car, takeaway bag in one hand and a few supplies from a nearby convenience store in the other. The man was a creature of habit. People liked routine, it made them feel comfortable. It also made them easier to predict. Loukas stepped over the dead pensioners on the floor —careful not to soil his boots in the expanding pool of blood — and walked out of the house. He left the front door open, uninterested if the bodies were discovered or not.

Barry fumbled for his keys. His wife's key was on his fob so he used that one to open the door.

'I'm home dear,' he whispered as he entered. 'Just a normal day.' Placing the bags on a small table, Barry closed the door behind him and turned on the lights. Sniffing the air, he smiled. The fragrance of the house was back in balance now.

Pulling a small bottle of perfume from the sideboard, Barry gave the room a single squirt of his deceased wife's favourite scent.

'I'm sorry dear, I must have let a cat in without realising' he apologised to the empty room. It had taken a thorough cleaning and disinfecting of all surfaces to remove the faint scent of urea.

Sitting in his favourite armchair, Barry stared at the empty counterpart that had been Irene's. 'I try Irene, I really do. Work's not the same anymore. Not since Martin was murdered. I think they will move me out soon, then it won't be the same. I will have lost another part of us, our routine. I miss you so much.'

The empty chair didn't reply, the food in the bag filled the room with the exotic fragrances of India.

Barry placed both hands on both arms of his chair, preparing to pull himself up, when movement in his room caused him to shout out in alarm.

'Jarrod! Mr Wentworth, what are you doing here, how did you get in?'

'No time Barry, I must get you out of here, now!' Jarrod gasped, blood spitting out of his mouth as he spoke.

'You look like death, Mr Wentworth!' Barry commented. With concern he suggested, 'Let me get you a cup...'

A sound came from the direction of the kitchen, the old hinges of the back door groaned as they turned slowly.

'Who...?' Barry began.

Jarrod grabbed the security guard's arm and Stepped them both out of the lounge before Barry could finish his question.

Barry fell backwards. Grasping hold of Jarrod's arm for support, he managed to pull his friend on top of him.

'Where? Mr Wentworth?' Barry attempted to rouse the unconscious man lying on top of him.

'Mr Hastwell?' Li leaned forward offering a hand.

'Yes,' Barry replied. Seeing a group of Chinese men dressed in black combat gear, Barry shot up and stood between them and Jarrod. 'You stay away! Do you hear? I'll kill the first man that touches Jarrod!' he bellowed in confused rage.

'Barry, you are a most fortunate man. Do you know that?' Li said as she waved at her men to move back. 'Jarrod risked his life to bring you here. He is beyond exhaustion and yet he could not let any harm come to you. You are in a small select group of people that he cares for.'

'How did I get here?' Barry asked, carefully looking around, not trusting the woman or men in front of him.

'You won't believe me if I tell you,' Li answered calmly, hiding the concern and urgency she felt for Jarrod on the floor. 'The idol that was stolen was demonic. Jarrod is a wizard, a sorcerer — call it what you will. He plucked you from your home and brought you here because he believed you were in danger.'

'Bullshit! You kidnapped both of us from my home, drugged us and I have just come to now.' Barry stepped towards the woman and attempted to grab hold of her. She was too quick and she disappeared behind him. Turning, he found her beside Jarrod, tenderly holding his head off the concrete floor.

'I said you would not believe me. Stand aside and let my

men attend to Jarrod or you will be tranquillised.' Li nodded in the direction of a man holding a bolt-action rifle with a wide bore barrel pointing directly at him.

A stretcher appeared and Jarrod was lifted onto it with reverence.

'Come,' Li ordered. 'You can stay with him. Give me your phone!'

Barry complied, bewildered at the turn of events. Li ripped the back off the phone, removed the battery and stuffed the pieces into her pockets.

'He might be tracking you,' Li warned.

'Who?'

'The murderer, Barry. Who else?'

'Mr Wentworth, you're awake.' Barry rushed to Jarrod's side. 'The Chinese woman said you should drink this when you wake,' he said, handing over a glass of green liquid.

Leaning up on one arm, Jarrod drank it with a shudder. 'Ah! That's worse than normal,' he mumbled as he slumped back onto the cot and fell asleep.

'He'll be like this for a couple of days,' Li informed Barry as she entered the room. 'He used up too much of his own energy destroying the chapel, then he foolishly used more rescuing you.' Li removed some fresh blankets from a nearby cupboard and covered Jarrod. 'I have fresh clothes for you. I assume you wish to get out of that guard's uniform? You will remain here until Jarrod recovers.'

'In this room? You can't...'

Li rolled her eyes at the man. 'In this facility, there are showers past the dining area. Breakfast is in half an hour. You are not our prisoner, Mr Hastwell. Jarrod wants us to protect you.'

'I'm sorry I don't understand. What is happening?'

'Come, I will show you.' Li grabbed the large man's arm and pulled him into a communal room. She spoke in Chinese, instructing one of the menfolk to display the footage of the previous night.

Four screens showed the footage from the two drones — the normal and infrared recordings. Other screens were tuned to the news channels. Barry stared in horror at the depicted scenes.

'Why's this one yellow and that one green?' he asked absentmindedly.

'Stained glass windows. It was a chapel.'

'Was?' Barry turned to Li, confused.

'Watch.'

'Oh God, no. They're killing them.'

'They're eating them, Mr Hastwell.'

'What are they?'

'Demons,' Li answered coldly.

'What! What's happening?'

'Jarrod froze the chapel, killing the demons inside.'

'You can't do that, it's to do with the laws of thermodynamics. I watched a documentary about how the vacuum of space would effect astronauts,' Barry argued, struggling to accept the horrors on the screen.

'Magic often stomps all over the physical laws as we know them. It can be frustrating at times,' Li confessed.

'Jesus Christ! He shattered them! How?'

Li smiled in silence as the images changed to local news footage, showing the sink hole and hundreds of surviving immigrants being released from shipping containers.

'He saved hundreds of lives and killed more demons in one night than I have seen in my lifetime.'

'Why come for me?' Barry sat down on a chair, his leg suddenly weak.

'I don't know,' Li confessed. 'The effort nearly killed him. Did you know he lost wife? It left him like you for many years.'

A man entered the room before Barry could answer. He carried a tray of food for the pair.

'Thank you,' Barry smiled at the man, unsure of the food in the bowl.

'Guilin rice noodles, a staple breakfast in south China. I am sorry, we are all vegans. There will be no meat while you stay with us.'

'Jarrod's always looked out for me. I never understood why. Lending me books, the special projects. Did you know he's had me learning Spanish?'

'He told me. He's going to Mexico later in the year and wanted to take you with him. Something to do with your late wife.'

'Irene,' Barry smiled. 'We were meant to visit Mexico for our anniversary. She always wanted to go there, she loved the Mexican culture.' Barry's voice trailed off as he thought of his departed wife. Returning his gaze back to the news feature, he asked, 'Did he really do all of that?'

Li nodded.

'With magic? Can you do that?'

'There are few practitioners left. My family are from a long line of protectors. Few are born with any overt abilities. I can sense a person's intentions, that is all. My father is the magician, though he is nothing like Jarrod.'

'I'm sorry, it's a lot to take in,' Barry confessed, staring at the bowl of noodles and vegetables.

'Did she tell you he's an alien?' Melissa said as she entered the room.

Barry choked and coughed out his mouthful of food. 'What?' He stared at the ragged looking girl for a second, then looked at Li for confirmation.

'This is Melissa, aka Hellcat. You know her as the person who stole Jarrod's statue from Caster and Randle.' Li held out a hand to instruct Barry to remain seated. 'She has seen the error of her ways and is on our side now.'

'We fought the badass demon that Jarrod killed last night. It was wicked. I got this,' Melissa pulled her top down a little to show her scar, flashing her bra in the process.

'We hope he killed her last night, but we're not sure,' Li corrected.

Barry blushed at the sight of Melissa's breasts. 'It... It looks painful,' he stammered.

'It is. Li applies her herbs every day, which helps.' Turning to the Chinese woman, she asked, 'Can you send someone out for a McMuffin? Please? I need some meat. Never thought I'd say that.' She giggled. Seeing Barry looking even more confused, she elaborated, 'I'm gay.'

'I need to call work, let them know I won't be in.' Barry looked at Li.

'Ah, yes... erm... no need for that.'

'Why?'

'Loukas burnt your house down and the police have you listed as missing, presumed dead,' Li explained.

'What, No...' Barry cried out, pain lancing through his chest at the thought of losing his wife's belongings. Barry placed the bowl of food down and hid his tears behind both hands.

'Way!' Melissa admonished Li, confusing everybody with youthful vernacular. 'Barry, it's okay. It's only a house.' She knelt next to the large man, placing her arm over one shoulder.

'No, you don't understand. All the memories I had of her were there.' Pulling his wallet out from his trouser pocket, Barry extracted a photo of his late wife. 'Irene's belongings, our life together, everything's gone.'

Melissa placed her other hand on the Barry's knee, not certain how to comfort the stranger. She shot a glance at Li as if to say, *Really, you broke the news like that?*

'Come on Jarrod, wake up.' Melissa talked to Jarrod as she wiped his brow with a damp cloth. 'We need you to wake up. Please.' She felt old and tired, the past couple of weeks had taken their toll on the young girl and now she was bathing the old man. Pulling the bed sheet down to his waist as she performed her rendition of a bed bath, she apologised. 'I'm sorry for stealing your statue, she was so beautiful. It called to me. I could feel it in the box. I don't know, I'm not making sense.'

Wiping Jarrod's chest with the cloth she paused. Tears ran down her face and she stared at Jarrod's face. 'I'm scared Jarrod. I'm scared all the time. Even before all of this. I... I need you. You make me feel safe. You're the closest thing I have to a father. I know that sounds stupid. That night after the demon attacked us, you held me and I felt you in my head. It didn't make sense at the time but I felt your concern. It was clean, you didn't want... You didn't...' Tears dripped from her cheeks to the floor. 'You didn't abuse me. Do you know how long it has been since someone didn't try to take advantage?' She sniffled.

Wiping the tears from her face with her sleeve, Melissa raised Jarrod's right arm to wash underneath when it suddenly became rigid.

'Jarrod?'

Jarrod's hand gripped her forearm, the pressure causing her to wince. He rose up, pulling himself towards her and she down to him.

'Is Arbon safe? Tell me, is my son safe?' Jarrod's eyes closed as the words passed his lips and he fell back into the army cot, unconscious once more.

Chapter 35

Loukas had returned to the site of the sinkhole, hopeful that someone from the congregation might have survived. He needed resources, money to hire more muscle and access to the police database. Not that they would have helped him willingly; if any member of the congregation had survived they would be in hiding by now. With Selgroch's demise, her spells lost all their power; once powerful and famous people across the globe were now in financial chaos with many facing criminal investigations. He found no one at the chapel site, none of Selgroch's surviving subjects came to show their respect. Once he had dealt with Jarrod, he swore that he would kill them all.

A man whimpered on the floor, semi-rousing from unconsciousness. Loukas jabbed the heel of his boot into the man's head, silencing him. Loukas was keeping the computer technician alive in case he needed him to enter more passcodes into the Metropolitan Police system. The man was a contractor working in the police IT department, so, was not accustomed to pain. It hadn't taken much persuasion for the nerd to enter the password. Loukas was unaware that by amending an extra two digits to the end of

231

his login, the computer technician had alerted the police to his coercion. An armed police unit was currently on route to the technician's home and the IT forensics department were attempting to trace the IP address of the internet connection. Fortunately for Loukas, he was in a neighbouring apartment using The Onion Router anonymising browser. Because of the inherent lag of the Tor network bouncing his connection between proxy servers, Loukas didn't notice that the police network was unusually slow.

Chapter 36

'How long?' Jarrod asked, yanking an IV needle from his arm.

'Five days,' Melissa answered. 'Li said you need to drink this.' She handed Jarrod an insulated travel mug.

'Urgh, not more of her herbs,' Jarrod groaned. Opening the lid his face beamed, 'Coffee?'

'She wants you to stay awake.'

Jarrod was relieved. 'What have I missed?' he asked, happily slurping the hot beverage.

'Hundreds of businesses and celebs are in the news after filing for bankruptcy. The press is saying they were duped by a global Ponzi scheme. Li says they were more than likely Selgroch's followers, which hopefully means she is dead. Erm... Loukas burnt Barry's house down and we have no idea where Loukas is.' Melissa moved to the doorway and called out: 'Li! He's awake.'

'Jarrod, you might want to cover yourself up,' Melissa advised.

Jarrod, noticing for the first time that he was naked, pulled the blanket over his lap. Jarrod turned to thank Melissa, which was dismissed with nonchalant wave.

'You have been unconscious for five days. Melissa, Barry and I have taken turns looking after you,' Li said, entering the room.

Holding out her little finger, Melissa crooked it back and to, 'Aliens, who knew,' she joked, mocking the size of Jarrod's manhood.

'Loukas?' Jarrod asked Li.

'Disappeared. That's why I wanted you awake. We need access to the police system to track him down.'

'Widcombe?'

'Yeah, we need her, too.'

'I put her out of harm's way for a reason,' Jarrod protested.

'You nearly stranded her there. If you'd have died, how would she have got back?'

'I left Swalon a store of energy. She's in no danger.'

'We need her. Sort yourself out then tomorrow you bring her and my sister back.'

'You have people in the police, Li, why can't they help?'

'Because a shit-storm has gone down and everything is locked down tight.'

Jarrod knew better than to argue with Li. 'I'm starving.'

'Melissa, you can help me in the kitchen while Jarrod takes a shower and gets himself dressed,' Li ordered. 'Father wants a word with you after.'

Jarrod smiled. The old Chinese mystic had saved his life once again.

'Detective Widcombe, it's nice to see you again.'

'Barry, what the hell are you doing here?' the detective asked.

'I have nowhere else to go,' Barry confessed in a

sorrowful tone. 'Loukas burnt my house down.'

Detective Widcombe looked at Jarrod and indicated towards Barry with her eyes.

'He knows. I had to Step him out of his house. He's part of the team now.'

'Barry, I am so sorry about your house.' Detective Widcombe hugged him and letting go she asked, 'Where's Melissa?' She was concerned at the girl's absence.

'She's fine,' Li answered as she entered the room. 'She's training with my men.' Li greeted her sister formally in Mandarin and then hugged her close. 'Welcome back, Xiu. How is Swalon?'

'He's fine. Jarrod alleviated the water problem for now and gave Swalon a store of energy. He was more relaxed than I have ever seen him.'

'Good. Sarala, has Jarrod explained why he brought you back?' Li asked.

'Intel. You need me to access the police system and track Loukas down.'

'Yes,' Li confirmed with a nod.

'My sick leave ends tomorrow. I'll see what I can do.'

Chapter 37

'Welcome back Sarala,' Sergeant Dowery greeted Detective Widcombe. 'I called at your place a couple of times to see if you needed anything.'

'I went out of town, Bob. I needed to get away for awhile,' she said. 'What's new?'

'We've had a spate of home killings,' Sergeant Dowery replied. 'A string of unrelated families found dead in their homes, nothing taken. On the plus side, since the home of Barry Hastwell burnt down, there have been no more sadistic deaths. Speaking of which, you haven't seen that Wentworth fellow have you? There was a bombing outside of his apartment building while you were off. Detective Jeffers believes the grisly murders, the stolen idol, Hastwell's house and the bomb are all related. That Jarrod fellow is involved somehow.'

'I've been away, Bob. I haven't seen anybody.'

'Do you know what's even more bizarre?' Sergeant Dowery prevented the detective from passing in the hallway. 'The sketch your man Jarrod drew of your attacker's accomplice? Well, he was seen in the crowd at the chapel sinkhole. Crazy, eh?'

'Crazy, ' Widcombe agreed, placing her hands on his shoulders and physically moving him out of her way. 'Have there been any other sightings of him?'

'Who, Jarrod?'

'No, my attacker,' Detective Widcombe shot back, a little too abruptly.

The sergeant's eye narrowed as he looked at his colleague walking down the corridor. 'There's a file on him in Jeffers's office. Be careful of Wentworth, Sarala. He's a hot potato at the moment. That IT technician that went missing, his login was used to access Jarrod's file. The brass at the top want answers, they've even ordered the fraud squad to look into Jarrod's finances. He's not your friend and he's not what he appears.'

Detective Widcombe turned to look back at the sergeant from the end of the hall. 'Men rarely are, Bob.'

'John.' Detective Widcombe greeted the tired man behind the desk.

'Sarala; been back long?' Detective Jeffers's face lit up as the station's most attractive detective entered.

'About ten minutes,' she answered.

'Hitting the ground running, eh?' He handed a file to Detective Widcombe from his desk's top drawer. 'I thought you might come by. This is everything I have on the perp who attacked you. It's the same guy who broke into Caster and Randle and killed most of the Razor Crew. The full list of crimes I can hook him to are on the second sheet. We have a group of local thugs who are willing to testify that it was this man, Lucas —' he pulled a photo from the printer and handed it to Detective Widcombe — 'who paid them to disfigure and disable people. Each of these heavies were incapacitated during the act by one or more Chinese ninjas.'

'Ninjas are Japanese,' Detective Widcombe corrected.

Dismissing his cultural faux pas with a wave of his hand, Detective Jeffers continued. 'Your report on Jarrod states that he trained with a Chinese woman. A martial arts expert.'

'She's a student and a pretty one at that. He's probably getting his jollies off by grappling with her on the floor. You're grasping at straws.'

'He's involved, Sarala. I don't know how or even if he is the victim here. But he is central to a lot of people getting hurt.'

'The statue is central to people getting hurt. Has it turned up yet?'

'No. You are right of course. Everyone involved with the statue has turned up dead. Did you know Caster and Randle installed a security system that exceeds their annual turnover? And that the directors have personal bodyguards? Jarrod's chauffeur had a near miss; the second guard, Barry, his house burnt down and he's missing, presumed dead.'

'And you think a relic appraiser did this?'

'No, not really. But Jarrod Wentworth knows something. Did you know he's rich? I mean *seriously* rich. His accountant is Price Waterhouse Coopers. Conglomerates use PWC, not antique dealers.'

'We need to find Loukas.'

'Loukas? You said Loo-kAAs not Lucas... why?'

Caught out by her slip up, Detective Widcombe fed Jeffers enough information to direct his investigation. 'Jarrod believed Loukas was part of a satanic cult and that he was after the statue.' Raising her hands at Jeffers, she added, 'I didn't believe it either. That's why I didn't put it into the report. Jarrod called the man Loukas, claiming he was eastern European. He blamed him for all the murders, starting with the original owner and the auctioneer.'

'No one fitting the man's description called Lucas or Loukas has entered the UK since the auction, so Loukas could not have been the murderer in Malaysia.'

'If he came in via the usual channels. You know as well as I do that anyone with a boat or a small plane can smuggle a man into the UK.'

'I do know that there is enough CCTV to put this man at the scene of a dozen crimes. I also know that you won't be allowed to work the case because he attacked you directly. You're too involved.'

Wafting the file, Detective Widcombe said, 'Thanks for this. I want to get this guy, John.' She turned to leave.

'Oh, Sarala. It's probably best if you don't mention the cult thing to anyone else. You know how they get.'

'Yeah, I know,' she replied, walking out of Jeffers's office. As soon as she was out of sight, she paused, listening.

'Get me all the information on that chapel that disappeared near Bolton. Oh, and run Lucas through Interpol. Try Loukas, possibly eastern European.'

Detective Widcombe smiled as she walked away. Men were so easy to manipulate.

Chapter 38

'Are you sure you weren't followed?' Li asked as Xiu and Detective Widcombe exited the car.

'Relax sister, I know what I am doing,' Xiu answered.

'You look tired.' Li commented on the detective's haggard look.

'Long day,' Sarala replied.

'And?' Li enquired.

'Loukas is officially Manchester's most wanted. Every police officer has been briefed about him and told to report but not to approach. If Loukas appears in public, he will have the armed response unit surrounding him within ten minutes.'

'So, they do not know where he is?' Li asked, annoyed at the lack of progress.

'He's moving around a lot. He cuckoos to avoid hotels.'

'What's cuckoos?' Jarrod asked walking into the garage area, Barry and Melissa following behind.

'He enters someone's house and lives there for a day or two. There have been numerous families found murdered in their homes. He's not torturing them, Loukas is killing them quickly.'

'He has no one to sacrifice them to,' Jarrod explained.

'So how are we going to find him?' Melissa asked, standing closer to Jarrod than the detective liked.

'We set a trap and I'm the bait, Jarrod huffed.'

'Jarrod!' Sarala gasped.

'He'll want to kill me upfront and personal. He'll want me to know it was him. He'll use a knife,' Jarrod predicted, profiling the murderer. 'His magic wards will be useless because they are tied to Selgroch's magic.'

'She might not be dead?' Melissa asked

'I believe she is,' Jarrod asserted.

'Where? How?' Barry interrupted.

'Where it all started, at Caster and Randle.'

Chapter 39

'Are you mad?' Johnathan Caster shouted.

'It's the only way, we need to capture the man.'

'No, the police need to capture this Loukas fellow,' Archie Randle replied. 'And from what you just told us, he's more dangerous than we thought. Certainly not! We will not support you in this foolish endeavour.'

'Archie, Johnathan, we have been partners for years, trust me.'

'Jarrod, this is not a film. You're not Harrison Ford. You're good at what you do, damned good. But you are not a hero. Let the constabulary deal with it,' Archie berated.

'I could rig up some gas canisters. Once he enters the building, I'll put him to sleep,' Matt Johnson, the head of Johnson Securities said, entering the room.

Jarrod stared at Matt, annoyed at the intrusion. 'Your services are no longer required, Matthew. You can take your men and leave.'

'And your apartment building? Are you going to put innocent bystanders at risk because of hubris? The taxi firm, Bert, Barry, Archie and Johnathan's families and the two dozen other concerns you have us protecting. You want us to abandon everyone?' Matt enquired, sarcastically.

'Jarrod, how much is this costing us?' Archie gasped.

'Nothing, Archie,' Jarrod confessed. 'This is my problem and I have covered the expense to protect you all.'

'And the Chinese?' Matt Johnson asked. 'I know they're working for you. Until recently they all lived in your apartment building.'

'Astute of you Matthew, but that's what I pay for I suppose.'

'That and confidentiality,' Matt beamed a disarming smile at Jarrod. 'Let me do what I'm paid to do Jarrod. We will capture Loukas.'

'He's not stupid. He'll know it's a trap,' Jarrod warned.

'And yet he will come for you. It's his nature,' Matt replied.

'We have closed the shop, locked the building up tight and sent the staff home,' Archie said in a worried tone.

'Not all the staff, Mr Randle,' Matt Johnson replied. 'My men will escort you and Mr Caster to your homes. Then you and your families will be taken to a secure location for a couple of days.'

'Is this really necessary, old boy?' Archie asked.

'Yes, Mr Randle. Now please let me do my job and go home.'

'It's OK, Archie,' Jarrod confirmed. 'We need him to come here. That means securing everything else while I act as bait.'

'I'll set up the gas canisters,' Matt confirmed to Jarrod.

Hearing Jarrod conversing with someone, Matt Johnson entered Archie's office and stared at Detective Widcombe and two Chinese women.

'How did you get in here?' he demanded.

'There are ways in that even you do not know of, Matthew.' Jarrod cut him off before he could reply. 'They are secure.'

'And off camera,' Matt complained.

'Any news?' Detective Widcombe asked.

Shaking his head, Matt Johnson replied, 'Nothing. It's too busy out there at the moment, schools are out and the roads are chaotic. A couple of hours, I'd say.'

'Are you sure he knows Jarrod is here?' Detective Widcombe asked.

'I walked in the front door, Sarala. He will have someone watching the building,' Jarrod confirmed.

The usual background rumble of traffic altered. They all darted to the window in time to watch a brick-carrying lorry gunning for speed.

'Oh Lord!' Archie paled as he saw the vehicle approaching.

'He's heading towards the Persian wing,' Jarrod shouted, mesmerised by the lorry as it bounced over the pavement. The engine roared as the driver increased speed.

Matt Johnson barked orders into the cuff of his immaculate jacket.

The brick-carrying lorry shook the entire building as it collided with the old stone wall of the Persian wing. The sound was deafening, made worse when the alarm systems began to wail.

Matt Johnson spoke to his cuff. 'Other units remain alert, this could be a diversion.' Then he ordered, 'Jarrod, stay here!'

Ignoring Matthew's instructions, Jarrod and the three

women ran from the room, along the corridor and down to the ground level. The front of the truck had penetrated through the wall, becoming badly mangled in the process. Bricks, shelving and antiquities were scattered everywhere.

Jarrod stepped up to the cab and moving the deflated airbags out of the way, checked the driver and shouted, 'It's not him.' Feeling for a pulse, Jarrod announced, 'He's alive, but barely.'

'Dad! Dad! Are you OK! Dad!' The muted sound of voices screamed.

'What? Li, check the passenger side,' Jarrod ordered.

Li managed to open the passenger door with the aid of Matthew's added strength. The door screamed in protest as it moved. Climbing inside the cab, Li retrieved the driver's mobile phone. The facetime call showed a family tied up. A woman's face was badly beaten.

'Help us!' the family shouted.

Loukas's face suddenly filled the screen. 'Is the driver dead? I should have forced him to disable the airbags, it would have been much more fun. SHUT UP!' He shouted at his captives behind him. 'Please excuse his family. Modern society breeds such weak peasants, don't you think Jarrod?'

'Loukas, I think we should end this, just you and me.'

'Oh, I agree. But that's not what you had planned, is it, with your small army of guards with you.' Loukas chuckled. 'I have sent a package for you to the loading bay. It will be arriving in a minute, so I suggest you act quickly.' Loukas pulled a thin spike from his jacket and turned towards the driver's family. They screamed and cried for mercy. Jarrod leaned over and disconnected the call.

'Watching them die will do nothing for them. Not witnessing it may deter him from killing them,' Jarrod declared sombrely.

'Look for a package at the delivery bay,' Matt whispered into his cuff microphone. At the sound of sirens approaching, he turned to Jarrod. 'Time for you to go. Use your secret exit before the police arrive.'

'I need to see that package first,' Jarrod shouted over his shoulder, running to the rear of the building.

✳ ∘••∘ ••∘ ••∘ ••∘ ◯ ∘•• ∘•• ••∘ ••∘ ••∘ ✳

Four security guards were searching the rear loading bay when Jarrod, Matthew and the three women arrived.

'Nothing, sir,' one security guard reported to Matt Johnson.

A mechanical whirr broke the silence and a small remote-controlled car appeared from the rear alleys. The toy vehicle drove straight up to Jarrod, crashing into his feet.

'Careful!' Matt shouted as Jarrod leaned over to retrieve a small box taped to the top.

Ignoring him, Jarrod opened the lid to reveal a photograph of school children in a bus. They all looked scared, eyes wide, mouths taped shut and their hands cuffed with plastic ties to the seat in front of them. A second photograph showed an old-fashioned candle clock, the hours of the day etched into the side of the wax. The candle sat upon an old-fashioned balance scale; being heavier than the counterweight, it was lower. A crude copper leaf switch sat beneath the dish containing the counterweight. A thick hose protruded through a small window opening, black tape sealed the gaps between it and the frame.

'Oh Jesus. Kids!' Matt exclaimed. 'Jarrod, we need to inform the police. We can't withstand this; the fallout will destroy us all.'

Jarrod unfolded a page of A4 paper. It contained the auction image of Selgroch's idol. Written across the top in red ink was, 'Meet me where you killed her in one hour. Alone!'

'I have to go!' He handed Matt the box. 'Do what you must with this. I have to go!'

Chapter 40

Jarrod Stepped himself, Xiu and Li into the rear cargo area of the chapel grounds, using the multitude of freight containers as cover from the houses across the road. Rain lashed at the trio as soon as they appeared. Unfurling his umbrella, Jarrod used it to offer some protection for his two would-be protectors.

'It's only rain, Jarrod.' Li pushed the hand-held canopy over the wizard's head. 'We'll find shelter and keep an eye open for Loukas. Keep it in your ear.' She tapped on her own blue tooth device. 'I'll set up a group call when I find shelter.'

'Be careful Jarrod. Loukas is insane.' Xiu hugged the wizard, pulling him in tight.

'As soon as I know where the bus is, he's toast.'

Xiu giggled. 'You're starting to sound like Melissa.'

'She's been quite an education,' Jarrod admitted.

Jarrod walked to the open central area for Loukas to see that he had arrived. The lorry driver's licence declared his abode to be a few streets away, so Loukas would be nearby, watching.

Jarrod waited for twenty minutes in the rain before Loukas contacted him. A phone, located in a small shelter between two containers, rang.

'Loukas?' Jarrod answered the device.

'Did you think I wouldn't notice that you brought your little helpers?'

'Where are the children, Loukas?'

'Patience, Jarrod. I'd like to know a little about you first.'

'You've read my police file, what else is there to know?' Jarrod tapped the Bluetooth device in his other ear as he spoke. Pushing it deeper into his ear didn't produce any sound. Li had not initiated the group call.

'They are not there,' Loukas informed Jarrod.

Jarrod turned around, surveying the areas beyond the two containers for Loukas.

'Yes, I am watching you. Don't worry. They are safe for now. I have a use for your two little Chinese girls,' Loukas chuckled.

'Loukas!' Jarrod's tone was stern with concern.

'How did you burn my talisman? The one Selgroch gave me for protection?'

'I don't know what you mean,' Jarrod lied.

'Tick-tock, Jarrod. The engine on the school bus will start soon, filling the cabin with fumes. Do you want the deaths of those children on your head?'

'Their deaths will tarnish your soul, Loukas. Not mine.'

'Soul?' Loukas laughed down the phone. 'The magic you cast has not been seen for a long time, Jarrod. The Church burned every practitioner they could find — the good, the bad and most of the time the innocent. How did you attain such power?'

'Is that it Loukas? Is that what this is about? Do you

crave power for yourself?'

'Tick-tock.'

'I have always had the power. I was born with it.'

'Impossible! You lie! Give me the talisman that you used, and I will spare the children,' Loukas shouted down the phone.

'There is no talisman, Loukas. I am naturally gifted and when I find you, you will feel how gifted I am.'

'Look down, Jarrod.'

Jarrod looked down at the metal grill under his shoes. Before he had a chance to react, electricity surged through his body. Then everything went black.

Jarrod woke spluttering as a bucket of rainwater was thrown over him. Iron shackles on his arms and legs were fastened to the grate on the floor. His back was leaning against another steel mesh. The rain lashed at the tin roof fastened between two cargo containers. Jarrod stared at his bonds, eyes wide, as if not comprehending why they did not fall away.

'Church blessed. Magically enhanced to prevent witches from escaping during their trial,' Loukas informed Jarrod. 'You will not break free. How did you destroy the chapel and kill my Mistress?' Loukas asked, pushing a long-bladed knife into Jarrod's shoulder, slowly piercing through to the other side, twisting the weapon as he withdrew it.

'God took her, Loukas. That sink hole was nothing to do with me,' Jarrod lied.

Loukas forced a small section of iron rebar into Jarrod's bleeding wound and pinned him to the metal grill behind. Standing clear, Loukas pulled the electrical lever on a nearby junction box and watched as Jarrod squirmed.

'You won't die, not yet. This isn't direct from the mains. I control the flow, the amperage and the wattage. I know how to make you talk.'

'She was weaker than you knew, she controlled you with lies and cheap parlour tricks,' Jarrod screamed as his body arched in agony.

'Liar! She was the most powerful of all the demons. She was a god!'

Jarrod laughed uncontrollably. Not the chuckles of a man but the hollow giggles of someone in pain. 'A god? You fool! She was nothing! A piss-poor demon, a con artist.'

Shutting the current down, Loukas approached Jarrod once more and pushed his knife through Jarrod's other shoulder. 'I have all night. No one can see you here. Where is the talisman you used to kill Selgroch?'

'I told you there is no talisman,' Jarrod said through clenched teeth.

'Liar! No one possesses magic such as that. You will give it to me!' Loukas demanded, pushing another metal bar into Jarrod's shoulder through to the grill behind.

'Where are the children, Loukas?' Jarrod pleaded.

'You'll never know. They will be dead soon.'

'Bastard!'

Loukas walked back to the end of the containers to flip the electrical switch, when suddenly something large collided with him, throwing his body towards Jarrod. For a brief second, Jarrod feared the murderer would become impaled on the rebars protruding out of his shoulders. Then Loukas tumbled to the ground at Jarrod's feet, his legs shattered, the man's head bleeding profusely from where it had hit the vehicle's windscreen. The car stopped and the driver turned the lights on, dazzling Jarrod. A figure stepped in front of the vehicle, a silhouette against the bright lights behind. Holding his arms up to shield his eyes from the light, Jarrod strained to identify the interloper.

As the figure approached, the characteristic shape of Detective Widcombe formed. As it came closer, she said, 'These electric cars really *are* quiet!' She held one hand to her head, slightly dazed from impacting with the airbags.

'Sarala, the children! He never told me where the children are!'

Crawling to one side, Loukas coughed blood and looked at Jarrod and the detective. 'You'll never find them!' he cackled.

'Erm, yeah we did.' Detective Widcombe placed her foot on one of Loukas's twisted legs and pushed. She felt the broken bones grate against each other. 'You should have been more careful, Loukas. Your first mistake was allowing us to see their school uniforms. The second, one of the girls pushed her phone between the seat's cushions, the "Find My Phone" app's a bitch, ain't it?' She pushed harder on Loukas's leg, annoyed at his lack of response.

'I am no stranger to pain, Detective. I have been broken and remade many times. Often by Selgroch herself, just for her amusement. You can do nothing she has not already thought of.'

'Thank God!' Jarrod sighed to himself at the news of the children. Sliding forwards to release the rebars from the grate, Jarrod stood. Chained and with the iron rebars still protruding from his shoulders, Jarrod asked through gritted teeth, 'Where is Li and Xiu, Loukas?'

'Why should I tell you?' Loukas snarled, surprised that Jarrod had the strength to rise.

Jarrod raised a hand to the man on the ground and invoked a spell.

Loukas laughed, the scarified sigils on his body changed

to deep red as the magic runes protected him from Jarrod's incantation.

'How?' Jarrod asked.

'I have magic too.' Loukas pointed his fist at Widcombe, a double-finger ring emanated a visible cone of distortion aimed at the detective.

Holding her arm up to her face as if to fend off a blow, Detective Widcombe stared down at her coat as runes of protection appeared on the material, glowing brightly.

Grabbing Loukas's arm, Jarrod moved the focus of the ring away from the detective before breaking the man's fingers to remove the magic talisman.

'How?' The detective looked down at her coat, brushing it with her hands, looking for signs of the now invisible runes.

'I wrote on your coat. I was worried about you,' Jarrod explained.

'Master Bargoch, I need you!'

The air next to Loukas changed, heat emanated from a shimmering portal. A hideous creature walked through and stared at Loukas on the floor and then at Jarrod.

'You're weak, Wizard. I can feel your overuse of magic from here.'

'Master, I have brought you Jarrod and his allies as promised. Alive, as you ordered.' Loukas looked at Jarrod, his eyes gloating. 'It was always a trap, Jarrod,' he sneered. 'Nothing you could have done would have saved you. Bargoch is going to torture you and your friends for eternity.' Blood spurted from Loukas's mouth, his wounds taking their toll on his body. 'Master, please.'

Bargoch stepped away from Loukas's grasping hand, uninterested in him. The grotesque body of the demon flickered and the equally twisted form of Swalon appeared.

'Swalon!' Detective Widcombe gasped. 'Why?' she cried.

Swalon caught the detective's fist in his hand and smiled. 'Jarrod knew Loukas would find another demon to serve. In the guise of Bargoch I contacted Loukas. Demons use a particular method of blood magic to ensure authenticity. This meant, of course, that I had to kill the real Bargoch to attain the creature's blood. Unfortunately, when I contacted Loukas, I could not locate his position. He knew better than to trust any demon until he had a sacrifice to offer.'

'Why? I trusted you.' Tears ran down the detective's face. 'After everything Jarrod did for you.'

'You never told her?' Swalon looked at Jarrod in anger.

'No, sorry.' Jarrod gave a cheeky, if somewhat pain-filled smile.

'Sarala, you must think me a monster.' Swalon clasped both of her hands in his. 'This was Jarrod's idea. He knew the only way to capture Loukas was a trap within a trap, within a trap... within a... I'm not sure how many withins... Wow! I'm rambling.'

'The ring?' Detective Widcombe asked.

'Oh, that was from Jarrod's collection, the Ring of Medicinal Sleep.' Swalon laughed. 'When I contacted Loukas, it was clear he desired magic of his own, a talisman of some sort. Loukas believed the ring to be a weapon. He was very thorough in hiding his whereabouts from me. I had the ring delivered through many intermediaries.' Swalon released the detective's fist.

'If you've finished,' Jarrod looked down at the rebars in his shoulders. 'If you don't mind.'

'My car! What have you done to my car?' Li shouted as she and Xiu approached the group.

'I'm sorry Jarrod,' Xiu apologised. 'We lost consciousness. He used something that bypassed father's wards.'

'Medicinal magic,' Detective Widcombe said as if she knew what it meant.

'Oh, clever. Yes, that would sneak under father's protection.'

'Sorry Li,' Jarrod apologised. 'It was the only way to prevent Loukas from killing you both. I knew you would insist on coming with me so, I asked Swalon to instruct Loukas to keep you alive and unharmed for future torturous events.'

'The children?' Xiu asked, alarmed.

'Safe. The police found them on their own.'

The group turned at the sound of sirens approaching.

'What are we going to do with him?' Swalon asked, looking down at Loukas.

The man's face was grey, his chest still.

Detective Widcombe gasped and tears ran down her cheeks once more.

'Sarala?' Li asked holding the woman to comfort her.

'I have never seen a person's spirit leave their body before,' she cried. 'It's beautiful, even stained as Loukas's is. Oh, he's... gone.' Sarala stared at the remains of Loukas on the floor. 'What will happen to his spirit?'

'We don't know, some... most of us believe he will be held accountable for his actions; why else hold a tally of one's indiscretions on your soul?' Swalon answered. 'At some point he will be reincarnated, and the cycle will continue until he has learnt what he needs to in order to move on to the next phase of existence.'

'Jarrod?' Detective Widcombe looked at the wizard for confirmation.

'We are all here until we learn our lessons, Sarala. Life only begins once we pass from this mortal environment. This is nothing but a training ground.'

Jarrod winced as he set fire to Li's car, exhaustion causing him to fall back to hand motions to invoke his spell.

'You two owe me a new car!' Li fumed.

'There can be no evidence of Sarala ever being here, you know that. Her DNA is all over the air bags, fingerprints...' Jarrod left the sentence hanging, watching the first of the emergency vehicles traverse around the sinkhole, blue lights casting shadows into the cavernous abyss. 'You should go,' Jarrod added, leaning on Swalon for support.

Swalon suggested, 'You could just Step out of here and burn the evidence,' as he assisted Jarrod back into his sitting position on the iron grating.

'No. This will exonerate me in the eyes of the law, a victim of a mad man. I'll say I didn't see who drove the car because of the lights and the pain. Go!'

Swalon Stepped away with Li, Xiu and Detective Widcombe, leaving Jarrod on the floor, metal rebars pinning him to the grating.

END

Author's Letter

I hope you enjoyed this novel. It is a strange thing being a writer as the story and characters live in our heads while we are writing. The worlds we create are as real to us as the keyboard I am typing on.

It is my that wife I feel sorry, I often hear an inward groan when she hears the phrase "I was looking something up...". Thankfully she still loves me for all my faults and her belief in me helps to me to write.

About the Author

P N Burrows was born in England and raised in rural Wales. Phil has worked in a variety of roles over the years from IT Consultant to a Business Advisor. In his spare time, he loves to read and particularly enjoys crime thrillers. He also enjoys working his way through a comprehensive bucket list that he and his partner have created; they can frequently be found dancing the Lindy Hop..

Web: www.pnburrows.com

FB: www.facebook.com/PNBurrows

Twitter: @pnburrows

Acknowledgements

I would like to thank the following people for helping to make this book happen.

Cath Burrows, my wife, for her continued support during the writing process, listening to me babble on about plot twists and for just being there.

A heartfelt thank you to my beta readers for the feedback they provide.

THE MINERAN BOOK SERIES
- AVAILABLE ON AMAZON -

BOOK 1 -MINERAN INFLUENCE

The story of an ex-soldier, Sam Shepard stumbles upon aliens in North Wales. He becomes embroiled in events that stretch across space, endangering Sam every step of the way.

BOOK 2 -MINERAN CONFLICT

Having enlisted with ISPAW's quasi-military Universal Police and trained with the Minerans for a year, Sam is sent on his first mission. 'It will be safe and easy,' they said. No it wasn't, and Sam's training didn't cover what happened!

BOOK 3 - MINERAN ASSAULT

While the team frantically search for Sam, he struggles to survive and to evade capture. The traitor and the truth behind ISPAW's mysterious and vengeful nemesis is uncovered.

BOOK 4 - MINERAN PURSUIT

Sam returns to Earth to locate the missing Dia Kuklos, where he discovers the truth about the Alien presence on Earth and their influences on humanity's development. Can Sam, Erebos and Apate survive the perilous journey to the ocean's depths and their encounter with ISPAW's nemesis?

BOOK 5 - MINERAN RESOLVE

In the final book of the Mineran series, we find the Inner Sphere of Aligned Worlds (ISPAW) being torn apart and at war. Dark forces move against the aligned planets, their nemesis threatens the existence of every lifeform within the Sphere. Amidst the chaos Sam and his friends are sent out to locate the source of the hostilities and ultimately, to find a resolution to the conflict by any means necessary.

A new book from P N Burrows…

Jarrod and the Dark Cardinal

The second book in the Jarrod Series.
Jarrod finds himself outside of his comfort zone, he is used to battling physical inter-dimensional demons. Flesh, bone and blood are easy to destroy, but this time Jarrod and Detective Widcombe find themselves battling an ancient evil, spiritual, non-corporeal beings.

Printed in Great Britain
by Amazon

82999563R00151